In Memory of

Henry Eckstein 1915–1942
Louis Eckstein 1884–1965
and
Esther Eckstein Lowy 1921–2013

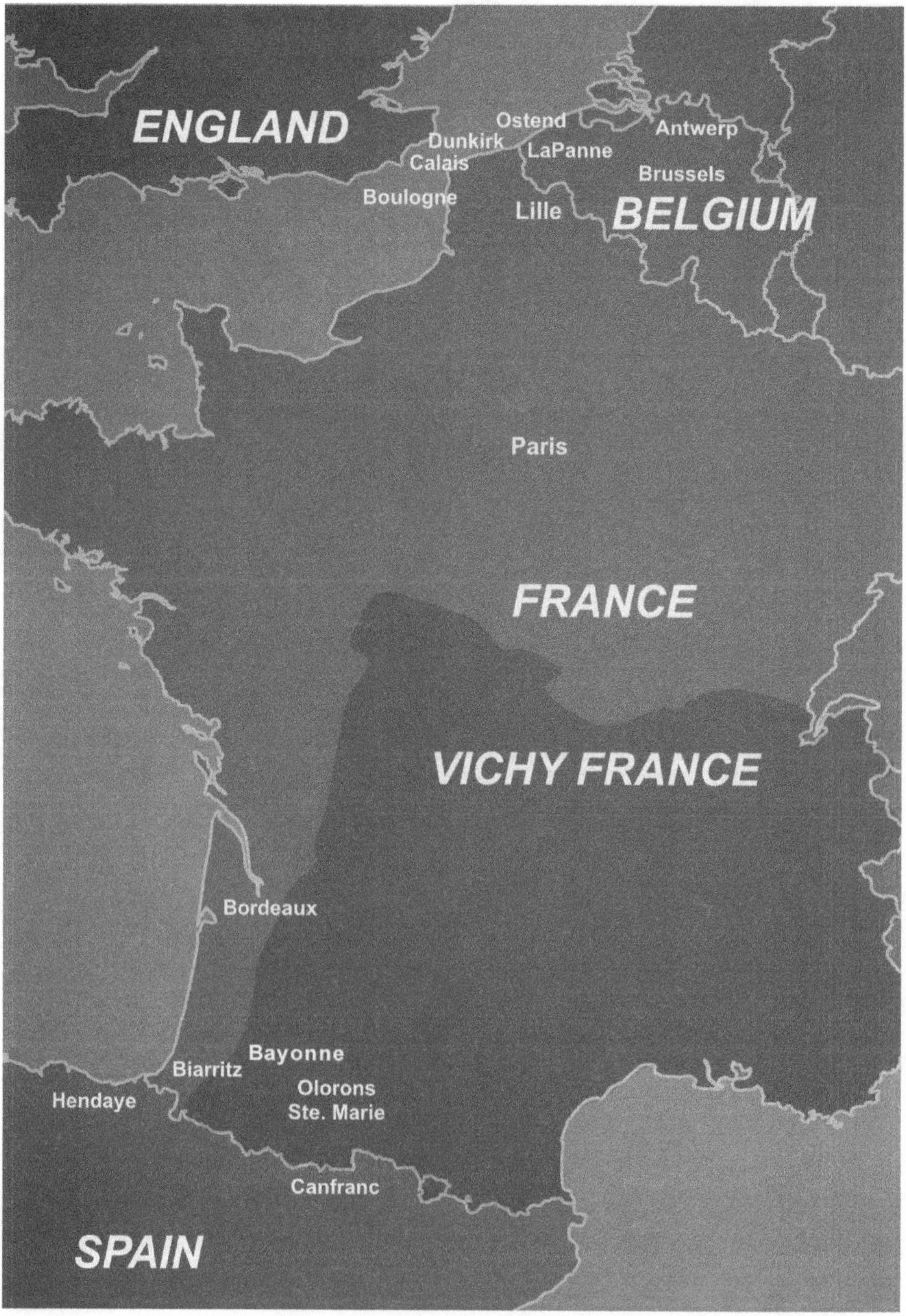
ENGLAND
Ostend
Antwerp
Dunkirk
Calais
LaPanne
Brussels
Boulogne
Lille
BELGIUM
Paris
FRANCE
VICHY FRANCE
Bordeaux
Bayonne
Biarritz
Olorons
Ste. Marie
Hendaye
Canfranc
SPAIN

a small door

Michele Shulamit Lowy

ONION RIVER PRESS

BURLINGTON, VERMONT

A Small Door *is based on a true story, and much research went into the writing, but it is a novel. The characters are fictional, and though their circumstances resemble those of the real people who inspired me, they are my creation. I have imagined incidents and, of course, conversations. Many of my cousins have been interested in the progress of the book, and I want to assure them that the foibles of my characters do not reflect on the real strength and courage of their parents. The book is dedicated to my grandfather, mother, and uncle, but the dedication could easily expand to Granny, Mark, Judy, Irene, Ruth, Menachem, and Uncle Elie. And to all the others, those who escaped, and those who didn't. I want especially to mention Mme. Bayens, the mother of my uncle's university friend, who risked her life traveling from Brussels to Antwerp each week to bring food to my great grandmother and great aunt. Mme. Goossens is based on her.*

1940

Fleeing from my fellow-countrymen
I have now reached Finland. Friends
Whom yesterday I didn't know, put up some beds
In clean rooms. Over the radio
I hear victory bulletins of the scum of the earth. Curiously
I examine a map of the continent. High up in Lapland
Towards the Arctic Ocean
I can see a small door.

—Bertolt Brecht

Prologue

Rachel ~ September 1939, London

On all her visits from Antwerp, she shared her cousin Irene's room. There was shopping and visiting and long walks where they talked about all the things seventeen-year-old girls talk about—the future, men, books, family.

But beneath it all, like a faintly off smell that people try not to mention but that no one can forget, there was the threat of impending war. It seemed as though everyone was expecting it; the whole country sitting at the edge of their seats waiting for some horrible performance to begin. Each evening they gathered by the wireless to hear the latest news, knowing that the same thing was happening in every home in the country.

Rachel found the received pronunciation of the BBC news readers soothing; it was like listening to her uncles and cousins. Not at all like the German broadcasts she heard at home in Antwerp. Though her mother didn't know much German, even she could hear the threat in Hitler's voice as he ranted on, and the unmistakable contempt and near hysteria as he repeated the word "Juden." Rachel almost expected the radio to start spitting as his voice reached a crescendo of hatred.

Night after night for six years, they had heard those frightening broadcasts, and terrible as it was, no one could stop listening. It was like a sore tooth that your tongue couldn't stay away from. Some evenings Mamma would just pick up her mending and leave the room, or Rachel would go down to the kitchen and out the garden door to breathe deeply and try to stop her inner trembling. It rarely worked.

"How can anyone believe what Hitler says? It's so outrageous," she asked at the dinner table.

"People believe what they want to believe," her father answered.

"But that Jews are responsible for everything that is wrong with the world? There aren't enough Jews for that to be true!"

"I know you don't like history, but it's been going on for centuries," her brother Alexander came back.

"I do know that! But this is the twentieth century!"

"Not for everyone," added Daniel, her other brother. "We know Jews who are stuck in the seventeenth century. Why shouldn't the goyim be equally backward?"

Before the teasing could continue, their father answered, "There's often no logic in what people believe."

"It's frightening listening to him."

"Be grateful we're in Belgium and not in Germany."

Disturbing as it was, the next night they would gather around the radio again to listen to another installment of the horrible real life drama coming from Germany.

But even the BBC uncles sounded almost shaken when they announced what everyone had been waiting for: the invasion of Poland, the ultimatum, and finally the announcement that war had come. Rachel was sitting next to Irene, their shoulders touching, listening to the King saying that Britain was at war with Germany.

Auntie Gert barely drew breath before she started talking about blackout curtains and gas masks and laying in supplies because there was sure to be rationing. Uncle Leonard told her to calm down, the Germans weren't here yet and there'd be plenty of time to get ready when official instructions were given. Auntie Gert paid no attention to him and went back to bustling around, talking nonstop. Irene and Rachel just sat, not knowing what to do or say.

The next day, they all went to Auntie Minnie's house. The family had gathered to decide what to do about Rachel, though no one had told her that. It was the largest gathering of Mamma's English family outside of a holiday—Auntie Minnie and Uncle Harry, Uncle Felix and Auntie Leah, Aunt Fanny and silent Uncle Bernard (none of the cousins had ever heard anything more elaborate than "yes" or "no" from him), Rose and David and John and Alice and Linnie and even Great Uncle Charlie. There was tea with biscuits and sandwiches and a sponge cake, but no one seemed to be eating, just pouring and drinking endless cups of tea.

"I hope tea won't be rationed again."

No one answered, but then no one ever paid much attention to what Auntie Gert said. Rachel was sitting with Irene and Rose, the cousins closest to her in age, when she caught her name and realized that she was the topic of the adults' conversation.

"She should stay here. After all, if the war goes on, Ernest and Freda will come here; they did in '14." That was Uncle Felix.

"Who knows what will happen? Maybe they'd rather have her in Antwerp," Auntie Minnie answered.

"It's safer here. Safety should be the first consideration." Auntie Leah always echoed Uncle Felix's opinions.

"Why is it safer here? Belgium isn't at war with Germany, we are. Belgium is neutral. She'd be safer at home," Auntie Minnie came back at her sister-in-law.

"In the Great War it didn't matter that Belgium was neutral; what matters is that Belgium is closer to Germany. She's better off here," Auntie Leah pushed her argument.

"Who knows how long Belgium will be out of the war? Before long the whole family might be here in London—Ernest and Freda and Eugene and the children."

"It's not so simple now. Business is just starting to improve, it's not a good time to leave—and the children aren't children anymore. Everyone won't be so quick to pick up and move. And it might never come to that. Maybe the war will be over in a few months."

"That's what they said last time, and it certainly wasn't true then."

"Maybe we should send a telegram to Ernest. Ask what we should do with her."

"The telegraph office will be a zoo today. Might as well wait a day or two."

She felt like a tennis ball being hit back and forth across the net as they discussed her fate. Only if it were a tennis match, they would have had their eyes on the ball, and she felt as though no one remembered she was even in the room.

Irene whispered to her, "It would be lovely to have you stay longer."

She didn't answer. She was angry. How could they talk about her as though she were a small child, or worse, not even in the room! She was ready to break into the conversation and say something she would be sorry for later, when Great Uncle Charlie, who had been sitting quietly in a chair drinking his tea, asked, "Why don't we ask Rachel what she wants to do? After all, she's not a child, she's seventeen."

The relatives were shocked into silence. It hadn't occurred to them to ask Rachel's opinion.

Uncle Charlie turned to her. "What do you want to do?"

She didn't hesitate. "I want to go home. Lena and Freddy are leaving for America. I want to be able to say goodbye. Who knows how long it will be till I see them again."

And that was that. They let her go back to Antwerp.

She left London two days after the gathering at Auntie Minnie's. Irene was sorry to see her go, but they expected to see each other soon; either back in London, or Irene would come to Antwerp.

From one day to the next, it was wartime in England. Everyone was issued with a gas mask and there were no public lights on at night. Black-out curtains appeared in all the windows, as though they had just been in mothballs since the Great War, ready to be put back up at a moment's notice. At Victoria Station, people looked anxious and grim, and the train to Dover was dark. Familiar, comfortable England had become strange and different overnight.

On the train, she heard a mix of ordinary chatter and rumors. It all seemed even stranger in the darkness of the blackout, as though every sound came out of a half-waking, half-sleeping nightmare.

"There's U-boats in the Channel, y'know."

"They'll not touch us. They'll be looking for Navy ships, military targets."

"These are Jerries. They don't care if they hit civilians or soldiers, not like civilized people. Remember what they did last time."

The crowd in the Dover station was much quieter than usual, with anxious voices and some tears.

On the night boat from Dover to Ostend, she sat with two Belgian businessmen and a girl who had been in school in England. The chatter from the train ran through her head as she watched the girl reading the safety instructions on the poster. She didn't, couldn't, really believe they were in danger, but it was all so ominous: the anxious faces; the windows blacked out; the pitching movement of the boat in the North Sea. The middle-aged man sitting across from them saw the girl reading the poster. Rachel caught the glimpse of a smile on his face before it took on a very serious expression.

"I hope they have enough lifeboats. They don't always." When the girl looked over at him, he continued, "Could be Germans in the Channel. U-boats." The girl clutched her bag tightly. He was speaking in Flemish. "But don't worry, women and children first if we have to go into the water." He smiled, showing his tobacco stained teeth below his mustache.

Rachel glared at him and turned to the girl, speaking in English. "He's just trying to frighten you. We'll be in Ostend before you know it." The girl looked from her to the man, trying to decide who to believe. "Where are you headed?" Rachel asked. The two girls started talking and the man got up and walked out of the compartment.

It was light when the boat docked in Ostend and it was as if she had entered a different world, not just another country. There were no signs of a blackout, no one was carrying a gas mask, and most of all, the faces held the full range of ordinary human expressions—not what she would come to know later as the "war face," an expression of grim caution, of someone who knows bad things are likely to happen and is preparing to face them. The familiar ride from the coast back to Antwerp passed quickly, and she sank back into normalcy, the only discordant note the headlines on the newspapers other passengers were reading, and her own thoughts.

Her older sister Lena, with her husband and two small children, left for New York the following day. No one knew when they would see each other again.

1

Rachel ~ May 10, 1940, Antwerp

Rachel sat up in bed, wide awake. Light was seeping in at the edge of the curtains; it was barely dawn. Too early. A sound like distant thunder, then footsteps running in the hall. No one ran at this hour of the morning. She put on her robe and slippers and opened the bedroom door. Mamma was calling to Pa downstairs. Why was anyone up? She ran down the stairs. The front door was wide open.

More thunder. No, it wasn't thunder, but explosions. Mamma, Pa, and Daniel were standing in front of the house, looking up.

Daniel came over and pointed. "German bombers." There was an explosion and a burst of something that looked like cotton wool in the sky. "Anti-aircraft fire."

She tightened the belt of her robe and looked down the road. In front of every house were the neighbors, still in their nightclothes, looking up at the sky. Even M. Goetelsmans, a middle-aged man who was never without his stiff collar, tie, waistcoat, and jacket, was standing outside in his dressing gown and slippers. Seeing Mamma in the front garden before she had put her hair up was almost as startling as the German planes flying overhead.

What could they do but go inside, get dressed, eat breakfast, and turn on the wireless? They drank their coffee, pretended to eat, and listened to the news that the country had been invaded.

Daniel put on his uniform and brushed off Mother's plea that he eat breakfast before he left. The door slammed.

"Where are the Germans?" Mother asked. Her very limited French meant she couldn't follow the news. Through the dining room window, they could see anti-aircraft shells bursting in the sky to the east. Why were they sitting at the breakfast table? Shouldn't they be running, or hiding?

"The wireless says they've come through in two places—at Fort Eben Emael near Maastricht and through Luxembourg. Still quite a ways from us," Father explained. He wiped his mouth and brushed the crumbs from his mustache.

"Then why are they flying over here?" Rachel asked.

"The planes attack ahead of the troops. They'll try to eliminate our planes and defenses on the ground before any ground troops get here."

"Should I go to work?"

"Of course not!" Mother answered.

Father shook his head. "Go to your job. We'll meet after I speak to Uncle Eugene and call at the bank."

"I think Rachel should stay here," Mamma said.

"We'll be home soon, Freda. Start deciding what we need to take if we leave. Expect to travel as lightly as we can. Rachel will probably not be at work for long, but it would be discourteous for her not to go in at all. I'll telephone if I can."

Mamma wouldn't openly disagree with Pa, but she wasn't pleased. Rachel should be at home helping her. She didn't like that Rachel had a job at all. Her daughter shouldn't be working at an office job. Lena, thirteen years older than Rachel, never had a job. She was home until she married at twenty. That was the way it should be. But that was before the Depression. She didn't complain when Rachel turned over her earnings.

As they walked to the tram, Rachel could hear explosions in the distance. She looked in several directions, trying to figure out where the noise was coming from.

"It will take them a while to get here," Father said. "Even if our army collapses, the Germans have to travel from the border."

"What about Daniel? Will he be back?"

"He'll probably be mobilized."

"And Alexander?" He was a student in Brussels, finishing the work for his PhD in chemistry, and had stayed with a friend from the university the night before.

"He'll most likely come home this afternoon."

The tram was crowded, as usual, but hardly anyone was speaking. They got off at the usual stop in the diamond district.

"I'm going to the bank to get cash for Bonmama and Tante Rosa. After I take the money to them, I'll go to my office. Meet me there in about an hour."

Rachel was a secretarial assistant, or as Alexander and Daniel said, a dogsbody, for M. Gutfreund, a diamond dealer like her father. She wasn't sure who to expect in the office, but when she arrived, both the bookkeeper and the secretary were already there.

"We were wondering if you would come," said Arnold Rosen, the young German refugee who kept the books.

"Good morning, Rachel," said Etta Zimmerman, M. Gutfreund's secretary, who was also a refugee. An invasion was not going to stop her from being polite.

Rachel answered in German, "Good morning, Frau Zimmerman, Arnold. Is M. Gutfreund in?"

"Rachel, is that you?" Her employer's voice, speaking French, preceded him into the room. M. Gutfreund knew her family well; his sons had been in school with Alexander and Daniel. "What is your father's plan?"

"I'm not sure. He told me to meet him at his office in an hour."

"Well then, you needn't stay. I'll see your father in shul. We'll all be going home soon. Good shabbos."

"Good shabbos." M. Gutfreund went back into his room. Rachel turned to the others. "What will you do?"

Frau Zimmerman shrugged. "Wait and see. Maybe the French and the British will push back the Germans."

Arnold snorted derisively. "That won't happen. We should all have gone to England. Or America."

They were silent for a moment.

"Well, I'll be going to my father's." She hesitated, not knowing what to say. Etta Zimmerman and Arnold had left their homes in Germany because of Hitler. They would probably have to leave again. "I don't know when I'll be back to work …"

"None of us do. Good luck, Rachel," Arnold said.

"Good luck."

Etta said nothing, just looked down at her desk.

"Good shabbos," Rachel said.

They nodded, and almost automatically answered, "Good shabbos."

It was hard to know what else to say.

A Small Door

At home, the suitcases came out and everyone began packing. Any small, portable valuables like jewelry and silver candlesticks were gathered at one end of the dining room table. What do you pack when you don't know where you are going or for how long you will be away?

After she had gathered the obvious—clean underwear and nightgowns, a few blouses and skirts, a cardigan and raincoat—Rachel looked around. What else to pack? More shoes? Rain boots? Books were so heavy, but she didn't want to leave them.

She heard another plane passing over the house and almost laughed, feeling ridiculous. The country was being invaded, and she was wondering whether to pack galoshes!

She looked around the room at the space that had been hers for more than ten years. The house had been built for the family before the Depression. The bedroom, with its built-in shelves and pale mauve marble fireplace, was designed for Lena, decorated for her fourteen-year-old tastes. However Rachel had tried to change it, the color scheme remained that of her older sister—you couldn't get away from Lena's purple. But it was now Rachel's private space, her refuge, with her books, old dollhouse, and belongings scattered around.

They had just finished eating lunch when Daniel came in. He was a sergeant in charge of a big piece of artillery, stationed less than a half hour from home.

"I don't know where I'll be sent—it's full mobilization, but they've let us come home to say goodbye."

"You'll ring us?" Mother asked.

"If I can," Daniel answered, though they all knew, Mamma included, he wouldn't be able to. Father gave him some money and vague instructions.

Rachel didn't know what to say. Do you say "good luck" to your brother going off to war? She had said "good luck" to Arnold and Frau Zimmerman this morning and that was inadequate. She would have liked to hold onto Daniel and say, "Come back to us. Stay safe." If you said that, did you make the danger more real? But it was real—this was war and the country was being invaded. She didn't say it. No one said it, and the words, like so many others, hung unspoken in the air as Daniel, the tallest of them at over six feet, leaned down and kissed everyone, then was gone.

Alexander returned from Brussels later in the afternoon, jacket open, light brown hair standing on end, with the same news they had heard already.

It was a strange Friday night. Rachel set the table with the white cloth and fixed candles into the silver candlesticks. There was chicken soup and brisket, cooked with Mother's usual skill. Mamma lit the candles and said the blessing, Father said kiddush over the wine and they passed around the challah Rachel had brought. But despite all appearances, it didn't *feel* like shabbos.

Usually it would take a life or death situation for her parents to go against the Sabbath commandments and use the electricity or the telephone, but Pa let the non Jewish maid turn on the radio so they could hear the news. It was hard to sort out what was happening. The Germans had invaded Holland, Belgium, and France. The Belgian government had declared a state of emergency and Luxembourg was occupied. In Britain, Chamberlain had resigned and Winston Churchill had become Prime Minister.

"That at least is good news." Father had had no patience for Chamberlain since Munich.

Even though the spring evening stayed light, no one knew what to do with themselves. Sitting in the garden waiting for more planes to come over wasn't a good idea, it was hard to concentrate on a book, and since it was shabbos, there was nothing useful you *could* do. They all went to bed early and Rachel lay awake, unable to sleep, finally drowsing off just before morning.

Saturday, they walked to synagogue together. Even before the service began, the old building was crowded. Women who never came to shul were quietly greeting each other while the men gathered in clumps, shaking their heads over the news. In the women's section, not even the most pious were following in the prayer books. Instead of the usual chanting of the familiar prayers with an undercurrent of whispers from the gossipers, the anxious murmurs overtook the prayer melodies. Even old Mme. Horenstein, who always reminded Rachel of a witch, was quiet.

She slipped out before the end. People were standing quietly talking in twos and threes on the sidewalk. Alexander was talking to school friends, David Edelberg and Yoska Nachman. David was a diamond polisher and Yoska worked in his father's business. Rachel walked over to them; they were sharing the latest news and rumors. Yoska had several newspapers with him.

"*Le Soir* says the French army has crossed the border and the King is in firm command of the 'brave troops.' And the *Gazet Van Antwerpen*, that pro-fascist rag, says the Germans will be in Brussels within a week."

"And what else is new? The one thing they don't have to say is that wherever the Germans, the French, or the King are, we're in the—," Yoska's next word was lost as Father came up and collected his family to walk home. Usually he stayed to visit, but today he wanted to go immediately. Uncle Eugene and the cousins were coming too, and the two men strode ahead quickly, talking quietly together, Maurice and Alexander behind them. Beatrice, Louise, and Rachel followed.

"Did you start packing already?" sixteen-year-old Louise asked. Rachel nodded. "Do you know where we're going? Uncle Ernest didn't say anything?"

"Not to me and not to Alexander."

Twenty-four-year-old Beatrice said, "Probably we'll go to England, like they did during the Great War."

Shabbos lunch was as subdued as dinner the night before had been. The adults felt no need to pretend a cheerfulness they didn't feel, since even Louise was old enough to understand the seriousness of the situation. The afternoon dragged even more than the usual late spring shabbos; though the weather was fine enough for a walk, no one wanted to go far. It felt strange—they were clearly on the verge of something big and important, and doing nothing.

Sunday morning, the news was grim. The Belgian army had blown up the bridges crossing the Meuse River and there was a battle raging in Hannut. No one expected the army to be able to stall the Germans for long. Soon the enemy would be in Brussels and Antwerp. There was no call from Daniel, and no one speculated about where he might be.

An early phone call to Uncle Eugene confirmed plans made the day before, and they all went to pack, this time seriously.

"There might not be any porters to be had—we have to be able to carry everything ourselves," were Father's instructions. They were ready before nine—wearing layers of traveling clothes, each with two suitcases and, except for Mamma, a rucksack. Some of the best silverware was parceled out among them; Father carried the silver kiddush cup and Alexander the best candlesticks. Mother wore her jewelry under her clothes, only her wedding and engagement rings were visible on her hands. Her diamond earrings were tucked in with her toothbrush. Father threaded the old gold coin and civic service medallion he usually wore with his watch onto a thin chain and fastened it around Rachel's neck.

"Gold is always useful. But keep it hidden." She tucked it under her blouse; the cold metal soon became warm from the contact with her skin. Father locked the door behind him and they walked to the corner to catch the tram to the station. Rachel looked back at the house one last time.

Then they stood on the platform at the suburban Berchem station. In a few moments they would be on a train heading for the Channel coast. In 1914, more than seven years before Rachel was born, her parents and Lena, then only five, had gone to London with Uncle Eugene and Auntie Emma, Mamma's sister. Alexander and Daniel had been born in England, and so had Beatrice and Maurice. The two families had returned to Belgium in 1919. Now, with Rachel and Louise, both born in Belgium, they would once again try to take refuge with family in England. Lena was in America with her husband and children, Daniel was in the army, and Auntie Emma was dead.

The train was filled with people like them, fleeing the Germans. Anyone who could, was trying to get away. A seat was found for Mamma, and the rest stood. Louise sat on her suitcase. At each stop, more people and luggage crowded onto the train, until it felt like every centimeter of space was crammed with something or someone. The train seemed to crawl along as they passed familiar stations. Antwerp Central, Sint Niklaas, Lokeren, Ghent, Bruges, Ostend.

Every summer of Rachel's childhood, even after the 1929 Crash made money so much tighter, had been spent at the seaside. Her family and Uncle Eugene's, along with several aunts and uncles and scores of cousins from London, had moved into adjoining apartments across from the beach at Ostend. Those were the best times—the hours spent at the beach with her brothers and cousins.

With longer stops, the trip stretched to two and a half hours. The train slowed as it pulled into the familiar station at Ostend. But instead of the usual happy crowds heading for seaside holidays, the anxious mob pushed and shoved, frowning as they surged out of the train and toward the exits. Rachel held on tightly to her bags and was grateful that Pa and Uncle Eugene were tall enough to be visible in the crowd. There were no porters and they moved slowly, weighed down by possessions. Everyone was going the same way, toward the docks; it would have been impossible to go in a different direction.

"There's no sense in all of us going to get tickets. Rachel, go with your mother and see if you can find a British boat we can get on. An English accent might get better results in this sea of Belgians," her father directed.

The first captain they approached just shook his head. "Sorry, ma'am. No room." The answer was the same at the second boat. Finally, at the third stop, the situation was explained.

"We've orders to only take soldiers. There's no space for civilians."

"We better head to the French border. Maybe we'll have better luck in Dunkirk," Uncle Eugene echoed everyone's thoughts. There was no motorized transportation; they picked up their luggage and began to walk.

Rachel had taken many long walks along the wide, flat beach in summers past, but this was a completely new experience—weighed down with luggage, in layers of traveling clothes, part of a mass of similarly burdened walkers. Though the noise at the station and the dock had been almost overwhelming, quiet soon descended on the crowd. Everyone was concentrating on putting one foot in front of the other, shifting their loads to avoid straining backs and shoulders. Only the children saw the trek as a lark, running back and forth, shouting and singing.

They reached De Panne, the last Belgian town before the border, by five in the afternoon, with only brief stops for drinks and the toilet. Instead of the usual customs officials and border guards, there were French soldiers manning the crossing.

"On ne peut pas passer. La frontière est fermée." *You can't cross. The border is closed*, the soldiers repeated as they stood on their side of the barrier—just a simple wooden gate.

Suddenly, a German fighter plane flew overhead. Another plane came into view, either Belgian or RAF, and the German plane was hit. It was pouring smoke and dipping crazily and, as they watched, the pilot jumped from the plane. Seconds later, his parachute opened. The pilot drifted slowly down into France and the plane plunged towards the sea.

The crowd cheered as though they were at a circus. People at the back began pushing and shoving, whether from excitement or panic, and the whole mass of people began shifting and moving forward, carrying everyone toward the barrier at the French border. The family moved in closer to stay together. Rachel couldn't shift her bags to grab onto Alexander or Mamma. There were bodies pressed against her, pushing her forward. She had to keep moving her feet or she would fall. The barrier broke and the crowd of Belgian refugees streamed into France. Rachel saw one of the French soldiers shrug and light a cigarette, an almost stereotypically French gesture, before she was carried ahead on the wave moving toward Dunkirk.

It was about a half hour past sunset, around 9 p.m., when they got to Dunkirk. Mother looked ready to drop and Alexander was carrying one of her bags. Rachel's legs ached from walking and her shoulders hurt from hauling the suitcases. All she wanted was a place to sit, and then a hot bath.

Coming into town, they were met by harassed looking officials directing refugees to shelters for the night. They were sent to a convent several streets away. Rachel had never been inside a convent, those mysterious places inhabited by Catholic nuns, a foreign species to an orthodox Jewish girl. Mother looked at Father with eyebrows slightly raised, but he shook his head and continued on in.

An official at the door told them where to go. The underground rooms of the convent, with their thick stone walls, were being used as an air raid shelter, and many people from the neighborhood had already come in and staked out a spot to sleep.

Once they found space, they put their bags down and laid out blankets to mark where they would sleep. The girls set out for a washroom. They had to wait behind a long line of women who looked as bedraggled and tired as they did. Finally, they could use the toilet and wash some of the grime off their hands and faces. It was a small blessing to have enough time for the necessities without rushing.

The washroom was at one end of a dimly lit corridor. At the end of the hallway was a closed door and, just as they approached, the door opened and out glided a nun. Silently, she shook her head at them, closed the door, and disappeared down another dark hallway. They giggled nervously.

"Shh. Stop being silly; they'll hear us." Beatrice pushed them back to the main room.

Makeshift bedrolls were laid out. Exhausted from the long day of travel, anxiety, and the unaccustomed walking, everyone lay down to try and sleep, or at least rest. Father was rubbing Mamma's feet and ankles, an oddly intimate gesture in such a public space. It was strange to lie down fully dressed in the middle of so many people. Rachel had never even slept in the same room as her parents or brother, and here she was surrounded by a crowd of strangers. There were people talking and whispering, babies crying, and the sounds of coughing. The light was dim but she could see the shadows and outlines of people sitting, lying down, and occasionally standing up.

From outside the convent, there were the sounds of bombing, even closer than it had been in Antwerp. But how close were they?

She whispered to Alexander, "Is the bombing right here in the town?"

"Probably the port mostly. And they're attacking the British and French soldiers. We should be safe here."

She thought about the soldiers, young men like Daniel. Where was he now? He wouldn't be safe inside like they were (if they were safe), he would be a target, along with many others. She thought she would never sleep, between the noise, the lack of privacy, and the fear, though she had never been so tired.

From the other side of the convent, sealed off by walls and doors, they could hear the nuns chanting and praying. No sooner did the noise settle into a dull pattern—the low thud of the planes and the murmuring of the nuns—then there would be a burst of shelling, an explosion, or the sound of dogfights between British and German planes, followed by the nuns praying louder, as though they were trying to make sure God heard them over the noise of war. Rachel would doze off, then be jerked awake as a bomb fell and the prayers rose in volume and intensity. Between the bombing and the praying, no one got much rest. The air battle continued all night, punctuated by the explosion of British bombs in the harbor. It only let up as dawn came.

Very early the next morning, they tiredly gathered their things and found a cafe not overrun with other refugees. While everyone else settled in for coffee and fresh bread, Rachel and her mother went down to the docks.

They got nowhere near the harbor. Fire trucks and ambulances were rushing down the narrow streets and there were soldiers everywhere. There was no way to get passage on a boat. They returned to the cafe. Father and Uncle Eugene would decide what to do next while they finished breakfast.

"We might as well continue down the coast. Maybe we can get on a boat in Calais." Father paid the bill and picked up his rucksack. Mother sighed and drank the last of her coffee.

Once again, they joined the hundreds, maybe thousands, of people walking along the coast.

Mamma's mouth was set in a grim line and she shifted her bags slightly in her hands. She was wearing thin cotton gloves. Mamma hardly ever went out without a hat and she often wore gloves. It was part of the way a "lady" dressed. Mamma was always a lady. But in this instance, the gloves had a practical use. Soon their hands would be blistered from carrying the suitcases and gloves gave some protection. Rachel wished she had thought to wear gloves too. She looked down at her mother's feet. She was wearing sturdy walking shoes, as they all did.

"Do your feet hurt?" she asked softly.

"A bit. It's all right." Mamma didn't smile, but her mouth relaxed momentarily.

The day before, the crowd had walked in relative silence, seemingly in shock. Today there was more talking. Children were complaining—their legs hurt, they were thirsty, they had to pee, when would they stop? The ones who were too old to be carried lagged behind, along with the old people and those who had run frightened from their homes wearing only their house slippers. Every time a German plane flew overhead, there were loud calls of "Sale Boche!"—the only anti-aircraft weapon available. They were out in the open with no place to hide.

The walk from Dunkirk to Calais took all day. Once again, they stopped only briefly for the most elemental needs. The whole time, they could hear the fighting, and knew that if it came closer they had no escape. Frightening as the sounds of bombing and battle were, it required so much effort to keep putting one foot in front of the other that there was little energy left for fear.

They reached Calais close to dusk and trudged down to the harbor, looking for a boat with space to take them. Mamma tidied her hair, pinned her hat on more securely, straightened her jacket, and walked up to the nearest boat. She smiled and asked to see the man in charge. "Always speak to the highest authority you can," she used to say. Something in her tone made the sailor turn immediately to get someone with more power. An officer came down to speak to her.

"I need passage for my family. There are nine of us." She might have been booking tickets at Victoria Station.

"I'm sorry, ma'am. We've orders to take only soldiers."

"What about British subjects with family in England?"

"Sorry, ma'am, only soldiers." The officer turned away and walked back to his boat. Mamma set her shoulders and they went back to Father.

"We should find shelter for the night."

She nodded and they began walking back toward the town. This time they were sent to an old factory. It had been converted into a barracks for British soldiers. Now the soldiers were gone, all except for one orderly who had been left in case the place was needed again. There were rows of cots and straw mattresses and the family was told to bed down anywhere, since they were the only ones there.

Rachel put down her luggage by a cot and slipped the rucksack off her shoulders. She stretched her neck and moved her shoulders in circles, trying to work out the knots and aches. Alexander came and stood behind her, rubbing the back of her neck and the spot between her shoulder blades where the pack had rested. It felt good.

Beatrice sat on the cot next to Rachel's, slipped off her shoes and began rubbing her feet. Louise was examining a blister on her palm. Rachel wondered whether she even had the energy to brush her teeth.

Alexander gave her a gentle poke and she looked up. Father and Uncle Eugene were seated on their cots but Mother was still standing. She had unpinned her hat, turned up the little veil, and carefully taken it off her head without disturbing her hair. She stood, hat in hand, literally, and looked around at the rows and rows of cots, just cots. Just as the family had all noticed her, so did the British soldier.

"Lady, whotcha want?"

"I'm looking for a chair to put my hat and clothes on," she answered, her familiar clear tones contrasting with his almost stereotypical cockney. He looked at her in disbelief.

"Lady, do ye think yer in Buck'n'am Palace?"

Maurice snorted, Louise and Rachel giggled, and before long they were all laughing, Mother and the soldier along with the rest. It was such a relief to laugh together and to realize that, even in wartime, Mamma was still Mamma.

The night in Calais was no quieter than Dunkirk. More bombing and dog-fights. But instead of nuns chanting prayers, they had their cockney guardian muttering curses at the Jerries because the shelling prevented him from getting across the road to the bar for a drink. The mixture of exhaustion, fear, and noise was like being inside a nightmare.

The next day, they tried again to get passage on a boat across the Channel, without luck. There was nothing to do but pick up and keep walking along the coast towards Boulogne. There were some cars and other vehicles (even horse and donkey carts), but they were all filled with passengers. The oldest and youngest among the refugees were given the few available seats. Alexander tried to find a ride for Mamma, but she refused, and anyway, there were no places. It was clear they would be doing a lot of walking in the coming days. The distance to Boulogne was slightly shorter than that from Dunkirk to Calais, but they were walking more slowly.

In Boulogne, they found a hotel with a few rooms. After taking Mother, Father, and Uncle Eugene to rooms downstairs, the concierge showed the rest of them to a room on the top floor with two double beds. Though it would be tight, they would get to sleep in real beds that night. They were just finishing supper in the hotel dining room when dusk fell, and with it the bombing began again.

"I think it'll be safer downstairs. You can sleep on the floor in our room."

"I'll take my chances," Alexander answered his father, "I want to sleep in a real bed tonight. And Rachel probably does too." Father frowned but said nothing when she followed her brother and cousins up the stairs to their "luxury" accommodations.

The door next to theirs was open, and the room seemed to be filled with people.

"Rachel!" a familiar voice called. It was Gabby Fishel, more disheveled than usual. Behind Gabby was her bro lensed glasses sliding down his nose.

"Rachel Brody," he echoed, "Is your brother with you?"

"Yes," answered Alexander, coming up the last sta Daniel's still in Belgium. The army. Who else is with you?" ejected the rest of its occupants. Along with Gabby and Izzy's cousin, Lena Blitz, were Bram and Ziggy Lichtman, Max Birnbaum, and Abie Shapiro, all of whom they knew from Antwerp.

They all settled in the larger room to exchange news and food.

"We left on Monday," Abie said. "The parents couldn't decide what to do about my grandmother, but they told me to go on ahead. I caught up with Bram and Ziggy at De Panne. What a mess!"

"It's a good thing it was a mess," Max broke in. "I wasn't sure I'd get across the border with my second class Polish papers. Not as kosher as you Belgians." He grinned at the others. Born in Belgium, with Polish parents, he had been caught up in a bureaucratic snafu which left him with a nearly useless Polish passport, now that Poland was occupied. "Have any of you seen David Goldstein?"

They continued to exchange information, trying to find out where friends might be and what news there was of possible escape routes. The Fishels, Lichtmans, Lena, Max, and Abie were traveling without their parents, who had all stayed behind in Antwerp, either to take care of aging and infirm relatives, or because they had little money and feared more for their children than for themselves.

When they finally talked themselves out, they fell exhausted into the beds, real beds, Maurice and Alexander in one, and Beatrice, Louise, and Rachel in the other. Though she woke periodically when there was an especially loud explosion, Rachel fell back asleep with the brief quiet that followed. The bombing was frightening, but if you were tired enough, you could even sleep through that. You could only go for a limited amount of time without sleep, and then your body took over.

That night of bombing had been fierce, and when they went out to find breakfast, smoke was still rising from the burning buildings.

"This bombing is only going to get worse," Father said as he waited for

.er to drip through the filter sitting above his coffee cup. "Since
. seem to get passage across the Channel, we might as well go inland.
.ould be safer there." Rachel could feel Mamma's body tense in the chair
next to hers. Inland meant farther away from England, and to Mamma,
England meant safety. But she didn't contradict Father. "We can leave some
of our heavier luggage in storage here at the hotel. That way we won't have
to carry so much."

The hotel owner was happy to let them store some luggage, for a price,
of course. They headed away from the coast, once again part of a stream of
people searching for any safe haven.

2

Alexander ~ May 1940, Northern France

Alexander looked back at Boulogne as they took the road east away from the city and the coast. Avoiding the main roads, they often traveled on unpaved farm tracks. There were farmhouses and barns, all of which seemed to be filled with refugees. Good sized barns were filled with forty or fifty people. In the village schools, each classroom was packed with refugees, along with the few belongings and meager supply of food they had been able to carry. They saw families bedded down in the cars and lorries that had brought them.

The sun was shining, the late spring wildflowers were blooming, and there were cows and horses grazing in the more distant fields. It could almost be an outing in the country. Alexander was walking with Maurice and the four young men from Antwerp they had met in Boulogne. Abie was a bit younger than him, Daniel's age. His father was a diamond cutter, and he had been learning that trade. The Lichtmans' father was a diamond broker; Bram, who had also been in Daniel's class, was working with him. Izzy Fishel and Max Birnbaum were younger, closer in age to Rachel. Rachel was chatting with Gabby Fishel and her cousin Lena. Gabby and Izzy's parents owned a small tobacco shop in the diamond district. Lena was an orphan whom the Fishels had taken in.

Mother was certainly not used to this amount of walking. She didn't complain, but her shoulders sagged and her face was set and tight. Uncle Eugene was walking with his daughters. They passed through a village called Carly—just a tiny church, a cafe, one shop, a market square, and a few houses. On the outskirts of Carly was a farm with the barn set far back from the road. It hadn't been sighted by other travelers and seemed empty. Pa and Uncle Eugene strode up to the farmer, who was watching the road, and the others followed.

The farmer looked at the foreigners suspiciously (anyone coming from more than five kilometers away was a foreigner).

"Can we shelter in your barn? We won't bother you."

"I need to ask my wife. She's visiting her sister in the next village." While Pa tried to think of a persuasive argument, Uncle Eugene, standing next to him, casually opened his billfold. He took out a bill and studied it, as if trying to memorize the serial number. Pa said nothing as Uncle looked at the money. The "patron" glanced at Uncle and scratched his head.

"My family is very tired. We've been walking for several days. We won't be any trouble in your barn," said Pa. Uncle made as if he was going to put the money back in his billfold. The farmer nodded his head and Uncle Eugene handed him the bill, shaking the man's hand as though closing a deal.

Pa put out his hand and introduced himself, "Ernest Brody, from Antwerp, and my brother-in-law, Eugene Langermann."

The farmer nodded again and said, "Jacques Marechal."

From the gate, a lane led to the farmyard, a slightly irregular square, three sides of which were house, stables, and barn. The fourth side was open, a big patch of grassland with a view far to the other hills and an expanse of countryside dotted with little houses. Behind the farm buildings in every direction were fields and meadows sloping downwards and then up again further away. Opposite the farm on the other side of the road was a dense wood, dark and forbidding.

Even on such a busy afternoon, there was little traffic on the road in front of the farm. They could see the larger roads further away, circling the spot they had landed, but "their" farm felt wonderfully separated from the rumbling of traffic on the big roads, peaceful and calm on the spring evening.

Like many others in that part of France, the barn was made of stone, with a steeply pitched tile roof. Under the roof was a wooden floored loft. The walls and roof sagged slightly but there were no obvious holes. In one corner was a pile of old equipment: a faded blue cart missing one wheel and some rusty metal farm implements.

Of course, there were no beds or furniture, but the barn hadn't been used for animals in a long time; it smelled of the hay being stored there and the fresh outdoor air. There was a pump in the farmyard, with a bucket next to it.

Louise went up to the farmer, who was watching them from his doorway. "Monsieur, please, where is the toilet?" she asked politely.

He looked at her, puzzled, then pointed to the field. "All of France is before you, mademoiselle."

Louise returned to her family, chagrined and surprised. "They have no toilet!"

Just then, four young men with rucksacks on their backs and bulging bags attached to their bicycles rode up. They would bed down in one end of the barn.

After putting down their bags, everyone stretched their arms and shoulders. It felt wonderful to be momentarily unencumbered. Alexander, Maurice, and Abie put together a makeshift table out of some planks resting on bales of straw. More bales would serve as seats. Mother, Beatrice, and Rachel laid out some of the food they had managed to carry with them. There were three long loaves of bread, some cheese, apples, and several packets of biscuits—the same selection they had eaten from for a quick lunch as they walked. There was water from the farmyard pump.

They ate sparingly; Alexander noticed that his mother ate only a biscuit and some water, his father not much more. He knew his father, ever the provider, was wondering how they would get enough food. Seven Brodys and Langermanns, plus the friends they had picked up in Boulogne. There was only one small shop in Carly, and they certainly hadn't brought much with them.

Though it was early, they were exhausted and were ready to settle down for the night. Alexander, Max, and Ziggy climbed up into the loft and tossed hay down into the lower part of the barn to be piled up and covered with coats for makeshift beds.

"We'll be like Heidi sleeping on hay," enthused Louise. Once they lay down, they discovered that hay sounded more comfortable than it was. The sharp stalks tickled and scratched their legs and arms, and Abie and Rachel seemed to take turns sneezing—as soon as one finished, the other started.

"Hay fever," said Abie apologetically.

Finally everyone settled down and there were just the usual sounds of many people sleeping in one place—sighs, snores, coughs, and the movement of straw as someone shifted in his or her sleep. They were getting used to the strange sleeping surfaces and lack of privacy—or maybe they were just tired enough not to care.

It was barely dawn when they were woken by the sound of a lorry at the gate. Pa and Uncle were first out of the barn, with Rachel and Alexander behind them. Two families with several children tumbled out of the lorry. They were haggard, drunk with fatigue, hardly able to stand on their feet.

"Can we rest here? We've been driving for the past two days, day and night, trying to get away, to get somewhere," one of the men asked.

"Of course!" Rachel led them into the barn, where the others were just waking up. Mother was repinning her hair.

"The roads are blocked, and there's no way to tell where you are. I'm sure we passed the same spot three times yesterday."

"Like rats in a maze."

Without another word, the newcomers slid down into the straw and were almost immediately asleep.

The others went outside to let the newest refugees sleep. The "patronne," Mme. Marechal, came out and gave them some milk, a welcome addition to a very meager breakfast. There was no point in sitting down to anything resembling a formal meal. Mother and Beatrice distributed food to everyone. They could hear Mme. Marechal clucking softly to her chickens as she collected eggs.

Pa, Uncle Eugene, and Alexander walked toward the road to discuss their options. Uncle spoke first. "There's no point in leaving until we know where the fighting is or we could just be walking straight into it."

"But we have to get more food. Maybe you should go talk to M. Marechal. He seems to like you."

"He likes my money."

Alexander wanted to laugh, but a look from his father silenced him.

"Well, I'm sure we'll have to spend plenty more to keep all of us safe and fed, but we should be all right in that department for a while." Uncle went off to talk to the patron and the other two continued to look out at the road.

The evening before, the wood across the road had seemed dark and mysterious, but empty of human inhabitants. This morning, it was bristling with life.

"French soldiers," Pa said.

A Small Door

"Coming or going?" Alexander's question was rhetorical.

There were all sorts of noises, shouts mingled with military commands. Army lorries rumbled along the road, stopping briefly and then leaving. Something was happening.

An officer came through the gate. He was shouting and gesticulating wildly. "Whose lorry is this here?"

Father went up to the officer. "It belongs to a family sleeping in the barn."

Alexander ran into the barn and returned with one of the refugees.

"You must get away! Get away at once!" yelled the officer.

Mother came and stood with Rachel. "What's he saying?" she asked.

"He's telling them to get away, that they must leave at once." They all looked across the road at the soldiers and the army lorries.

"What's happening?" Rachel looked at her mother and shrugged.

Father turned to the officer and asked, "We came on foot. Should we be leaving too?"

"No, you can stay. Stay where you are."

Rachel translated for her mother, "He said we should stay since we're on foot."

Louise frowned. "That doesn't make sense. Why are we safer because we're walking?"

Meanwhile, the rest of the refugees from the lorry had stumbled out of the barn, the children drowsy and the adults looking drawn and frightened, and got back into their ramshackle vehicle.

Father walked over to the driver, his family right behind him. "Can we come with you? We don't have a vehicle."

The man shook his head. "We would take you, but there are eighteen of us. We barely managed to squeeze all of us in."

By this time, Uncle Eugene and the Marechals had joined them and everyone was out of the barn, standing around and watching to see what would happen next. The four cyclists packed up quickly and rode off.

It was obvious the French troops were clearing out of the wood. Equipment was being loaded onto lorries and the men were marching away. Were they going towards the front? Or ... were the Germans coming here and the French retreating?

"Maybe the officer just wanted the lorry out of the way," Rachel suggested, but no one answered.

The patron stood in the farmyard, watching and smoking while his wife went about her morning chores.

From nearby, there was shouting. "Depechez-vous! Hurry up!" From a distance they could hear again, like an echo, "Dépêchez-vous, dépêchez-vous!" There was a shrill whistle and the last of the soldiers disappeared around the bend. Guns were booming in the distance; the fighting wasn't far off. Everywhere there was activity and movement, and they did nothing; what should they do?

Pa was pacing back and forth by the gate. They were all watching him. He and Uncle spoke quietly for a few moments.

"We're caught. This is insane."

"If we wait here the battle will just come to meet us. We've got to go."

"But where?"

"Anywhere at this point."

"We're not going to stay here and just wait for them to come for us. We must get away. We must at least try!"

They gathered their things and picked up their bags once again. It felt better to be doing something, rather than being immobilized in the center of a maelstrom.

Pa and Uncle went over to the farmer.

"Thank you for your kindness."

M. Marechal, who only yesterday had seemed reluctant to house them without Uncle's cash, suddenly seemed an old friend.

"If you need it, the barn is yours," he said.

They shook hands and the refugees walked out onto the road. They had just reached the bend when a swarm of airplanes appeared over their heads. There were rapid bursts of gunfire. They threw themselves into a ditch by the roadside.

Alexander was with his father; Mother, Rachel, and Beatrice were just behind him. Rachel's calf was skinned and Beatrice was rubbing her knee. Mother's stocking was ripped and her skirt was covered with grass. They kept their heads down and barely looked at each other, reluctant to see their own fear reflected back.

Rachel took her mother's hand. Alexander slowly hitched his body up so that he could look over the top of the ditch. Another burst of gunfire and he slid back down.

"Machine guns, I think," he whispered. Again, he straightened his legs and craned his neck. After a few moments, Rachel dug her toes into the side of the ditch a few inches from the bottom. She pulled herself up till her eyes were level with the top of the ditch.

"Get down," her father hissed at her, as he pulled himself up to see what was happening.

They could *hear* fighting from all sides, but could see nothing. The guns were booming, much louder, much nearer. There was machine gun fire sounding incessantly in what seemed like every direction, behind every hedge and bush. Mother and Beatrice remained curled in the bottom of the ditch, but Pa looked out and saw Uncle Eugene watching on the other side of the road.

Finally, Uncle stood up and gestured. They all ran back to the farm, Rachel and Alexander half-carrying, half-dragging their mother between them. They didn't stop until they reached the barn, where they leaned against the rough stone walls, breathing hard.

"Lovely outing. We should do that more often," said Alexander. They settled back into the safety of the barn and stayed inside until the sounds of battle dimmed and they felt they could go out into the air.

It was that evening, in the strange half-light of dusk, that they saw the conquerors for the first time. They heard a special kind of rumbling, different from the noise of city traffic—the rolling of a long motorized column.

Standing behind the shelter of the hedge, they saw them pass: tanks, each with a man sticking out on top; cars with officers standing up in them holding guns; lorries full of men, some with small anti-aircraft guns pointing upwards; and many covered vans. It was getting too dark to distinguish details. Not a word was spoken, there was no human sound of any kind, just the rumbling of wheels and the whirring of motors. It looked like a host of terrible ghosts.

When they had passed, they noticed the patron standing nearby, watching from behind a tree.

"Did you see?" he said, in a voice full of awe.

The next day, they passed again. The heavy rumbling had become so much a part of the background noise that no one noticed how close it was until the first tank came into view. Within moments, they were in the barn, silent, barely breathing. Soon, another sound was added—airplanes flying directly overhead.

Crash, bang, heavy explosions. Shrill yells and screams, hard, guttural shouts of command. The column seemed to come to a standstill. A long, drawn-out swishing whistle passed over them and there was a terrific crash, worse than any that came before. The whole barn shook as though it would collapse, heavy clouds of dust were flying everywhere, coming through the chinks in the walls, and they could hear the screeching of the terrified chickens in the yard. Alexander and Abie stood, as if they were going to check what was happening. Uncle Eugene, sitting close to his nephew, reached out and grabbed his arm. He shook his head and the two sat down again.

It finally became quiet outside, but it wasn't until M. Marechal came, over an hour later, to tell them it seemed to be over, that they ventured out of the barn. The dust had begun to settle, and the patron pointed to a deep, wide hole in the field just one hundred and fifty yards from the barn, where a bomb had fallen. They walked over to it and stood gingerly on the edge, looking into a huge crater.

"Probably an English attack on the German troops," said Uncle. Pa nodded as Mother shivered.

Over the next few days, there was almost continuous fighting, sometimes nearby, at other times further away. They couldn't see anything, they only heard it, the uninterrupted booming of the guns. They could see planes, swarms of them, coming and going and fighting overhead. The dry cracking rattle of machine guns, somewhere very high up, was the constant background sound. They couldn't stay inside all the time, it was maddening. Besides, there were times when nature called.

Because the farm was one of the highest spots in the neighborhood, they could see a wide stretch of the countryside, even to Boulogne, twelve kilometers away. One afternoon, Maurice, who had taken to watching the airplanes, trying to keep track of the battles in the air, called out, "Boulogne is being attacked!"

A Small Door

Everyone ran out to see a large number of German planes, Stukas, high up in the sky, flying westward. One of them made a sudden swoop down, deep down, disappearing from view, and then came up a fraction of a second later in a graceful curve, almost immediately followed by the crash of an exploding bomb. One after another, each of the Stukas did the same, swooping down and up again with beautiful precision, always followed by a resounding explosion. Later in the evening, there was a thick cloud of black smoke on the western horizon.

M. Marechal pointed to it. "That is Boulogne, burning."

3

Rachel ~ May 1940, Northern France

It was evening. The distant sound of shelling finally stopped. They had spent the day in or around the barn; one never knew when the shelling, or even soldiers, might come closer. Rachel was restless and she had cramps. Her back ached and there was no real privacy for "not feeling well" in the barn. Mamma had been able to find some clean rags, and promised they would be able to rinse them before bedtime.

The light summer rain had stopped and the sky was clear. If you didn't think about the earlier noises of war, you might have found it was a perfect May evening in the French countryside.

Rachel, Beatrice, Gabby and Lena went to take a walk. They slipped away before the parents could tell them not to go, and strolled to the path between two fields. On the left, sugar beets were growing, the broad leaves shading the bulbous white roots barely poking above the ground. Beyond the beet field was a row of pollarded trees dividing the field from the apple orchard. On the right, stretched a large field of "colza"—rapeseed, the brilliant yellow blossoms seeming to go on forever to the horizon. Once, when she was little, Rachel had been walking in the country with her nanny and had picked some of the bright flowers. She had crushed the flowers and leaves in her hand and tasted them when Nurse wasn't looking. The unexpected bitterness made her exclaim, and earned her a scolding from Nurse for being foolish enough to taste an unknown plant. But now, after the rain and the noise of the guns, the clear yellow of the field lifted her spirits, despite her physical discomfort.

Freed from the constant company of parents and brothers, they could complain about the minor irritations of life—Uncle Eugene's snoring, the scratchiness of the straw they slept on, the teasing of Bea's brother Maurice, Abie's all night sneezing.

All of a sudden, Beatrice gasped. A long silvery snake slipped out from the field on the right. Rachel held Bea's elbow and stayed completely still, watching the snake. It continued into the beet field, its shiny scales disappearing into the shade of the leaves. Even after it had passed, they stayed still. Rachel felt an odd reluctance to go beyond where the snake had passed, as though it had marked a boundary. But she didn't want to admit to such a silly feeling, even to herself, and she didn't want to go back to the barn yet. She let go of Bea's arm and started to walk again; Beatrice and the other two girls followed.

Their eyes were on the ground ahead of them, watching for another snake. They ignored the clear blue of the early evening sky and the yellow of the blossoming field in favor of scanning the path immediately before them. The walk was now much less pleasurable, but they weren't ready to go back yet. They were so intent on looking for snakes that they were startled when a much larger shadow fell across the path.

Three German soldiers stood in front of them. The girls immediately stepped closer together, as though they could become more formidable by melding into one person.

"What do we have here?" one of the soldiers said in German.

Rachel was paralyzed. Should she act as though she couldn't understand German? Would Beatrice be able to pretend? She sent her cousin a silent message, repeating it in her head as if that would help communicate with Bea and convince herself. *Don't speak English. Don't know German. Don't speak English. Don't know German.* Lena slipped her arm through Rachel's and squeezed gently -- from fear or to strengthen her.

"Schoene, die Franzosischen." One of the soldiers gave her a look and another laughed, an unpleasant sound. He continued in German, "You've wandered far from the house, haven't you?"

"They don't understand. Silly French girls. They can't speak German."

"Not yet."

"Maybe we can teach them."

"That would be fun." The three men laughed, and the girls struggled not to reveal they understood.

"I'll take this one. She's prettier, though very skinny. Nice tits though."

He grabbed Rachel by the waist and pulled her roughly to him. His free hand roamed over her breasts, fondling and squeezing. He smelled of sweat. Her body stiffened, she felt nauseous and wanted to cry out, but couldn't.

"Don't worry, you'll love it. French girls are just dying for a strong German man to show them who's master."

Now she was so terrified she couldn't make a sound. He hiked up her skirt and grabbed at her panties.

"Ugh, she's wet! Blood!" He shoved her away and she fell into the field.

The two others laughed.

"Let's try this one. Maybe she's less 'ripe.'"

They grabbed Gabby, who whimpered once and then was silent. Rachel couldn't see what was happening to her, the men stood between them. All she could see were legs—the uniformed legs of the three soldiers, and Gabby's pale, stockingless legs, which buckled under her as they slid her to the ground. Rachel closed her eyes but she could still hear the men grunting and breathing, interspersed with unfamiliar German words.

After a while, the men let go of Gabby. Laughing, they picked up their gear and walked away. When she was sure they were gone, Lena crawled over to her cousin, who was lying on the ground, crying quietly. Gabby was coiled in on herself, making soft sounds somewhere between moans and sobs.

Beatrice put her arms around the two girls. With Rachel's help they managed to straighten Gabby's clothes and help her stand. They walked slowly back to the barn, stumbling occasionally. Rachel didn't know what would have happened if one of her parents or Uncle Eugene had been the one to see them approach, but it was Alexander.

"I was just coming to look for you." Arms entwined, they slowly came close enough for him to see their faces. "What happened?" The sight of her brother standing there, his hand reaching for her, dissolved something within Rachel. The strength that had enabled her to help support Gabby back from the field was gone.

"German soldiers ... out there ... grabbed ..." She didn't have the right words to explain what had happened. Who knew how to say such things?

"Did they ... did they hurt you?"

"Not me." She looked at Gabby, not meeting Alexander's eyes. And then he took over.

Rachel never knew what he told the parents, but Mamma took Gabby to wash and lie down, and Uncle Eugene didn't say anything to them about how they shouldn't have gone off on their own, though he looked ill. Izzy looked furious, and was only kept in the barn by the combined persuasion of Alexander and Uncle Eugene. And even more surprising, her father put his arms around her and held her tightly, which he hadn't done since she was small, stroking her back and murmuring something incomprehensible into her hair.

For the next few days, the other girls watched Gabby, pale and quiet, hardly eating. Finally, Rachel asked her, "How are you?"

She answered with a shrug, and a bitter, "How should I be?"

Rachel could see her mother watching silently. Maybe Mother could help Gabby? "Maybe Mamma—" she didn't have time to finish the sentence.

"No! I know she means well, but she's not my mother."

The next day, Alexander and Rachel walked along the road that marked the border of the farm. They were silent, an odd situation for the two most talkative members of the family. Rachel had nothing to say. Or nothing she felt she could say. How could she talk about what had happened? Other than a terribly sick feeling when her mind, against her will, went back to the experience, and a cold dread of going anywhere without Pa or Alexander in sight, she wasn't sure what she felt, or what she should feel. Her feelings, her fears, were beyond words—or beyond any words she knew.

Though Alexander was six and Daniel four years older than her, Rachel and her brothers were close. Father was strict and demanding, and Mother was very conventional, falling back on the phrases "People like us do this" or "People like us don't do that." Rachel could complain to her brothers and they understood. They shared a similar sense of humor. Alexander often told them funny stories of professors or fellow students in Brussels. But now the two of them just walked.

She tried to stop reliving the encounter with the German soldiers. Was there something else she could have, should have, done to help Gabby? She couldn't have stopped the soldiers and yet she felt guilty that she had done nothing and guilty it hadn't happened to her.

She shouldn't have suggested taking a walk, but how could she have known what would happen? It was stupid to take a walk with fighting so nearby, but they were so restless cooped up in the barn. It all went round and round in her head. She glanced at Alexander. Did he blame her? Did Gabby? Did Izzy? He had looked so angry, and Lena so fragile. She would never ask.

"Listen!" In the distance was the now familiar rumbling of motor traffic. They quickly moved to the side of the road and no sooner were they half-hidden by a tree with their backs against a hedge than the first in a column of British army lorries passed.

Was it possible? Had the Germans been beaten back? Rachel felt a surge of excitement. The second lorry was almost even with where they stood when she looked over to the one at the front. She could only see the back of the driver, but his uniform was unmistakably German. A wave of disappointment washed over her and fear clutched at her stomach. The British soldiers and their vehicles were prisoners, not liberators.

They stood silently, watching the lorries with their beaten crews passing by. As the column neared its end, she noticed one of the British soldiers, the Tommies. He looked to be barely older than her. It was the expression on his face that caught her attention, a mixture of despair and the stoic resolution not to show "them" what his feelings were. Her eyes met his. At that moment, they each lifted their right hand and thumb in an immediately understood gesture: "They will not beat us!"

The lorry passed and the moment was over, but the expression in the young man's eyes stayed with her. She thought of the boat captains who had told them they were only taking soldiers across the Channel. These must be soldiers who, like Rachel's family, had not been able to get on a boat. She wondered what their fate would be.

Father frowned as he listened to them describe their encounter with the column of captured British lorries and soldiers upon their return.

"We need to be as inconspicuous as we can."

4

Alexander ~ May 1940, Northern France

But the need for bread made it impossible to stay hidden at the farm. By careful management, they had stretched out the three loaves of bread brought with them from Boulogne. An amount had been allocated for each day and divided by Alexander, with his chemist's skill at measurement, into eleven mostly equal parts, one for each of them.

Alexander, Maurice, and Abie set out early the next morning on a hunt for bread. Carly had no bakery, and a shopkeeper told them to go to Samer, three miles west southwest. The bakery in Samer was open for business and had fresh bread, but they weren't the only customers. The queue started at the bakery door and went past the cafe, the post office, and the mairie.

The first batch of bread from that day was sold out. There was not a crumb left; the people who came earlier had bought even the stalest of the stale. They had to wait in the queue for the next loaves to come out of the oven.

Some people got annoyed at having to wait, or having to stand next to whoever they were standing next to. And of course there ended up being some pushing and people trying to get in front of others or claiming that someone else was taking their spot. Eventually some minor scuffles broke out. The whole time, there were German soldiers looking on, watching the "natives" fighting in a line for bread. Finally they got into the bakery, but only were able to buy two loaves.

The next day, they had to walk back to Samer to get bread again. Since they left earlier and didn't detour through Carly, the wait was shorter and they were back at the farm earlier. They had news too.

"The Germans have taken Amiens."

Uncle Eugene said, "It won't be long before they're at the Channel."

Mother took the bread over to the makeshift table, her shoulders slumped. With the Germans at the Channel, there was no way they could get to England.

The patronne provided them with eggs and milk. Once a week, she made butter and gave them a supply. It was clear that the Marechals had other food stores, but with the future so uncertain, they weren't going to reveal them, even for cash. But gradually they warmed up to "their" refugees and produced some potatoes and even a few woody carrots. They let Mother use a pot and cook on their stove. With her usual skill, she managed to make a stew. They had no plates, but Mme. Marechal had lent them tin bowls and cups and they had the silverware they'd carried from Antwerp. There weren't quite enough utensils or dishes, but they shared. The table was short, both in length and height, and the eleven of them were jammed quite close together. Mother dished out the fragrant stew and Alexander carefully divided the bread.

Father picked up his bread and took a deep breath, relishing the fresh, yeasty smell. "With good bread, everything else is possible."

Uncle Eugene murmured the blessing over it, and they all answered, "Amen," before beginning to eat.

They settled into a kind of routine. In the morning, Rachel shook out the bedding while Louise helped Mother get breakfast ready. Each day, two or three of them went to get bread, first at Samer, and later at an old bake oven that had been reopened to serve the population swollen by all the refugees.

One day, Alexander and Abie walked and hitchhiked to Boulogne. Izzy would have gone with them, but Gabby and Lena looked so fearful at the possibility of being separated from him that he stayed back. There was not much traffic, but after a half an hour of walking they were picked up by a farmer going to get his aunt in Boulogne.

"My aunt's a stubborn one, but my mother insists I go get her. Petrol is so scarce I wouldn't go if Maman hadn't been so forceful."

"Wouldn't your aunt rather be safe in the country?" Abie asked.

"I hope so. I don't want to hear what my mother will say if I come back alone. Where are you from?" Alexander introduced himself and Abie and explained that they were refugees from Belgium, staying at a farm near Carly. "The Marechals?" Alexander nodded. The driver introduced himself, "Louis Blanc."

"We want to see if there is any food for sale in Boulogne."

"Good luck. Between the bombing and shopowners keeping goods for their families and regular customers, there might not be much in. Prices will be high too." He glanced over at them to gauge how well off they were.

As they approached Boulogne, the signs of the recent battle were visible. There was the haphazard rubble of bombed buildings and vehicles, even a ruined tank. Many buildings that were still standing had broken windows and debris piled in front of them. Their driver let them off near the center of town.

"If you meet me here in two hours I can give you a ride, though you'll have to sit in the back." They thanked him and he drove away.

It was difficult to find an open shop; many were closed, if not destroyed. But they finally found one that was open. They bought whatever was available and easy to carry—jam, sardines, a few packets of biscuits, soap, and powdered coffee. They just had time to stop in a cafe for a cup of coffee before they met Louis Blanc. In the front seat of the car was a neatly dressed woman in her fifties.

"These are the men I told you about, Tante Emilie. M. Brody and M. Shapiro. My aunt, Mme. Durand."

It seemed strange to be introduced so formally, but they understood when Mme. Durand said, in a disapproving voice, "Shapiro? Brody? Those are not French names."

"I explained, Tante. They are Belgians, Belgian refugees." "Yes, madame. We are Belgians. I am a student in Brussels," Alexander explained, thinking that a student from Brussels had to be better than a Jew from Antwerp.

"Brussels, yes, Brussels," Mme Durand repeated, and settled back in her seat. Abie and Alexander climbed into the back. They were silent during the journey, as Mme. Durand complained about the inconvenience of having her city bombed. They got out at the turnoff to the Marechal's farm, thanked the driver, and took their purchases to the barn.

The rest of their time at the farm, they cut wood and helped M. Marechal stack it in the cellar for the winter. It was monotonous, but for the moment, safe. News drifted in—there were nuggets of truth among the wildly swirling rumors, but who could tell one from the other? The Germans had moved across northern France to the Channel, they had seen that for themselves. With the sound of gunfire now coming from the south, the Germans must have reached the Somme. Refugees trying to go south came back and reported that all the bridges over the river had been blown up. By the French? Or the Germans? Nobody knew. The sound of heavy fighting and explosions could be heard from the north, towards Boulogne, and even further, in Calais and across the border in Belgium. How long could they stay in the barn? If they left, where could they go? The refugees were trapped between the Somme and the coast, with fighting and soldiers on all sides.

One morning, Rachel and Beatrice were in the farmyard shaking straw out of the bedding when a battered car, riddled with holes, sputtered through the gate. A familiar face leaned out of the window.

"Dr. Strauss!" Rachel exclaimed. The others came out of the barn to greet their friend.

Dr. Strauss' suit was rumpled and his face was drawn, with dark circles under his eyes. He was alone.

"There was an incredible crush of people between Calais and Boulogne," he told them, sitting on a makeshift bench. "When the airplanes started coming over, the crowd panicked. Leah's hand was pulled away from mine and she and Annie were swallowed up by the mass of people. I tried to turn back and find them, but the crowd kept pulling me away."

"Where are you going now?" Father asked.

"A doctor I know in Boulogne gave me his car so I could look for them more easily. I stop wherever there are refugees to see if they've landed there or if someone has seen them. I've met many people I know from Antwerp, but not Leah and Annie. I'll go a bit further along this road and then circle back to Boulogne. They can't have gone far, Annie's only eight."

"I'm sure you'll find them. They might already have made their way to your friend in Boulogne."

The doctor gave them a tired smile, as though to say thank you for the kind words, however little they were believed. He said goodbye and went off on his search.

"Do you think he'll find them?" Louise asked. No one answered.

"We should have stayed in Antwerp," Beatrice said bitterly, glancing at Gabby.

"But there are Germans in Antwerp, or there will be soon," Louise answered.

One day, news came from the village. The German "Kommandatur" had ordered that all refugees must return to their homes. The fighting had stopped, at least for now, and the occupying German army was settling in. The next day, groups of refugees, on foot and traveling in an assortment of vehicles, began to pass by the farm on their way back to Boulogne, to Calais, to Dunkirk, and to Belgium.

"If the Germans are here too, we might as well be at home," they said. "There's no getting away from the Germans."

But Father and Uncle Eugene weren't convinced.

"If we go back to Antwerp, we'll be trapped."

No one said what they all thought, that they were already trapped. No one asked where they would go if not back home. The men would talk about it, and maybe Mother too, and then they would tell the rest of them what they had decided.

That night, the sirens sounded several times. Motorized columns were passing on the road again, heading toward the coast.

In the morning, the patron came with news. There would be a train for refugees leaving from Samer at eleven a.m, German time. It seemed the decision was made. They would take the train.

"But where is the train going?" Louise asked. "I thought we weren't going back to Antwerp?"

"We don't know where the train is going, but we can't stay here," her father answered.

They would move on with no clear destination. The barn was clearly temporary. Everything was temporary. And everything they had taken for granted in Antwerp, even after the business had lost so much money in 1929—good food, beds, clean clothes, baths, indoor plumbing, privacy— were longed for luxuries.

They packed their remaining food, shouldered their rucksacks, said goodbye to the Marechals, and set off to walk the three miles to Samer.

As they approached the town, Father reminded the others, "No speaking English. We are ordinary Belgian refugees."

Alexander and Rachel walked with their mother, who spoke no French. The caution was wise; the town was crowded with German soldiers. There were more Germans in the station. It felt uncomfortable to be in their midst. This was their first "official" contact with them.

There were people waiting on the platform, though the ticket window was closed and the announcement board had clearly not been changed in several days. The station clock seemed to display the wrong time. They heard someone say that it had been changed to show Berlin time. The benches were already filled, so they sat on their luggage. The presence of other passengers convinced them that a train might really appear. Finally, they saw a train being shunted to the platform.

And not just a train, but one with brand new Belgian express carriages, first and second class only. There were no conductors, no porters, no tickets, nothing to pay. Passengers just surged onto the train and sat where they liked. Alexander and Maurice led the rest of the family to two first class compartments and they all settled in. The German soldiers on the platform just watched, amused. One young soldier walked up to a carriage and handed a basket of strawberries to a young girl sitting by the window.

The train jerked and began moving. Slowly, slowly they left the town. It never picked up much speed, and it soon became clear why. They were traveling through what had been, until very recently, the front lines. At times, the train slowed to a crawl as it passed over temporary rails that had been laid on top of the ones damaged by explosives. Torn telegraph wires hung down, tangled in knots on poles and in trees. It was like the pictures in newsreels, but right in front of them.

They passed through some villages where only one or two buildings were left standing, and others which looked intact except for a single house completely in ruins. The train slowed and nearly stopped as it went through a railway junction. Along the intersecting track were two wrecked trains. Charred carriages sprawled behind a still smoking engine, litter and the scattered contents of burst suitcases were everywhere. Destruction, but no people, alive or dead.

They relaxed in the forgotten comfort of soft cushioned seats. The soothing effect made it difficult to connect with the reality of all the terrible sights outside the train.

A Small Door

Still no railway employee had come through the train, either to collect tickets (which they hadn't been able to buy), or tell them where they were going. The train passed through obscure towns; everywhere they stopped, more passengers got on, though no one left.

Where was the train going? Lille? Armentières? Some tiny border crossing? Would they be allowed to leave before it got there? Should they try to get off before the train reached the unknown destination? They stopped at St-Omer, but away from the passenger platforms in a shunting yard, and then at Hazebrouck, a small town not far from Belgium. A few passengers left the train. Should they get out as well? Before they could decide, they were moving again. A quarter hour later, the train stopped suddenly at a level crossing with only a small guard house in an otherwise open field. Was it the end of the line? They had no idea what town they were near.

They waited for the train to start moving again. Or for an official to come through with some kind of information. After another quarter hour, they saw passengers from other cars getting off the train.

Uncle said, "This must be the end of the line."

He got up and the rest of the family followed him, gathering their bags. The train emptied and everyone stood outside—families with small children, old people, with as much luggage as they could carry.

Some local people walked over to the passengers. "This is Nieppe. It's about three kilometers to Armentières. We can show you the way."

They walked, and the crowd of refugees followed. But they were somewhat rested and had become much more used to walking long distances. "The German inspired fitness program," Alexander called it.

Father said, "Armentières is only a small town. It probably doesn't have too many hotels." They walked faster, overtaking some of the stragglers.

About halfway there, they came to a river. In it were the bombed remains of what had clearly been a fine modern bridge. Large lumps of concrete, looking as though they had been torn apart by titanic hands, were lying in the water; others were poking up into the air with ripped lengths of steel wire sticking out. Just beyond it, a temporary wooden bridge had been erected and was being used for motor and foot traffic. At the end of the wooden bridge was a sign with the name of the bridge and the fact that it had been constructed in two days by a certain engineering regiment. The sign was in

German. Alexander wondered about the purpose of the sign. Propaganda?

Three kilometers wasn't far, and they were soon approaching Armentières. It was evening but not yet dark. Looking around, their spirits sank. The town was well known for its fate in the Great War. There had been a punishing battle here in 1914, and in October 1918, the Germans shelled the town with mustard gas. Much of it must have been rebuilt, but everywhere they saw evidence of more recent bombing. More than half the buildings were in ruins. Some buildings were partly destroyed, with pieces of furniture and household articles hanging against the walls where the upper floors had been. Of other buildings there was nothing left but a huge heap of rubbish, masonry, wooden beams, and bits of furniture all mixed up together.

There were no hotel rooms available and very few people walking in the desolate streets. They asked the people they met if anyone knew of a room in a private house for just one night. Nothing. Every spare bed and private floor space was taken up by townspeople returning to Armentières who had found their own houses destroyed. Finally, someone told them to ask the local priest, who was in charge of finding shelter for refugees. Alexander and Maurice went off to find him.

They all agreed they could use a hot drink, and walked another block to a square where there were two cafes facing each other. One looked a bit less shabby and they went in. It was filled with German soldiers, drinking, singing, boasting.

"In eight days we'll be in Paris. In two weeks we'll have the whole of France, and then the war will be over."

They slipped out of the cafe as quickly as they had entered, shaken.

As they walked, Alexander caught sight of a poster on a brick wall, a picture of a fat, ugly, and bloodthirsty John Bull, symbol of England, with the text in French, "It is all his doing." A wave of disgust washed over him. The Germans expected this propaganda to be taken seriously. They really imagined that the cultured people of Western Europe could be convinced by such crude and clumsy methods.

They spent the night in a school building that had been turned into a shelter. In one corner of the courtyard was a pile of dirty straw, smelling none too fresh. Each person took an armload of straw to spread on the stone floor of a classroom. The desks and chairs had been pushed aside and piled on top of each other; classrooms had become dormitories. They had come early enough to get a section of a classroom for their group, and they spread blankets and traveling rugs over the straw. They tried not to think about what was in the straw, lay down on the blankets, and covered themselves with their overcoats, hoping, rather than expecting, to get some sleep.

More and more people came in and tried to find a spot. Eventually there were close to forty people squeezed into the room. Someone even had a dog they insisted on keeping with them. Four cyclists (their bicycles propped against the piled up furniture) had arrived earlier and were fast asleep, rolled up in their blankets and snoring loudly. Though the windows were shut, the door was wide open, letting in a welcome cool breeze. It began to rain.

"Close the door!" a woman who was close to it demanded.

"We'll suffocate," came from a man huddled by the piled furniture.

"It's raining in, and we're freezing over here," complained the occupants of the doorway spots.

After some more back and forth, the door was shut. The room quickly became stifling hot, but they were tired enough and they fell into a fitful doze until they were woken suddenly by shouting.

"Laisse-moi! Je t'en prie!" A woman was having a nightmare, arguing with someone in her sleep.

When she realized that no one was being attacked, Louise began giggling.

Beatrice elbowed her sister. "The poor woman. Don't laugh."

Someone woke the dreamer and she quieted down.

Alexander dozed again but was woken before long. This time it was the dog howling piteously in its sleep. In wartime, even dogs have bad dreams. The owner took the animal outside.

"Maybe now we can get some rest," Uncle grumbled. But no sooner had he said it than a man and his wife on the other end of the room began quarreling—something about who had more blankets that descended into a litany of marital recriminations. When they were silenced, someone started coughing. The sufferer coughed on and off for the next hour or so; no sooner had one dozed off than the next fit of coughing began.

A little later, the cyclists got up. They washed themselves in a miniature basin with a few drops from a water bottle. They had their breakfast and rearranged and repacked their luggage, talking the whole time. Even Mother's glare didn't silence them. By now, everyone was awake, watching the cyclists, waiting for them to leave so the others could go back to sleep.

When they were almost ready to go, a second group got up and started the same morning ritual of eating, rearranging, and packing. The family lay on their makeshift beds, wide awake, waiting patiently. Soon a third group rose, and before long, the whole room was a busy hive of preparations.

"Maybe when everyone leaves we can have a short sleep," Father said hopefully. But a bit later it was obvious there would be no sleeping. They got up and put their luggage back together.

Outside the building, Father took one look back. "No bombing, no shooting, no air raid, and that had to be the worst night so far."

"Bombing is definitely better than nightmares, domestic disputes, and overeager cyclists," agreed Alexander with a straight face. Everyone smiled tiredly and walked away from the building.

The next challenge was how to get to Lille, about ten miles away. Even though no trains seemed to be running, the station was still a transportation center. Private cars, taxis, and lorries gathered at the station, selling their services to the crowd of refugees. Father managed to hire a small, old and ramshackle car with room for four passengers and most of the luggage. Mother, Beatrice, Rachel, and Louise would go in the car. Uncle Eugene and the other young people would catch a ride on a German military lorry. Father could not bring himself to ask the enemy for a lift. He and Alexander walked.

They made good time, just the two of them without any luggage, and the walk was uneventful. They walked mostly in silence, occasionally remarking on sights that they passed, but not speaking about what was uppermost in both their minds—the uncertain future.

Outside of Armentières, they passed a vehicle cemetery full of burned and charred tanks and cars. After that, the landscape was untouched and peaceful until they reached the outer suburbs of Lille, where they saw the remains of recent battles. Some houses had been completely destroyed by bombs, and most of the others had pieces torn from the walls, the windows shattered, with some already replaced by wooden boards. Garden railings were broken and thrown over. Everywhere there were the marks of moving tanks, aerial bombardment, and machine gunning.

The center of the city had been spared most of the fighting. But many buildings had signs chalked on their doors, saying "This house is inhabited." Some of the nicer houses had had their locks broken open, and on the doors were posted notices, in French and German, with the words "Occupation forbidden. Reserved for Army Authority."

Alexander pictured the same thing happening in Antwerp. He thought of their home, with the same sign on its door. He pushed the thought from his mind and went to meet the rest of his family and find lodgings for the night.

5

Rachel ~ June 1940, Lille

They spent the first three nights in Lille in a shelter for the city's newly homeless and refugees. It had been a student dormitory, with many small furnished rooms. Each single room held one family—they had two rooms for the eleven of them. Thin mattresses were laid on the floor—three sleepers for every two mattresses. But there was running water and indoor plumbing, though no bathtubs or showers, and they didn't have to share with strangers. It seemed almost luxurious. By now, Rachel could fall asleep with many people around her, and she was getting used to sharing a bed with Beatrice and Louise.

There was good bread, and they still had some of the provisions they had brought. But to get a cup of coffee one had to walk a half hour into town and then find a cafe willing and able to serve that "luxury."

Rachel sat at a table in a dingy cafe with Alexander and her cousins, hands cradling their precious coffee cups. She hadn't washed her hair in over a week (and even then it had been with cold water at the farm), and hadn't had a proper bath since they left home. Her shoes, which had been new in April, looked as though she had had them for years. Alexander's shirt collar and cuffs looked almost gray, and he badly needed a haircut. Though they had washed out their underclothes, she didn't have a single clean handkerchief. She hoped they would be able to get laundry done here.

Louise's thoughts were clearly the same. "Just a few weeks ago, I took so much for granted. Bread and butter, hot tea, shabbos cake ..."

"Marmalade, chocolate, more than one cup of coffee a day," added Maurice.

"Clean clothes," that was Beatrice's contribution.

Rachel added, "A proper bath in a real bathtub."

They all sighed.

After a brief pause, Alexander said, "But they say that travel broadens the mind. We've seen places we never expected to visit—Dunkirk, Calais, Boulogne, Carly, Armentières! We have actually visited the historic town of

Armentières! And now we are lucky enough to be in lovely, scenic Lille."

Rachel tried not to smile and chimed in, "Well, it's good we're broadening our minds, since we're not likely to broaden any other parts of ourselves!"

"It's the German weight loss plan," said Maurice.

"Goes along with their fitness program," added Alexander.

At that moment, Father burst into the cafe, a broad smile on his face. "We have an apartment!" he announced.

It was small, but clean, furnished, and reasonably priced. It had a bedroom for the parents and a kitchen big enough for a couch, where Rachel would sleep. They rented three other furnished rooms nearby, one for Uncle Eugene, one for Beatrice and Louise, and one for Alexander and Maurice. They could all eat together, either in the apartment or at a restaurant.

Izzy announced that he, Gabby and Lena were returning to Antwerp. "We're not getting anywhere safer, and the parents are still there. They're going to need us." Before they left Gabby took Rachel and Beatrice aside and gave them the news they had been waiting for -- she wasn't pregnant. "All" she would be left with was a dark memory.

Normal life in Lille had been completely disrupted. The trams didn't run. The gasworks had been damaged by bombardment, so there was no gas. The central telephone exchange had been destroyed by bombs and fire, so no phone service. All the banks were closed. The Germans had ordered all the food shops to open, but there was little to buy. Supplies didn't seem to be coming into the city, and most of the inventory had been bought up by the first customers. There were things on display, like bottles of vinegar and pots of mustard, but the few useful provisions left in the shops were probably hidden away and only brought out for the regular customers. There were long lines outside all the bakeries. If you waited long enough, you could get good bread, or good bread by the new wartime standards.

Two days after they moved into the apartment, Alexander came back from the morning hunt for bread with news. "There's going to be food rationing. We have to go to the mairie and register."

"Will they give us ration cards? Or will they only be for residents of Lille?"

"We are residents of Lille. We live here. We pay rent. Or at least Father and Uncle Eugene do."

The trams were still not operating, but luckily the apartment was close to the center of town. As they approached the building, there was a long line snaking out the door and down the street.

"We'll be here all day!" Louise moaned. "The whole town must be here!"

"The whole town has to eat, don't they?" Maurice answered. They took their places at the end of the line. Alexander and Rachel stood with their mother between them.

When they saw there were no German soldiers in sight and they were completely surrounded by family, Alexander spoke quietly in English. "When we see how quickly the line is moving we might be able to find a cafe and have a cup of coffee." No sooner had he finished speaking than three German soldiers passed on the sidewalk, barely looking at the crowd. Even the low murmuring of the people in line became quieter. Rachel moved closer to Mamma and Alexander.

The line inched forward. Maurice scouted out a cafe nearby and they were able to take turns going to have coffee and rolls. After an hour and a half, the line was getting restless. They could hear grumbling, but the words were indistinct. The German soldiers strolling on the sidewalks looked more like tourists in uniform than enemy occupiers, but no one wanted to test the limits of their patience, and the complaints never rose above a low mutter.

Finally, they reached the big heavy doors of the mairie and then the smaller door to an inner office.

Father offered his identity card to the official. "Ernest Brody, Belgian, from Antwerp. And my family."

Rachel thought they would ask why a Belgian was living and registering in Lille, but she realized that there must have been plenty of Belgians before them. It was obvious why they were here.

Mother stepped up beside Father and silently held out her identity card. "My wife," Father said.

When it was Rachel's turn, she handed over her card and gave her name. The clerk barely looked at her, just glanced at the identity card and then at her face. He wrote her name on the ration card and handed it to her. She was now entitled to buy rationed food in Lille.

Those hours in line for ration cards were an introduction to life in Lille. Their main occupation was gathering food. But rather than a primitive band foraging through woods and meadows for nuts and berries, their hunting grounds were the shops of Lille. Each morning, they set out in twos and threes, in different directions, searching for shops with something edible to buy.

Vegetables were brought into the city and sold off barrows in the street. There were plenty of vegetables, but they were mostly useless since the kitchen of the apartment had a gas stove and there was no gas. Every shop selling electric appliances had a big sign in the window saying "No electric cookers." Alexander, used to heating his chemical experiments with methylated spirits, went to a druggist where he found another big sign: "No methylated spirit." Though there were coal mines less than fifteen miles from Lille, they couldn't get any coal.

After one fruitless morning, Alexander and Rachel returned to the apartment to find M. LeBrun, the landlord, triumphantly hoisting a small stove into the back garden.

"Found it in the rubbish," he announced. Rachel went up to fetch her parents and they all watched, fascinated, as he propped up the stove on some stones and attached a rusty stovepipe. He had even found a bucket of small, egg-shaped coal brickettes left over from the previous winter. "Voila, monsieur. Madame, you can cook now." It was fortunate her mother spoke no French; Rachel could imagine her response to the expectation that she would be able to cook whole meals on an old stove that could maybe boil an egg.

After locating some matches, Alexander succeeded in lighting a fire in the stove. Rachel rushed to fill a pot with water and they managed to make tea. It was smoky, and there was neither milk nor sugar, but it was tea. Now, in addition to searching for food each day, they searched for fuel.

She was grateful that foraging gave her an occupation, and a chance to get out of the tiny apartment and away from her mother. It wasn't that Mother did anything to annoy or upset her; it was her silent anxiety about Daniel. She didn't worry with words, at least not in front of Rachel. The worry was in the set of her mouth, the slight frown that was always on her face, the frequent trips to the toilet down the hall. When Rachel was with her, she couldn't get away from thinking about Daniel, wondering where he was. He was a constant presence, without his name being mentioned. She worried enough when she was lying on the couch in the dark, trying to sleep.

One day, Alexander and Rachel set out for a shop on the other side of town that was rumored to have tea and jam. It was a good long walk but the weather was lovely.

"All the walking we've done since we left home, we're in great shape."

Alexander raised an eyebrow at her remark and she knew a tease was coming.

"Maybe we'll walk all the way to America."

"What about the ocean?"

"A small problem. We'll figure it out when we get to the shore. You can charm a ship's captain." He continued in a high pitched voice, "Oh please, sir, won't you take me and my family on your ship to New York? We're all quite thin and won't take up much space. And my rich brother-in-law in America will pay you when we arrive."

"And you'll all just hide behind the luggage so he doesn't see how many of us there are?"

"Of course."

"At the last minute you'll all just pop out and dance onto the boat, like in Gilbert and Sullivan."

"With our sisters and our cousins and our aunts!" Alexander sang out. A very proper looking Frenchwoman, all in black, glared at him. All of a sudden, he became serious. "I forgot we shouldn't be speaking, or singing, in English." They looked up and down the street. "No soldiers in sight." From then on, they spoke only in French outside of the apartment.

The oddest thing about being in Lille was how often they ran into people they knew. It seemed as though a whole section of the Antwerp Jewish community had been picked up as they were strolling on the Belgielei or the Pelikaanstraat and dropped in Lille, where they continued to walk, with only a slightly confused expression hinting at their displacement.

One morning, Rachel was waiting in line with Beatrice at a grocer's when a familiar voice called out her name. It was Lillie Goldblum, who had been in school with her.

"I didn't know you were in Lille too," Lillie said. She was with her father. "Papa, this is Rachel Brody."

"Hello, Monsieur Goldblum. This is my cousin, Beatrice Langermann."

"Are you Brody and Langermann's daughters?" Father and Uncle Eugene were business partners, and other diamond people knew them by the firm's name. They chatted and exchanged news while they waited their turn.

Back at the apartment, the parents were interested to hear about the meeting.

"I heard that Goldblum was here, but I hadn't run into him. Old M. Tenenbaum told me that he was here with his sister and her husband, Bernard Levy. The Levys said the Goldblums are going back to Antwerp. Did they say anything about that to you, Rachel?" When she said no, Father was silent for a moment. "I'll try to contact him anyway. If they are going back, they can take a message for Daniel."

"Do you know where Daniel is?" she asked. She had been afraid to ask, though Alexander had said the parents would have told them if they had heard from Daniel.

It had been more than three weeks since they left Belgium. With the Germans in charge, it was hard to tell what was true. Some cafes had radios broadcasting the news, but everyone assumed it was censored.

How could you know which information to trust? Everyone spent so much time standing in line at the shops, so there was plenty of scope for rumors. Sometimes a person near you in line told you about something they had actually seen or been told by a relevant official, but usually the news was something they had heard from their second cousin who lived in a village nearer the front, or you caught part of a conversation from the knowledgeable looking man who was several places ahead of you.

There were newspapers for sale, but they were sure they were censored either by the German authorities or by the publishers themselves, who didn't want to get in trouble with the Germans. They didn't have a radio, but sometimes they were able to visit someone who had one. The local radio news was censored too, of course, but you could get the BBC or the Swiss radio news, which broadcast in French.

It was in a cafe that they heard that Antwerp was captured. None of them said anything. What was there to say? Since they arrived in Lille, Rachel had seen German soldiers up close. She could easily picture them marching down the Avenue Elisabeth in downtown Antwerp, peering into shop windows, laughing at the girls going home from work. They hurried back to the apartment to tell the parents.

Mother gave a small cry. "What will happen now?"

Father answered, "It will be like here. The Germans will be in charge. Life will go on, but with more rules, more difficulties."

On May 28, Beatrice and Rachel were standing in line outside a shop that was rumored to have milk and butter, when they overheard someone ahead of them reading from the paper.

"The Belgian Army has surrendered. The King is suing for peace. Unconditional surrender."

They left the line and hurried back to the apartment, milk and butter forgotten. Maurice had gotten hold of a newspaper and everyone was huddled around him as he read out the news.

Louise was translating for Mother, and she stopped to ask, "Unconditional surrender, what does that mean?"

"It means that the Germans can do whatever they want with the soldiers," Maurice answered before he was silenced by a look from Uncle Eugene. Mother said nothing and no one dared to say what was on all their minds—what about Daniel?

"The Germans won't want to take too many prisoners. They'll disarm the soldiers and send them home." Rachel wanted to believe what her father said, but she was realizing more and more how much of what he said was to reassure them when he really knew no more than anyone else.

"What will happen to the King?" That seemed a safe question.

"He'll be a prisoner, either in Belgium or in Germany, but a pretty comfortable prisoner. The government has already left for London."

"The French people in the streets are saying the Belgians let them down by surrendering."

"They would be foolish to think the Belgians could fight on. They had no chance to win, so the King must have decided to save the men."

"Thank God," Mother finally said.

"I assume Daniel will be demobilized and will go home. If we meet anyone going back to Antwerp, we must tell them that if they see Daniel, or anyone who might have contact with him, they should tell him we're here."

"Can't we just send a letter?" The words were out of Louise's mouth before she thought. "Oh, there's no post."

"And where would we send the letter?" Maurice asked. "To an empty house? Or a defeated army?"

Uncle Eugene frowned at his children, and no one answered. Mother went into the bedroom. So many things one couldn't say, either in public or in private. They spent so much time together as a family, much more so than in Antwerp, and yet rarely talked about their real thoughts. That was probably true before too, but Rachel hadn't noticed it, or cared. But she did have Alexander and her cousins to talk to when they were alone.

Daniel did get word that they were in Lille, and he arrived the first week in June. They had just finished breakfast when the door opened and there he was. Almost before he had his rucksack down, Mother had her arms around him, holding him tightly. She didn't say a word, but tears were running down her face. Father, Alexander, and Rachel huddled around the two of them. Finally, Mother let go and led him to the table.

"Are you hungry?" she asked. "We can't make coffee but there's bread and even some jam."

Daniel smiled wearily at her. "I'm all right."

Rachel looked at him. He looked tired, very tired. There were dark circles under his eyes and he needed a shave. He wasn't wearing his uniform and his civilian clothes seemed to fit him poorly.

"So, tell us," Alexander prompted.

Daniel sighed and began his tale. "When we heard that the generals had surrendered we didn't quite know what to do. They don't go over that in training. But soon we were marched off to a temporary prison camp. It was actually one of our own barracks, but we were crowded in with twice as many men as the place was built for. It wasn't comfortable, but it wasn't terrible. They fed us and didn't mistreat us.

"They separated us according to which part of the country we were from. The men from French speaking areas were put on trains and sent, I think, to prisoner of war camps in Germany. The Flemish speakers were released and told to go home. We had to hand in our military equipment and sign an oath that we wouldn't fight against the Germans."

Maurice scoffed at that. "Do they really believe that?"

"Why not? Many of the Flemish are pro-German," Uncle Eugene said.

"What then?" Alexander asked.

"I hitched a ride on a lorry back to Antwerp. They actually dropped me at the end of our street. Mme. Goetelsman saw me as I came down the street and ran out. Of course, she asked if I had seen Jan, and I told her that he would probably be home soon since we were all being let go. She told me that you had left, which I expected, and that the house had been broken into."

"Oh no!" breathed Mother.

Daniel nodded and went on, "Well, when I went into the house, it wasn't just broken into, but completely cleaned out. Anything that wasn't hidden or too big to move had been taken. Even our clothes were gone. I couldn't find a pair of trousers or shoes to change into. I went back to Mme. Goetelsman and she gave me some of Jan's civilian clothes to put on so I could take off my uniform.

"I had been told to register with the local authorities in Antwerp, so I took a tram into town. I went to see Bonmama and Tante Rosa." He turned to Father. "They're well, though of course very anxious about what will happen next. Uncle Itzik wants their sons to leave Antwerp and I told him I thought that was the right thing to do. They had received your letter; that's how I knew where to find you."

During the evening, while they ate and afterwards, he shared more of what he knew about friends and relatives still in Belgium.

Once everyone had gone to bed and it was dark, he began to talk again. There was no room or bed for him, so he slept on the floor next to Rachel's couch. She couldn't see his face, she just heard his voice, that so familiar voice, telling her things she could never imagine.

"Do you remember when we read *All Quiet on the Western Front?*" They had both read it and been deeply affected. She'd had nightmares afterward and Father had been annoyed at Daniel for giving her the book without thinking whether it was appropriate. "Real war isn't like the book. If I read it now, it wouldn't seem any more real than *Alice in Wonderland.*

"We were with the British troops defending, or supposedly defending, Louvain. At first we were just waiting, waiting for orders, or for the Germans. Jojo, Claas, and I took turns sleeping. We were sleeping on the ground, since of course we couldn't leave the gun. I thought I wouldn't be able to sleep, I was so keyed up, but of course, eventually I slept.

"We never did fire the big gun at Louvain. We could hear some fighting beyond the city, but it was over before it reached us. The Germans were coming into the city and night was falling. We got the order to move to the next line of defense. We walked all night, as silently as we could, dragging the artillery along with us. You can't imagine how hard it is to walk with all your gear, pulling a heavy gun, without making a sound. But you can do a lot of things when your life depends on it.

"We rested and waited during the day, hiding, or hiding as well as an army can hide in the flat openness of Flanders. Belgium is a country made for marching through on the way to somewhere else, not a country for hiding and ambushes.

"The next night, we walked again, and the night after that. Staying hidden during the day and walking only at night, you lose the sense of where you are and where you're going. We tried not to go through towns when we could avoid them. Every once in a while, we saw a road sign and I would try to orient myself, picturing the map in my head."

Rachel broke in, "Didn't you have maps?" Surely soldiers carried maps.

"Yes, of course. But we didn't need to use them while we were traveling. There were so many of us moving together, we just had to follow the soldiers in front of us. And of course, we couldn't have a light. We were trying to travel undetected.

"At last, we reached the River Lys, where the higher ups decided we were going to dig in and defend ourselves. Defend ourselves! As though the Belgian army with a few tanks and some old planes could put up much of a fight against the Germans."

"But you said the British were there?"

"They were, but not enough. We were all spread out so thinly. It was like a fishing net with holes big enough for most of the fish to swim through. It's impossible to tell you about the battle in any kind of orderly way. I don't know how novelists and war correspondents are able to put everything into a clear sequence. When I think about the battle, it's just a series of horrible and ordinary pictures jumbled together with no real sense of time—everything either happens incredibly quickly, in a flash," here she could imagine Daniel's face, "or time seems to stand still. The individual pictures are all so clear to me. The screaming shells, much closer than what we heard on May tenth at home, explosions, men moaning, crying, screaming, and some of those screams sounded barely human, though I knew they came from men, cursing, and more cursing, almost as though the men had no control over the words coming out of their mouths.

"You'd see someone just ahead of you, leaning over their gun, concentrating on their shot, and then all of a sudden he'd be pulled up into the air like a marionette and dropped flat on the ground, and you'd know he was hit, even dead. Or you'd hear an explosion and see a flash of light, and when it stopped, there'd be an arm or leg lying on the ground in front of you, just an arm, separated from the rest of a person, and it would be no more startling than seeing a lost glove on the ground, because there were so many of them ..."

Her mouth was dry and her stomach rolling, but she couldn't say anything. It was horrible to listen to Daniel go on and on, but she knew he had to talk, had to tell someone, and she knew she had to listen, because she hadn't been there, he was her brother, and she hadn't had to see and experience what he had, so she had to be silent and just listen. When they had heard the sounds of battle from a distance, hiding in the barn in Carly, and even when the German soldiers had attacked Beatrice, it had been terrifying, but she knew it could have been so much worse.

"And the smell. I can't describe the smell. It was more horrible than anything I'd ever smelled before and I couldn't get away from it.

"And then a soldier not two meters away from me was hit. I happened to be looking right at him. At first he looked surprised, and then he looked down to where he had been hit, and when he looked down, I did too, and there was blood, only blood, where his leg should have been." Daniel was silent for a moment, and she swallowed hard. Then he began to talk again.

Rachel was awake long after Daniel had stopped talking and fallen asleep. When she finally slept, she dreamt she was walking in the dark with Daniel and he kept telling her to be quiet, and at the same time he was reassuring her that he knew exactly where they were going. Then they were on the beach somewhere, still in the dark, and she knew she had to find the captain of a boat and ask permission to come aboard. Just as she was about to board the boat, it turned into their house in Antwerp, completely dark inside, darker than it had ever been in real life. Rather than reach for a switch to turn on a light, she turned to Daniel, to ask him if he could see where anything was. He wasn't there anymore, but she could see now, and as she walked through the house, she saw that it had been looted, with drawers pulled out, books emptied from the shelves and strewn on the floor, and fragile ornaments broken. A vase of flowers had been overturned on a small round table and she thought, Mamma will be upset, the water will make a mark.

Still in her dream, she walked to the window, but instead of seeing the back garden, she saw the battlefield as Daniel had described it, with men in uniform marching toward her, the same soldiers who had attacked her and Beatrice. Suddenly there was a loud explosion and she sat up in bed, awake.

Daniel leapt up. They stared at each other, wide eyed, until they realized that someone was banging on the door.

It was Alexander, waving a newspaper.

"The Germans are at the Marne!"

It was soon clear that, whether the paper had been censored or not, it was true that the Germans were advancing toward Paris. Now that the fighting was over in Belgium, some of the people they knew were planning to go home. The Fishels—Gabby, Izzy, and Lena Blitz —had gone back. Bram and Ziggy Lichtman were going to try to get to Switzerland, where they had an uncle. Max Birnbaum and Abie Shapiro were headed for Marseilles; they hoped to get on a boat out of Europe. Father was adamant that they would not go back to Antwerp.

"Live under Hitler? No."

Daniel was safe, and with them, and their house had been looted. There was no reason to return to Antwerp.

But Lille was not someplace they could stay. There was no work, the city had been bombed, they couldn't even all live together. Mother wanted to go to England (they all wanted that), but there was no way to get there. The Germans occupied all the Channel ports.

Father had written to old family friends in Paris, asking for advice. The Bernheims had answered right away, saying come, come to Paris. In the big city, refugees were less conspicuous, they could find a way to live. Father and Uncle Eugene talked it over and announced their decision. They would go to Paris.

6

Alexander ~ June 1940, Paris

It was one thing to decide to go to Paris, it was another to actually get there. The trains were running, but a train journey seemed too dangerous. There might be German soldiers checking papers and asking uncomfortable questions. They were Belgians heading away from Belgium. Alexander, Daniel, Beatrice, and Maurice had been born in England, and Daniel was a demobilized Belgian soldier. They needed to avoid official scrutiny if possible.

The parents left with a Parisian who was driving home, and the rest of them headed south on foot.

"Six of us together is too many, we need to split up," Alexander said

"Two groups of three, or three pairs?"

"What if a car has only room for two? Then someone will be left on their own," Rachel added.

"She's right. Cars won't have room for three people. We should be in pairs. And not two girls together. But the girls should be the ones with their thumbs out."

So they walked to the road which led southwest out of Lille. They spread apart by the side of the road, Beatrice with Maurice, Alexander with Louise, and Rachel with Daniel.

A farmer's lorry filled with bags of potatoes stopped first. It was going as far as Amiens but only had room for two. Maurice and Beatrice climbed in with the potatoes. The others stood by the roadside for another half hour before a German military lorry stopped.

"Where to?" one of the soldiers asked in French.

"Paris," Alexander answered. The soldier gestured for all four of them to get into the back of the lorry, his meager French exhausted. Alexander was next to Rachel and could feel the tension in her body; he squeezed her shoulder gently.

The back of the lorry was lined with crude benches. Two of the soldiers slid off their seats onto the floor so that the girls could sit. Alexander and Daniel sat on the floor in front of them.

A burly blond soldier across the way grinned at Rachel. Alexander noticed and resisted the urge to glare at him. A couple of the soldiers tried to talk to them, asking if they spoke German, what their names were, where they were coming from. Though they all knew German, they shook their heads, and Louise said in French, "I don't understand. We don't speak German."

One of the soldiers began to pantomime, pointing first to himself, and saying, "Hans." He pointed to the man on his left and said, "Fritz," and then to his right, saying, "Gunter." Then he pointed to Alexander with an exaggerated questioning look on his face.

"Alexander." Alexander pointed to Daniel and Louise in turn. "Daniel. Louise." Then he pointed at Rachel, "Charlotte." That was her middle name, and not an obviously Jewish name.

"Charlotte," the young soldier next to her said softly. Some of his fellows laughed. Rachel hunched into herself. Alexander was glad Beatrice wasn't with them.

It was a long ride. Alexander and Daniel sat awkwardly, their long legs folded into the space on the floor. About an hour and a half into the journey, Louise whispered to Rachel in French, "Do you think they'll stop at all? I have to pee." Clearly the word "pipi" was universal enough. The soldier on Louise's other side grinned at her, pointed to his watch and made a gesture indicating that it would be just a little while until they stopped.

The lorry parked by the side of the road for a few minutes. The engine was going already when the girls came back and, as soon as they sat down, they set off.

When the lorry reached Paris, they thanked the soldiers for the lift and moved to the sidewalk, swinging their arms and shaking their legs to stretch cramped muscles.

Alexander started walking down the Quai de la Marne, away from the knot of soldiers gathered by the Porte de la Villette, where they had entered the city. They were to meet the rest of the family at the home of their family friends, the Bernheims. Father had made them all memorize the address in case they got separated. He had also told them in which quartier it was and near what big streets, so they could ask directions without sounding so ignorant that they called attention to themselves. He had gone over the instructions so carefully and repeated them so many times that Rachel had said afterwards to her brothers that maybe he should pin a note on the front of their clothes: "If found, return to ..."

As usual, Daniel and Alexander walked quickly. Louise and Rachel were looking around, excited despite their fatigue to be in Paris. It didn't look very impressive though. The girls looked disappointed.

"We're only on the edge of the city. This isn't the real Paris," Alexander said. The Porte de la Villette was at the northeast edge of Paris, and the meeting place was in the direction of the Gare Montparnasse, in the southwest. They would have to cross almost the whole city to get there. Once they were far enough away from the soldiers, Alexander took out a small folded map and they planned their route.

"It's a long way," Rachel said as Alexander pointed to where they were and where they needed to go.

"Your map doesn't show trams or buses," Louise put in. "And the underground," she added, remembering that Paris, like London, had this.

"Metro," said Daniel, "Here it's called the metro." Louise glared at him and he grinned.

"We'll find it as we go," Alexander said with his usual confidence. He shouldered his pack, picked up his bag, and started walking. With mixed feelings of apprehension and excitement, they were off.

Eventually, they took the metro. The station names were tantalizing. Here were the famous names they had read in literature or history, but instead of seeing the places, they were underground. Alexander promised himself that he would go to all the places he had read about. They were here because of the war, but he would get something good out of it.

After getting out of the metro, they crossed the Seine and saw the book stalls on the quais and the boats on the river. Then over to the Ile de la Cite. Alexander pointed to Notre Dame Cathedral in the distance.

They became part of the crowd walking down the Boulevard St Michel, and then at the edge of the Jardins du Luxembourg. After Boulogne, Carly, and Lille, Paris seemed strangely untouched by the war. Of course, it hadn't been bombed, which made it look more normal. There were German soldiers in the streets, swastikas on public buildings, directional signs in German, but none of the destruction they had seen in northern France. It felt strange to be even slightly removed from the war.

Mothers and nursemaids were watching children play, couples were strolling arm in arm, old people were walking carefully on the park's paths, enjoying the summer afternoon. Only the passing soldiers with their spider-like swastika armbands disturbed the ordinariness of the scene. They noticed that the Parisians seemed to take pains to not look at the soldiers, as if by choosing not to see them, they might disappear. Maybe they could learn to do that.

Alexander had never been in Paris before, but it was impossible to be educated in French and not to feel as though you knew the city. Everywhere they turned were reminders of the history, literature, and culture they had been taught all their lives. With their small map, he and Daniel easily found their way to the family's meeting place.

The next morning, at the Bernheims', Alexander hovered at the edge of different conversations, itching to be out exploring the city. Mother was delighted to be with an old friend, speaking English. Father and Uncle Eugene were getting advice on where to look for lodging. Daniel was reading a book he had picked up from a side table. The family always joked that Daniel was attracted to print like a magnet. If nothing else was available, he would read the information on packages. The girls were talking to the Bernheim daughters. The older one, about Alexander's age, was a pretty, elegant woman who was married with a small child. The other daughter, Elise, was Rachel's age.

Alexander wandered over to look at a painting on the wall, idly listening to Louise's eager questioning of Elise.

"I'm studying at the Sorbonne. Medicine." Alexander turned to look at her. There were of course women at the university in Brussels (though hardly any in physics or chemistry), but the girls he knew in Antwerp, the Jewish ones, didn't go to university. And they certainly didn't intend to become doctors. Elise didn't look like what he might expect a female medical student would look like. As soon as that thought came into his mind, he mentally shook himself. He had no idea what a female medical student should look like.

Elise was tall, almost as tall as he was. She was pretty, with large light eyes and regular features. She spoke rather quietly, but didn't seem particularly shy. Alexander found himself drifting closer to the group of girls. Rachel shifted on the sofa to make room for him and he sat down next to her.

"Alexander's a student in Brussels," she explained to Elise, who turned to face him.

"I've just finished my doctoral thesis. I have my defense left."

"In?"

"Chemistry."

"One of the subjects they use to torture medical students." She smiled as she said it.

"You don't look like the torture has scarred you too much."

"Hidden scars. Subtle but painful."

"The torture he inflicted on me was anything but subtle," put in Rachel.

"That's because you're my sister. Brothers are required to torture their little sisters."

Louise added her complaint, glancing over at Maurice, "Some of them enjoy inflicting torture."

Elise answered, "Then I should be grateful I have only sisters—the worst they did was ignore me." His father called for Rachel and Beatrice to accompany him in the apartment search. Alexander was left alone with Elise.

"I'd like to visit the Sorbonne while we're in Paris. Maybe drop in on the chemistry faculty."

"I could show you around if you'd like."

"I would. Since we have no fixed commitments, just tell me when would be convenient for you." They arranged to meet in two days.

Alexander said goodbye to Elise without referring to the plans they had made. She said only, "I'll see you again soon."

Louise answered for all of them, "Yes!"

It took some planning for Alexander to go to the Sorbonne on his own. All his cousins and siblings were eager to explore that part of the city. But when he announced at breakfast that he was going to look in on the chemistry department at the university, and might be there for several hours, no one asked to accompany him. He had been waiting for a quarter hour at the arranged corner when Elise arrived.

"Sorry I'm late," she apologized.

"You're not late, I'm early. I wasn't sure how long it would take me to get here."

"The metro can be unreliable lately." He didn't answer. The metro had been very efficient, but he wasn't about to let on how eager he had been to see her.

"Would you like to see a bit of the quartier?"

They strolled down the famous streets, the Boulevard St. Michel, Rue St. Jacques, Rue de la Sorbonne. Alexander listened to her pointing out buildings and cafes along the way. They ended up on the quai where the Boulevard St. Michel met the Seine.

"How about a coffee?" Alexander asked. Elise agreed and they stepped into a cafe. It was full of students like themselves, some sitting with friends, some alone with their books. They found a table tucked away in a corner. Without "sights" to view, they slipped into more personal conversation.

"What made you decide to study medicine?"

"I did well in school, and wanted to go on. I didn't want to get a job to just fill my time until someone came along and I got married, like many of the girls I went to school with. I want to do something real, something practical, and I've always been interested in people and in biology. Medicine seemed like a good choice."

"And your parents, they approve?"

"Why wouldn't they?"

He was taken aback. "I didn't mean to offend you. It's just ... my parents would never let my sisters study at university ... I don't think it would even occur to my sisters, or my cousins."

"Don't worry, I'm not offended. My parents are much less ... 'traditional' than yours."

"I realize that. In our thinking, Daniel, Rachel, and I are less 'traditional,' as you put it. But we don't always share our views with the parents. It sounds like you and your parents are closer in your thinking."

"Maybe. And in France, you know, many Jews are not observant."

"There are Jews like that in Belgium too, but not my parents. Antwerp is a small community in many ways. Everyone knows about everyone else, at least within the Jewish community and the diamond business. There are the chasidim who only speak Yiddish and live in the seventeenth century; 'Westernized' observant Jews like my father, who have a secular education and act like other bourgeois, only Jewish instead of Catholic; and secular Jews who reject the religion and yet aren't completely accepted by Belgian society."

"And you, where do you fit?"

"I'm a scientist. I've spent most of my time the last few years in Brussels living an ordinary student life. What my father doesn't know can't upset him." He smiled. "But I want to know more about being a medical student in Paris."

They talked, drank their coffee, and walked some more. Before they parted, they made plans to meet again when she was free next.

Alexander went to the chemistry faculty office and spoke to the secretary there. He found out which professors he might want to meet and when they were in. He would have another excuse to come to the Latin Quarter, alone.

By Friday, they had a place to live and Father had found the closest synagogue. The August evening was still full light when Ernest, Eugene, Alexander, Daniel, and Maurice set out to walk to Friday evening services. The synagogue was small and simply decorated, but full of worshippers. Most of the men were neatly but not expensively dressed. Shopkeepers and artisans. They heard French, but more predominantly Yiddish mixed with German, Polish, Czech, and Russian.

As soon as the service started, Alexander could see his father relax into the comforting familiarity. The old words and melodies surrounded him, almost cradling him. Alexander stood beside him, saying the prayers by rote, his mind detached, roving beyond the small building to the streets of Paris.

As the prayers came to a close, the rabbi, speaking in slightly accented French, reminded the congregation that the shul was not a wise place to speak of politics.

"We have not had any difficulties with our 'visitors,' but we must continue to be vigilant. Don't linger on the street in front of the shul to chat. I'm sure your wives will be happy to have you home more promptly than in the past." At that, there was a sprinkling of nervous laughter. Alexander pictured the street in front of the Antwerp shul; the men milling about before and after the service on Friday night and Saturday, visiting and exchanging news. But the rabbi was right—a sidewalk gathering of Jews would just attract German attention. It was a quiet walk back in the dusk to the Sabbath meal.

After breakfast on Sunday, Alexander went out with his father and uncle to visit a cafe where Belgian and Dutch refugees congregated. As soon as they arrived, they spied a fellow diamond dealer from Antwerp, Srul Edelman. Edelman was the kind of man who, wherever he went, immediately made all the right connections and knew exactly how to get things done. Just who they needed. Srul motioned them over to his table. They ordered coffee and exchanged greetings. After sharing stories of how they had ended up in Paris and reporting on the health of various family members and friends, Uncle Eugene got to the point.

"We need someone who can help with identity papers."

"Aren't you Belgians?" Belgian citizenship and the corresponding identity papers were considered "safe," unlike the papers that marked their bearers as coming from Germany, Austria, or worse, further east.

"We are. But we have children who were born in England."

"Ah. Not the best."

"No. Now that the British are at war with the Germans, it would be better if they could just be Belgian."

"So you need someone who can fix the identity papers so that your Belgian children were actually born in Belgium."

Father nodded.

"I think I know just the man." Edelman looked around the cafe. "Do you have the papers with you?"

"Yes."

Edelman saw the man he had been looking for. "Wait here." He got up and walked over to a man reading a newspaper on the other side of the room. While they waited, the three men looked at the other patrons. There were some who were obviously Parisians, and then a mix of foreigners. Before the war, they would have assumed they were travelers here on business or to see the city. Now they suspected most were, like them, refugees.

Srul returned to the table accompanied by a middle-aged Frenchman, who was introduced to them as M. Mayer.

"I understand you need some identity papers corrected," he said.

"Yes. My two sons, my niece, and my nephew are Belgian citizens, but their papers say that they were born in England."

"How unfortunate."

"Can you help us?"

"It shouldn't be a problem. Give me the papers." They handed them over, and he glanced through them. "Alexander Brody, Daniel Brody, Beatrice Langermann, Maurice Langermann. This looks quite simple. But there will be some expenses ..."

"Of course. How much?"

He named a sum and Father counted out the bills and gave them to M. Mayer.

"I'll meet you here tomorrow, at about two o'clock."

"Thank you, monsieur."

Three days after they arrived in Paris, Jewish shops in the Champs Elysees had their windows broken by rock throwers. Not shops that they, in their current circumstances, could afford to patronize, and they hadn't been in the city long enough to even window shop. Each time they heard the news, the details were slightly different. The concierge said with conviction that it must be communists. The owner of the "tabac" where they bought the newspaper said it was German soldiers looting. And a woman farther back in the queue at the boulangerie said it must be the Jews trying to get sympathy.

When Louise repeated what she had heard at the bakery, the older people just looked at each other. "It makes no sense. Why would they think Jewish shop owners would destroy their own property?" she asked.

"Antisemites just hate, they don't use logic," her brother answered.

"I thought things like this happened in Russia or Poland or Germany, not in France."

"The Nazis changed that," Daniel said.

"Was it German soldiers who attacked the shops?"

"There are French antisemites and Nazi sympathizers too," said Alexander. Louise looked at her father. He nodded. "Remember Dreyfus," Alexander added.

August 12 was Tisha B'Av, the day for mourning the destroyed Temple of Solomon in Jerusalem. It was a day of prayer and fasting. They walked to the synagogue in the morning. Along with the prayers, the biblical book of Lamentations was read. They listened to the chanted words with new understanding. The third verse was:

"Judah has gone into exile with suffering

and hard servitude;

she lives now among the nations,

and finds no resting place;

her pursuers have all overtaken her

in the midst of her distress."

The text went on to speak of the people's sins, which had brought God's wrath upon them. As usual, Alexander's mind wandered during the service; he could chime in when necessary without giving his full attention to the prayers. But that line caught him. When they were walking back to the apartment afterwards, he asked his father about it.

"Pa, do you believe that all the bad things that have happened to the Jews are God's response to their misdeeds?"

Uncle Eugene gave Alexander a look, as though wondering if the question was asked in mockery. But his nephew looked serious.

Father said slowly, "I've heard, over the years, of the many calamities associated with Tisha B'Av, the ninth day of the month of Av, besides the destruction of the First Temple by the Babylonians and the Second Temple by the Romans. Some scholars said that the First Crusade of 1096, during which many Jews were slaughtered, the expulsion of the Jews from England in 1290, from France in 1306, and from Spain in 1492, had all occurred on Tisha B'Av. It's difficult to believe all these events were divine punishments.

"And over the past seven years, I've met and helped many Jews coming to Antwerp, first from Germany, then Austria, then Poland, and heard their horrific stories." Alexander and Daniel nodded. They had often been listeners when those experiences were recounted. "Why is it all happening? We don't know. There are many things that happen in this world that are beyond our understanding. You, as a scientist, know that."

"But science questions, explores, seeks to find answers."

His father's tone was the kind that ended discussions, and was also sad.

"There may be questions we can never answer."

Alexander and Elise met more and more often, and somehow never got around to telling their families. Alexander stopped thinking of excuses, he just went off on his own when he was meeting Elise. In between, he stood in queues at shops, took long walks with Rachel, Daniel, Maurice, Bea, and Louise, read, or went to the cinema. The museums were empty and closed. It was a strange time. He had no work, no lab or classes to go to, no experiments to perform or write up. He wrote to Lucas Goossens, his university friend, and tried to find out what was happening in Brussels. Lucas wrote back, but it was hard to read between the lines and figure out what was really going on. The newspapers were worse than useless, and the BBC news, which they listened to regularly at the Bernheims', said very little about what was happening in Belgium.

He and Daniel, only two years apart, and sharing the top floor of the house in Antwerp, had always been close, and they continued to spend time together comfortably. He enjoyed walking and talking with Rachel. She was six years younger than him, and it was only now, when she was eighteen, that he was getting to know her as more than just a "little sister." But if it weren't for his growing relationship with Elise, he would have gone crazy with the uncertainty of his life.

He didn't stop to think about where the relationship was going. He had gone out with other girls before, of course he had, he was twenty-five! But he hadn't been serious about them—serious was his work, his studies. He had no thought of getting permanently involved, let alone married, until he had his doctorate and was settled in a job. But now? Everything was in limbo. He had finished his thesis, but until he defended it, he had no doctorate to show for all that work. As the war went on, it seemed less and less likely that they would be returning to Belgium any time soon. He knew his father wanted to get them all to America, but did he want to go?

He pushed away all the questions and avoided being alone. That was easy—he shared a room with Daniel and Maurice, and he spent his days with them and the girls, or with Elise. He didn't have to think.

One rainy afternoon, he and Elise were sitting in a cafe when the others came in. The cousins were in high spirits after being at the cinema. It wasn't the film itself that was responsible for their mood, it was what had happened during the obligatory propaganda newsreel. The defeated British soldiers in Hong Kong had sung "Tipperary" and the French audience had sung along with them.

"The official at the cinema was so annoyed," Louise crowed. "They stopped the newsreel before it was over and made us all quickly leave the theater. It was wonderful to see how mad they were." The others smiled, and Rachel gave him a quizzical look. He smiled back at her, ruefully.

The next day, it was Alexander and Rachel's turn to stand in the bakery queue. It was early and they were quiet as they started walking down the street. They were almost at the bakery when Rachel turned to her brother.

"The parents don't know, do they?"

"Until yesterday, you didn't know. I'm not sure I knew."

"What do you mean? How could you not know? Haven't you been meeting her for weeks? All those times you go out alone?" Rachel wasn't the little sister he could treat like a child anymore. She was eighteen. And even if she might have still been ignorant and naive when they left home in May, she wasn't now.

"Of course I knew I was spending time with her. But I didn't think about what it meant. If I did think about it, I would have told myself it wasn't important, just a pleasant way to pass the time." He caught sight of Rachel's face. "No, I don't mean that in a callous way. I just didn't know how important it was until yesterday. When I saw your faces, and then Elise's, I knew it was more than I had realized."

They arrived at the queue. Anyway, there wasn't much more to say. Alexander was thinking about Elise. Rachel was thinking about Alexander. He knew he could trust his sister to keep his secret—if it was still a secret.

7

Rachel ~ June 1940, Paris

After the attacks in the Champs Elysees things seemed calmer, and Rachel began her main occupation in Paris: walking. Sometimes alone, sometimes with Beatrice and Louise or Daniel or Alexander or her father. She walked to the shops, where she stood in long lines waiting to buy what was for sale, which hopefully was what they needed. She walked to the cafes and restaurants where they met friends from Antwerp. She walked to see the city and to keep busy.

She thought that if she could add up all the steps she took during that time in Paris and stretch them out in a straight line she might have walked all the way to wherever it was they were going. When she said that to Alexander, he laughed and said that as usual her math was wrong. He tried to explain to her why she hadn't really walked that far, but as always when he tried to explain something mathematical, she stopped listening. But she didn't stop walking.

Even though there were German soldiers in the streets, and German signs next to the French ones, and the curfew and rules about which streets and areas were closed to civilians changed randomly, she felt more free than ever before.

She expected to feel worse, and there were times she was scared or angry, but still ... she could walk without meeting anyone who knew her, her parents or Lena, Alexander or Daniel. No one would remark that her skirt was too short, or what would her grandmother say that she was walking alone down that street, and what a shame it was that she wasn't as pretty as her sister. She could look in shop windows for as long as she liked without Mother telling her that something was not really in the best taste or was probably too expensive. She could walk into a restaurant and order something that wasn't kosher and Father wouldn't know about it. She could walk along lost in a daydream in which she wasn't Rachel Brody, a Jewish war refugee whose life, both present and future, was in suspended animation. She was walking the streets of Paris, and in her mind, she could be anyone.

When she was tired of walking, or if it began to rain, there were places to stop and rest. If she was with her brothers or cousins, they would go into a cafe and order something to drink. They could sit for as long as they liked with a cup of tea or a "cafe filtre" or a cold drink. There were the people passing by on the street to watch if they were at an outside table, or the other patrons of the cafe if they were inside. She would watch the casually elegant Parisian women, who even held their coffee cups with a graceful gesture, the students scribbling away in their notebooks, the small groups arguing, their heads wreathed in pungent cigarette smoke.

If she was alone when she needed shelter from the weather, she went into a church. You could walk into any church, and if you were tired, you could just sit in the back and no one would bother you. She had been in churches in Antwerp with her father, to hear a concert or look at the paintings. He was not the kind of religious Jew who wouldn't go into a church, he thought that was superstition, and besides, it was in churches that you could hear wonderful music and see beautiful paintings, all for free.

Here, in the quiet dark weekday churches, she could sit and rest or think. There were other people in the churches too. Some, like her, seemed to be just seeking temporary shelter. Some, though not many, came to look at the paintings. There were even some German soldiers who came in to look around. And some people came to pray.

The worshippers usually chose to sit or kneel near the front of the church or in one of the little side chapels. Some of them were men, their hats clutched in their hands or resting on the seat beside them, but most were women. Rachel was intrigued by the women who came to pray.

They were so different from the women in shul in Antwerp, separated from the men behind the mechitza, the barrier that divided the sexes. Except on Yom Kippur, very few of them were actually praying. They might have a prayer book open in front of them, and they knew when to stand up and sit down, but that seemed to have little to do with their reason for being there. Many of them couldn't read the Hebrew of the prayer book; they knew by heart the words of the prayers they needed to say, and their worship was in the chanting, not the words, which they didn't understand. Some talked quietly to their friends, and others let their minds drift.

Rachel could imagine what her mother was thinking about on the occasions she was at services. She was observing the other women, their hats, their clothes, noticing an elegant cut, a jaunty tilt, an attractive new shade, and storing it away for future use in her own dressmaking or hat designing. Or maybe she was planning the week's menus or writing letters to her sisters in London in her head. Rachel was sure she wasn't praying.

And Rachel wasn't praying either. In shul, she was either bored, eager for the service to be over so she could do something more interesting, or daydreaming. As long as she stood up and sat down at the right times, her mind could go anywhere, and no one knew or really cared.

But the women she saw kneeling in the churches of Paris, their heads covered, their lips moving silently, were not daydreaming, they were praying. Some of them seemed to be crying as they knelt, or they looked up at the statues or paintings of Jesus or the Madonna as though they were really communicating with them. Rachel could easily imagine what they were praying for—an end to the war, enough food to feed their families, the return of a husband or brother or son imprisoned in Germany. Did they feel that they were actually speaking to God or Jesus or Mary? Was it like a real conversation? She couldn't imagine that experience, though it seemed more possible in the church than it ever did in shul. In shul, she was only aware of all the people around her and the timeless Hebrew words chanted and mumbled like a collective act of breathing, not personal conversations with God.

Returning from one of her solitary walks, she walked down a street where a detachment of German soldiers was quartered in a requisitioned hotel. Ordinary people were not allowed to use the sidewalk in front of the hotel, which was patrolled by sentries. Passersby had to cross the street and walk on the other side. Rachel always tried to walk without looking across at the hotel or the sentries, as though she meant to be on that side rather than being compelled. But this time, her eye was caught by a man about her father's age, nicely dressed, who either didn't know about the regulation or was just lost in his thoughts and hadn't noticed where he was. The sentry, a soldier barely older than Rachel, started yelling at the man to get off the sidewalk, asking rudely if he was a half-wit. As the man crossed to Rachel's side of the road, she caught sight of his face, his expression a mixture of anger and humiliation. She hurried on her way with a queasy feeling. What did it mean when a boy her age could humiliate a man old enough to be his father, someone Mother would call a "gentleman"? You weren't younger or older or respectable, you were German or French, or worst of all, Jewish.

Another day, she was walking back from the bakery, eager to get back to the novel she was reading, not paying close attention to her surroundings. She was waiting to cross the street when a voice interrupted her thoughts.

"Are you going this way?" a young German soldier asked in careful French, pointing. She looked at him briefly, but didn't answer. He repeated his question more slowly, perhaps thinking she hadn't understood his accent. What should she say? Should she lie, but he might follow her, and then what? She nodded, not wanting to speak out loud. "May I walk with you?"

No! she wanted to yell. *And if you knew who I was, you wouldn't want to walk with me!* But of course, she didn't say that. She didn't speak, just shrugged. He crossed the street with her. She should have said no, politely, she thought. But could you refuse an occupying soldier, no matter how politely you spoke? She continued walking in silence. He didn't seem dangerous like the soldiers at the farm, and anyway, there were other people on the streets—surely they would help a girl who was attacked? She didn't want to think about that.

He tried to make conversation, commenting on the pleasant weather, telling her how beautiful he thought Paris was, and how different from Frankfurt, where he was from. He didn't ask questions, as though he knew she wouldn't answer, but kept up the one-sided conversation. He seemed a bit nervous, but whether it was because he was speaking a foreign language or he was shy with girls, she had no idea.

She was nervous. They passed the tabac on the corner and the man who sold them the newspaper most mornings gave her a disapproving look. She wanted to say to the whole street, "I didn't ask him to walk with me! We're not having a conversation!" But of course, she didn't.

Finally, they reached her door. Rachel didn't look at him; she just turned into the building. She could hear him say goodbye, but she didn't answer or turn around.

When she got upstairs and put the bread in the kitchen, Mamma said, "Are you all right, Rachel? You look flushed."

"I'm fine," she said, and went into the room she shared with her cousins.

Beatrice was there, darning some stockings.

She looked up, saw Rachel's face, and said, "What happened?"

She sat down on the bed. "A soldier tried to chat me up." Bea put down her sewing and waited. Rachel swallowed hard and then told Beatrice exactly what happened. "Should I have said something to him? Told him to leave me alone?"

"Noooo. I don't know. What could you say? I wouldn't have known what to do either."

"You should have seen the way the newsagent looked at me. Like I was 'consorting with the enemy.'"

"Well, you weren't. You know you weren't."

"But he didn't know that! Anyone who saw me would think I liked having a German soldier walking with me!"

Beatrice half-smiled. "I don't think so. When something or someone annoys you, it's all over your face. Even when you think you're hiding your feelings."

"But that's bad! We should be hiding our thoughts and feelings now!"

"Well, you can't have it both ways."

"But that's what I want—hiding my thoughts from the Germans but letting the others see the truth!" They looked at each other.

Mother knocked lightly and came in. "I'm going to start dinner. I need one of you to help me."

A few days later, it was Rachel's turn to go to the bakery again. When she left with the bread, the same soldier was waiting for her. Didn't he have a job, or whatever soldiers called it? Once again, he walked next to her back to the apartment. Of course, now he knew where she lived. She thought of going somewhere else, but where? She didn't want to lead him to the home of friends, like the Bernheims, and he could follow her into public places. He didn't seem to mind that she was silent. He went on chatting, about Paris, about his home in Germany. Nothing about politics or the war. He didn't ask questions, except rhetorical ones. He told her his name was Erich. Again, the newsagent on the corner gave her a look. Now he really had suspicions—twice walking home with the same soldier!

She was shaking when she got inside. She stood at the bottom of the stairs for several minutes, calming herself. Should she tell her father? What

A Small Door

could he do?

She would ask someone to go with her next time she went to the bakery. Not Beatrice or Louise either, one of her brothers.

Daniel looked surprised when she asked him to go with her to buy bread, but he didn't say anything. They often went out together when they wanted to talk away from the parents. He waited until they were on the street before saying, "What's up?" She told him about the soldier. "And you didn't tell him off like you did Marcel Goldstein? Or Sylvain Kahn?" Though perfectly polite with her elders and strangers, she had a reputation for being blunt, to say the least, with some of their peers.

"I'm not an idiot!"

His face became serious. "I know you're not. It was a bad joke. You were right to be careful."

"I couldn't think of what to say or do. I still can't. "

"Alexander or Maurice or I can go with you. You probably shouldn't go alone." She sighed. She hated needing an "escort." But she didn't want to deal with Erich again. Not Erich—the soldier. She wouldn't even think of him by his name.

"What about the tabac on the corner? He thinks I'm going out with Germans!"

"It doesn't matter what he thinks." She glared at him. "Anyway, if it doesn't happen again, he'll forget about it." He paused. "Did you tell the parents?"

"I told you before, I'm not an idiot! Of course not, I only told Bea."

The soldier was waiting for her at the bakery. She didn't look right at him, but out of the corner of her eye she saw him walk away, a bit dejected, when he realized she wasn't alone. *Good,* she thought, *that's that.*

It was strange to have nothing to do. Of course, that wasn't literally true; there were things to do—buying food, because of rationing and unexpected shortages, took an inordinate amount of time. There were household chores to help with—despite the smallness of their quarters, Mother didn't relax her standards, whether they were standards of cleanliness, kashrut, or just "the way people like us do things."

But Rachel didn't have school or a job to go to. And neither did anyone else in the family. Father and Uncle Eugene didn't have an office to go to each morning. Alexander wasn't taking a train to the university in Brussels to work in the lab. Daniel wasn't going to training or to his diamond cutting job. Since they didn't know how long they would be in Paris, Uncle Eugene decided that sixteen-year-old Louise wouldn't be enrolled in school. Beatrice and Rachel weren't going to work or looking for work, and Mother had only a few small rooms to organize instead of a big house. For a few weeks, Beatrice and Louise took lessons in lace tatting at a nearby convent. Bea taught her father to knit; he needed some occupation to calm his restlessness.

Like many other people in Paris, they did a lot of waiting. Waiting in queues to buy food. Waiting at the post office or the railroad stations for news. Waiting at consulates and embassies for papers, or more frequently, information about papers. Waiting in cafes to meet friends from Antwerp, or each other, reconnoitering after doing their waiting in other places.

Though shopping for food involved so much tedious queuing, there was more enjoyable shopping to be done. By the time they reached Paris, their wardrobes had shrunk to a few bare necessities. The clothes they had left at the hotel in Boulogne were gone. Some other things had been lost in other places. Daniel had almost no clothes. And the clothes they had were not warm enough for the coming winter. But the famous big stores, Printemps and Au Bon Marche, were open and not yet depleted by wartime. It took only a few trips to replace what they had lost with newer, and more fashionable, clothes.

Mother had always been an exceptionally skilled shopper. She had a sharp eye for a bargain and impeccable taste. She could find several pieces of clothing that looked like nothing much, and with a few minor alterations, put them together to make an elegant and individual outfit. She had always made hats, and even without the sewing box and bags of trimming that had been left behind in Antwerp, she was able to work her magic. But shopping with her in Paris was a challenge. Speaking only English or Yiddish, she had to be silent in public so as not to draw attention. Louise, Beatrice, and Rachel became expert at speaking for her without it being apparent that she wasn't actually talking. Mother would catch sight of a garment and hold it up to one of the girls. They would comment, speaking enough to create a buzz of conversation around their little group. Rachel was able to read Mother's most

A Small Door

subtle expressions and then express the opinions behind them as her own. The shopping, though exhausting, was successful.

As Louise said with delight, pirouetting around the kitchen in a new outfit, "Now I look really French!" The unspoken side effect—they would be less conspicuous in new French clothes.

As in Lille, they had to go to the local mairie and sign up for food ration cards. Everyone had to be there and register in person, so it was a kind of dreary family outing, one that filled up the best part of a day standing in a queue.

It was in that queue that Rachel realized what about her father was different from the other "adults." He was looking around with an expression she had come to recognize. Mother looked anxious, though she tried to hide it, and Uncle Eugene looked resigned sometimes, and often impatient. Father looked ... interested. He seemed to be watching what was happening around him and taking note, and not just to be able to make decisions. Every once in a while, he would share his observations—wondering why one bakery seemed to have bread more frequently than another, or why there was a longer line outside of that particular grocer's even though he seemed to have fewer goods for sale. He noticed where there seemed to be more German soldiers, and would often comment that some of them looked very young, or that they acted like poor boys who had never been so far from home, which they were.

When he said that, Mother looked at him as though she couldn't understand how he could sound almost sympathetic about the young Germans. To her, they were all the same, all the enemy, only some were more dangerous than others. She couldn't understand how in the midst of this total disruption of their lives, her husband could take an intellectual interest in the experience, but that's what he seemed to be doing.

Rachel mentioned it to her brothers.

Alexander laughed. "Maybe when the war is over Pa can write a book about the economic effects of rationing on the general population."

Daniel added, "I wouldn't be surprised."

Visiting the Bernheims was another diversion that broke up the time. Mme. Bernheim was someone Mother felt comfortable with. She spoke English and her father had been friends with Mother's father before the Great War, even before the turn of the century. Mimi Bernheim was one of the few women, outside of family members, whom Mother called by her first name.

Of the three Bernheim daughters, only the youngest, Elise, still lived at home. The fact that Elise was studying medicine at university fascinated Rachel. She had no desire to do that—other than in literature and languages, she had only been a passable student; she had no interest or ability in math or the sciences. But even if she had, Rachel couldn't imagine Father letting her study medicine, or anything, at university.

It wasn't just about money. Daniel would have gone to university, and Father would have sent him. But after 1929, there was only enough to send one child to study, and Alexander was older and therefore came first. But girls didn't go to university in Father's world. He was more advanced in his thinking than many of his business friends and relatives, his daughters went to high school and studied Latin and Greek like his sons, and they had enough of a Jewish education to read and write in Hebrew and understand the reasons for many of the laws and customs. But not university. Not careers.

Lena had been twenty when she married Freddy Kelman. Rachel had only been seven and didn't know how it came about. But she knew Lena wasn't happy in her marriage, not the way Rachel wanted to be. Lena had been a better student than Rachel. She loved to draw and sing, was more skillful with a pencil and had a better voice than Rachel, but still she was married at twenty and now had two children and an underlying sadness.

Rachel didn't think she wanted to go to university. She didn't know what she really wanted, but she did know that whatever she did, it had to be something she could put her whole self into. She wasn't going to marry someone suitable she just "liked." She wasn't going to spend her life doing only what she was expected to do, doing what "people like us do," whether she wanted to or not. She wanted to really live, and she wasn't going to let her parents dictate what her life would be.

Elise was the same age as Rachel, but she seemed both older and younger than her. Going straight from school to the Sorbonne, she had never had a job, whereas Rachel had been working, helping out the family, since she left school.

For well off Parisians like the Bernheims, the war had so far been frightening, but nothing like what Rachel's family had experienced. Rachel felt she had aged several years in the less than three months since they left Antwerp. Elise had a home, an occupation, a purpose, and a future. At eighteen, Rachel was unsure of all of those.

But it was fun to listen to Elise talk about her professors and fellow students. She was an excellent mimic and storyteller, and the people came alive as she talked about them. Sometimes Elise joined them in a cafe, and she lent them books. Reading kept Rachel sane.

Her father had taught her to read in English before she went to school. She used to stand next to him as he shaved in the morning, holding a book and asking him to tell her what the different words were. She read whenever she could, even when she was supposed to be doing something else. She sped through novels as quickly as Mme. Bernheim, Elise, and her sister Juliette provided them. It was bliss to escape the confines of their small apartment or the uncertainty of their life as refugees. They passed the books around and shared their impressions over meals. Father, who preferred reading history and economics, and Alexander, who up until now had had little time to read fiction, were drawn in and read the same novels.

During the second week in September, the BBC news became more frightening. The Germans began bombing London. They sat huddled around the radio at the Bernheims, listening to the news readers talk about houses destroyed and fires burning in the streets. There were few details about where in London the damage was. Rachel sat holding Mamma's cold hands. Father tried to be reassuring.

"The family might not even be in town. People with means have probably removed to safer locations—the country, or Cambridge." Some of the cousins lived in Cambridge.

Mamma was not really comforted. Night after night, they heard reports of the Blitz, as the BBC was calling it, and there was no way of knowing if their London family was safe. Rachel realized that this was what Lena and the rest of the family were experiencing thinking about them, and she tried to explain her thoughts to the others.

"We're worrying about them, and they're worrying about us. But we know that we are all right, so maybe they are all right too. Just because we don't know, doesn't mean that they're not all right."

Mother gave her a little smile, recognizing the attempt at reassurance.

One morning, Beatrice and Rachel went to queue for butter. They left the hotel very early, as soon as curfew ended, to get a spot in the line. By the time the shop opened, there were at least a hundred people waiting patiently, two by two. The crowd was quiet, most people having exhausted their capacity for conversation after the long wait. As the line finally began to move forward, Bea moved closer to Rachel. She was standing a bit straighter, her face set, yet almost deliberately expressionless.

Two German soldiers had stepped in front of the crowd. They hesitated for a couple of moments, looked over the waiting Parisians, and then walked briskly into the shop, ignoring the queue. Within moments, they came back out, each carrying half a pound of butter. There were whispers from the crowd, but no one spoke loud enough for the soldiers to hear them. It took another three quarters of an hour before the girls got their butter.

It was a rainy afternoon, and Daniel, Bea, Louise, Maurice, and Rachel went to the cinema. They were showing an old French comedy they had already seen in Antwerp, but it was still funny. They needed the comedy to drown the taste of the German newsreels that were always shown with the main feature. They were clearly the same newsreels that were shown in Germany. The Germans seemed to think that the French would cheer for Nazi victories the way the homeland audiences did. But on this occasion, they were mistaken.

The same music introduced all the German newsreels. As soon as it began, Rachel felt her stomach clench, ready to hear the announcement of another glorious victory for the Fatherland over the evil forces of Bolshevism and Jewish bankers and thieves. The words flashed across the screen as the newscaster spoke.

"Hong Kong. The British surrender to the invincible Germans and beat a cowardly retreat." Hong Kong harbor came into the picture, and then lines of British infantrymen marching toward the ships at dock. As the Tommies were boarding their ships, they began singing "Tipperary."

To Rachel's surprise, the singing came not just from the newsreel, but from all around her. The French audience was singing along, loudly and enthusiastically.

They were hurried out of the theater by the authorities. Everyone was more cheerful, even without having seen the comic movie. The British may have suffered a defeat, but the Parisians had given the Germans a poke in the eye.

They ducked into a cafe for a warm drink, full of good spirits. Maurice was the first to catch sight of Alexander and Elise sitting at a table in the back. He strode over to them, the rest of them straggling after him. Bea took Rachel's arm and gave her a "look." Rachel just shrugged, but remembered how often she saw the two sitting together talking when the families were together, and wondered if Alexander was meeting Elise when he went out on his own.

She didn't know if the parents had noticed. Elise was eighteen (her age) to Alexander's twenty-five, which wasn't a huge gap, but she had other drawbacks (from his parents' point of view). Despite their long-standing ties to Mamma's family, the Bernheims were very "French," Mother's careful way of saying they were too assimilated and not observant enough for "people like us."

Rachel wasn't going to talk to her parents about Alexander, and she was sure Daniel or Beatrice wouldn't either. Father was quite strict about many things, and Mother was not the type one confided in, so they were used to only sharing certain aspects of their thoughts and feelings with their parents. Maurice was the one likely to give something away, either because he might decide to tease Alexander or because he just blundered into saying something revealing.

Soon after, Beatrice and Rachel were alone in the apartment. Rachel was at the sink, washing stockings and underclothes. Beatrice was hanging them up to dry on a rack Uncle Eugene had rigged up and checking to see if anything needed mending.

"What do you think of Elise?" Rachel asked. Beatrice quirked an eyebrow. "No, I don't mean Elise and Alexander, though of course that's interesting. I mean what do you think of Elise?"

"She's nice. What do you mean?"

"Would you like to be able to go to university like her?"

"Not especially. I certainly wouldn't want to study medicine. I don't know what I would want to study. What about you?"

"I don't know if I'd want to be at university. I certainly wasn't a great success at school. It just seems nice—"

"To have a choice?" Beatrice broke in.

"Yes. I mean, what were we doing in Antwerp? Working to help out at home, waiting until we married?" Beatrice was nearly Alexander's age, five years older than Rachel.

"I don't expect to get married."

"Why not?"

"Who would want me?"

Rachel put down her washing, wiped her hands dry and turned to her cousin. "Of course someone will want you!"

Beatrice shrugged. "Maybe. But not necessarily someone who I might want. I'll end up taking care of my father and Maurice and Louise, at least until Maurice and Louise marry."

Rachel didn't know what to say, it sounded so sad and dreary. Suddenly, she giggled, "Who would want to marry Maurice?" Maurice was a terrible tease, and they loved to tease him back; his looks did suffer by comparison with Alexander and Daniel, especially Daniel. "I do want to make my own choices. But I guess none of us have much choice until the war is over."

"Maybe. But it would be nice to not have one's life path all laid out … though whatever might have been laid out is gone now." They heard footsteps on the stairs.

Rachel reached out for Beatrice's hand. "Someone *will* want you," she said softly before the door opened.

Even though Paris was a big city, much bigger than Antwerp or even Brussels, they kept meeting people they knew, just as they had in Lille. There were certain cafes where, at almost any time of day, you could run into someone from Antwerp. One of them would pass by these cafes almost every day to see who was there and get the news. It was from one of Alexander's old schoolmates that they first heard of the regular "traffic" between Paris and Belgium.

Daniel and Rachel had stopped in for a coffee on a chilly September morning.

"Daniel!" a voice called as they looked for a free table. It was Nussbaum, who had been in class with Alexander. Not a friend, really, just a classmate. Nussbaum hadn't been much of a student, and his family had very little money. He had left school before finishing and gone to work. No one ever called him anything but Nussbaum; he had some awkwardly long and Jewish first name like Itche-Mayer. Rachel and Daniel went over and sat with him. These kinds of meetings all had the same pattern—each side explained how they had gotten to Paris, where and with whom they were staying, and what other mutual acquaintances they had seen. After that information had been exchanged, Nussbaum casually remarked that he would be going to Antwerp the next day, but should be back in Paris in about a week.

"Why are you going back?" Rachel asked. Nussbaum had already explained that his mother and two sisters were in Bordeaux, further south.

"Business."

Daniel lifted an eyebrow. "Business?"

Nussbaum explained further. "It's easy to go north—you just say you're a returning refugee. All you need is a Belgian passport. You can even go for free on the train. But nowadays the train takes up to twenty-four hours. So instead you pay a driver at the Gare du Nord, and you pay a bit extra to ease your way with any officials you might meet along the way. There are lots of useful things one can get in Paris that have become unavailable in Belgium. There are no customs inspectors at the border anymore, and with so many refugees crossing, they couldn't possibly inspect all the luggage anyway. I've been repatriated twice already. This'll be my third time."

"And I suppose the exchange rate doesn't hurt business either," Daniel added.

"Not at all. Well, I have to be off. Is there anyone you'd like me to look up in Antwerp?"

"No, but thank you. Take care."

"I will." And with that, he was off.

Rachel was puzzled. "What did you mean about the exchange rate? Doesn't everyone in occupied territory, Belgium and France, have to use the German mark? How can there be an exchange rate?"

"In Belgium, twelve and a half francs are worth one mark. But in France, the value of one mark is twenty French francs. By bringing marks from Belgium, buying merchandise in Paris, and bringing it back to Belgium, you can make a profit."

"Isn't that dangerous?"

"Of course. But all business is risk—here the risk is to more than your money."

"I don't think I'd want to go back to Antwerp now."

"No, I wouldn't either. But we have our whole family here—or at least the closest part of our family. Think of Abie Shapiro and Gabby and Izzy Fishel, whose parents are still in Antwerp." Gabby and Izzy had gone back to Antwerp from Lille. Abie's parents had sent him a message that he should try and get out of Europe and they would follow him later; he had gone south.

They were both silent for a few moments before Daniel said, "Let's go over to the Gare du Nord. We're not far."

As usual, the cafes around the station were busy. Now that they knew what to look for, they noticed that at each cafe there was at least one table occupied by someone with a sheaf of papers and a pencil, with travelers waiting to speak to him. The "travel agent" was booking seats for the passengers. All the other tables were filled with people waiting for their rides, with bags and packs and parcels piled all around them. There were groups of all sizes standing on the pavement with their luggage in heaps, blocking the way. Vehicles of all descriptions, from nice cars to buses to lorries and even a moving van, were parked by the curb.

They watched as one of the larger lorries was being loaded. First the luggage was taken on board. Each passenger was allowed an unlimited amount, so there was a mixture of genuine refugee belongings, and then parcels, sacks, and bales of merchandise to be sold or bartered. Some packages were even tied onto the roof. Whatever was left was pushed into every nook inside the vehicle that wasn't suitable for a human being. Then they began to pack in the passengers. These vehicles were only supposed to carry returning Belgians, but there were two French women desperate to return to their home in the north of France. They were seated in the darkest part of the lorry, surrounded by a screen of real Belgians packed in like sardines. When every centimeter of space was filled with either a person or a package, the lorry departed. The loading process took more than two hours.

They didn't see Nussbaum again until October, in a different cafe. He had grim news from Antwerp.

"They've been taking Jewish businesses, the ones they think they can run at a profit."

"Who's taking them? The Germans?"

"The Germans, the Flemish goyim, the government. Who cares who it is? Dettmar's hardware—taken. Zeilberger's shoe store—taken. How are the Dettmars and the Zeilbergers and the people who worked for them supposed to live?"

There was no answer to that. Rachel thought about Gabby. Her father owned a tobacco shop near the diamond district. They weren't as poor as some Jews in Antwerp, but she didn't think they had much besides the shop and the little house they lived in.

"The tobacconist near the Pelikaanstraat? Has that been taken over?"

Nussbaum looked at her. "The Fishels' place? Yes. I saw Izzy before I left. They were going to leave too but his mother got sick. Very sick."

After a silence, Daniel asked Nussbaum what his plans were.

"I can't go back to Antwerp again. They're tightening the regulations, making it hard for people to go back and forth. I'm going to join my mother and sisters in Bordeaux."

One morning, Daniel came back from the trip to the bakery with news. "There are notices up everywhere. A new German order." He paused. The others waited. "All Jews must register at the police station or the local sous-prefecture."

"What does that mean?" Louise asked.

"Just that, all Jews must register with the police," Maurice answered.

Louise threw an impatient look at her brother. "No, what does it *mean*."

Father understood what she was asking. "It means the Germans are really here. Really in charge. It begins now."

Rachel asked, "Must we do it? We're not French, we're not immigrants. Maybe they won't know we're here."

"Of course we must. It's an order." That was Beatrice.

And Alexander added, "They know we're here. We have ration cards. We had ration cards in Lille. The Germans are nothing if not efficient."

"But we have to register with the French authorities, not the Germans."

"The French authorities have no authority," Alexander quipped, and then turned serious. "The order comes from the Germans, and they're the ones in charge."

So they registered. Even the Bernheims, who had lived in France for several generations, spoke no Yiddish, didn't keep kosher, and rarely set foot in a shul, had to register.

"At least we don't have to wear the star," said Louise.

No one said, "For now."

Everyone who had decided not to return to Belgium was pooling their information towards the same goal—how to get out of Europe, or if that wasn't possible, how to find a safe place to live out of the way of the Germans. The first step was to leave occupied France for the free zone. Father explained the situation to his family.

"If we get a legal German "laissez-passer" or permit, we can take the train to the free zone, openly and safely. But, and this is a big but, we wouldn't be allowed to take any money or valuables with us." Beatrice voiced the obvious problem. "Without money, how would we live?"

"Or continue traveling?" Louise added.

"Exactly. There is another alternative."

"Which is?" asked Maurice.

"We smuggle ourselves illegally across the line."

"How?" asked Rachel.

"You find, by listening to the right people, where the likely crossing places are. Obviously we want the safest and least uncomfortable route, not one where we have to walk for a long way or wade across a river or spend the night in the woods. We have to figure out how to take our luggage with us. We need to deal with the French authorities on the other side, and some are more sympathetic to refugees than others. The mairie in the free zone has to give us a "sauf-conduit" to allow us to continue traveling on in free France. We have to get visas, and finally, permission to leave France from the Vichy government."

Mother said, "It sounds both risky and hard to achieve."

"It is. I think we try to get the laissez-passer first."

Eugene and Maurice went to meet "someone" at a cafe who knew "someone with connections" who might be able to help with the laissez-passer. They came back very excited. At least Maurice was excited; Eugene, as usual, was more restrained.

Two young men, one Dutch and the other Belgian, had crossed (most likely illegally) into the unoccupied zone. Once there, they had seen the Belgian and Dutch consuls, gotten new passports, and then visited another consulate where they had gotten visas for someplace at the other end of the world (they didn't say where—to protect the consuls). They crossed back into occupied France, which was even more difficult than the opposite direction. With their new visas, they were able, in Paris, to get transit visas to somewhere in South America, and then Spanish and Portuguese transit papers to get to South America. With all those papers, they managed to get into the German permit office and convince the officials there to give them the "permis de sortie" which would allow them to leave France and enter Spain. Maurice finished the tale with, "So, you see it is possible! We can do it too."

Father was interested, but more cautious. "It could be they were lucky. To cross twice without getting caught ..."

Daniel broke in, "But don't you see—it's not hard to pay for a laissez-passer just to get across to the free zone. Then you just have to go to Marseilles, where the consulates are, and do the rest. No need for sneaking across the line at all."

Daniel and Alexander heard that one of their friends from Antwerp, Lucien Hauser, tried the same tactic. He bought a laissez-passer for the unoccupied zone, went to Marseilles, got the passports and visas for his family, and returned to Paris. He used a professional "negotiator" to get the permis de sortie, and he and his family left France.

Uncle Eugene and Father were still not sure whether to follow the same plan. They could see all the risks. What if whoever went to Marseilles was stuck on that side? What if they ended up with visas for someplace they really didn't want to go and were forced to use them only for that destination? The argument went back and forth. Daniel, Beatrice, Maurice, and Rachel were all for sending someone (one or two of them) to Marseilles. Mother was fearful of the risks. Louise was told (by Uncle Eugene) that she was too young to go and therefore should stay out of the discussion. Alexander was, unusually for him, quiet.

The cafes where the Belgian refugees met were full of plans, rumors, and news, and every evening at dinner the family discussions continued. Then they heard a new and alarming rumor—in thirty days, the consulates in the unoccupied zone would be shut down. Only thirty days! Father and Uncle Eugene decided they had to make an attempt through Marseilles. But then came another hitch—no more laissez-passers available, even with the "negotiator."

Beatrice and Daniel met the son of an old family friend, Duvcha Stern, on their afternoon cafe visit. He was leaving in two days, sneaking across the demarcation line and traveling to Marseilles. Beatrice offered to go with him. Uncle Eugene was against it, preferring that one of the boys go instead. Beatrice insisted, and Duvcha, who had come to the hotel to make arrangements, suggested that she would look less suspect. Uncle didn't like it, he even hinted that Beatrice had some "romantic" interest in Duvcha, but at twenty-four, Beatrice could make her own decision.

That night, as they were getting ready for bed, Beatrice was almost giddy with excitement.

"Aren't you frightened?" Louise asked.

"Maybe, a bit. But finally I'm doing something besides going to cafes and teaching Dad to knit. I'm tired of waiting for something to happen or someone else to decide what to do." She looked at Rachel. Rachel wasn't sure she would have volunteered to go if Beatrice hadn't, but she understood why Bea was going. She needed to do something to change their lives instead of waiting for others to decide. They were learning that the "adults" couldn't manage the situation or protect them. They might as well try on their own. She nodded at Beatrice in understanding. Beatrice left the next morning.

While Beatrice was gone, the food situation in Paris got worse. Rationing was extended to more things, and aside from rationing, there were periodic shortages. Lines got longer and often what they were looking for ran out before they reached the front of the queue. At the market, there was a separate queue for each stall, and they spent an enormous amount of time just waiting. Sometimes they would see a long line near a shop. If they asked one of the hopeful customers what was on sale, the person would shrug; they didn't know, but it might be something useful. They joined several of those queues, waiting for a while until they found out whether the shop was selling something they could use.

Small luxuries like canned foods, chocolate, and tea disappeared from the shops. Adults were no longer allowed milk; special ration tickets for milk were issued for children and invalids. Then potatoes were rationed: two pounds per person per month. Meat was rationed and fish became scarcer. Shopping became more and more disagreeable, and hunger became more frequent.

There were more incidents at the cinema and other public places where Parisians expressed their dissatisfaction with the German occupiers. In response, the Germans put in new regulations and tightened existing ones. And of course, the first to be targeted were Jews.

The antisemitic campaign in the newspapers was ramped up. Soon after the order for all Jews to register (which included detailed instructions on who was to be considered a Jew), a new order was put forward, and all Jewish identity papers were stamped "Juif" or "Juive" in big red letters. Then all Jews were compelled to hand in a statement of their financial situation, listing all their possessions as well as details about direct and indirect partnerships and investments abroad. All Jewish businesses had to prominently display a yellow sign, inside and outside their shops or offices. The sign read, in French and German, "Entreprise Juive" and "Judisches Geschaeft."

Many of them put an extra sign next to the regulation yellow one that said that the owner of the business was a Frenchman who had served his country, or that his sons had done so and had been either killed, wounded, or taken prisoner. Some gave details about medals and distinctions on the battlefield, with details of military service to France by members of the family dating back to Napoleon.

Within a week, the "extra" signs were ordered taken down. But despite the yellow warnings, customers continued to give their business to the Jewish shops, and even some German soldiers were seen shopping there. Though they stayed in business, the signs made the shops look isolated and vulnerable.

The next, even more alarming rumor came from Belgium. It had been decided that the repatriation of refugees would be finished by the end of October. Anybody who hadn't returned to their home by that time would be forbidden to do so.

A decision had to be made—would they go back to Belgium while they still could, or continue on and try to leave Europe, as they had intended? And then Beatrice and Duvcha returned. They were greeted with hugs and kisses like returning heroes. When Beatrice was finally able to sit down, she began to explain why it had taken so long.

"It took us three tries before we could get back across into the occupied zone. Twice we thought we had found a way and then discovered that it had been blocked. I felt like a mouse looking for a hole in the wall."

"What about the papers, were you able to get the papers?" Maurice asked impatiently.

"I have the passports." She began pulling them out of her rucksack. "But we had a lot of trouble getting visas. The more exotic consulates aren't giving them as easily, at least not without the kind of connections or money we didn't have."

"So, no visas?"

"We got visas, but for the Belgian Congo."

Louise didn't understand why that was a problem. "What's wrong with visas to the Congo? We aren't going there anyway. We just want to get out of France. Then we'll go to America."

Daniel explained, "The Germans are less likely to let us out to go to the Congo; it's enemy territory."

"Oh."

Beatrice said, "I'm sorry, Dad, Uncle Ernest. We tried. But it was the best we could do without staying away much longer, and even then ..."

They reassured her and told her she had done a great job and they were proud of her. But they were clearly worried. It was another obstacle to deal with.

With all the new restrictions on Belgian refugees and Jews, it seemed more and more dangerous to stay in Paris and wait for the papers that would allow them to leave France. Every day, they heard of more refugees who were leaving Paris, either to return to Belgium or go further south. The adults were up late trying to decide what to do. They agreed that going back to Antwerp should not be seriously considered.

A Small Door

"We left to get away from the Germans; it would be foolish to retrace our steps and end up deeper in German territory. Besides, the house has been emptied," Father began.

"I wish ..." Mother began and then trailed off. They knew she wished they could go to England. But that was clearly impossible.

"But if we leave Paris without the right papers, we might end up stuck. Maybe we need to stay here to be near the offices that can grant us permission to leave the country?" Uncle Eugene asked.

The conversation went back and forth between the two men, with Mother listening anxiously. There was danger in staying in Paris and danger in leaving. How to keep safe and get the papers allowing them to leave?

The next day, Father went back to the cafe where he had met Srul Edelman when they first came to Paris three months before. Edelman had left Paris, but his contact, M. Mayer, who had fixed the identity papers for them, was there. He gave Father the name of someone at the department in charge of alien affairs at the prefecture. He vouched for his honesty and said he could be trusted to give fair advice.

Rachel went with her father to see the official. She listened as Father explained their situation.

"We are Belgian citizens with valid Belgian passports. We have visas, but are waiting for permission to leave the country. Our applications are in, but we haven't heard yet. What should we do to be as safe as possible?"

The man seemed friendly enough and listened carefully. As he listened, he glanced repeatedly at a typewritten sheet of paper in front of him. His latest official instructions? It was just far enough away that Rachel couldn't read what was written. He hesitated briefly, and then spoke, looking directly at them.

"You should not stay in Paris. If you do, you risk being arrested and sent to a detention camp."

Father stood up and said, "Thank you, sir. We appreciate your advice."

The official nodded, and they left. Rachel could see her father was shaken. She said nothing; she was old enough to know not to ask Father for reassurance that he couldn't give.

"Let's walk a bit," he said. It was cool for October, and clear. They were near the Luxembourg Gardens. The leaves had turned and some of the trees were already bare. The children playing, the mothers and nursemaids watching them, the couples strolling hand in hand, all wore jackets and coats. She put her hands in her pockets.

"You need gloves," her father said.

"I have some, but I left them in the apartment. I thought it would be warmer." They stopped for a moment to listen to a man playing the accordion. There was a wooly caterpillar on a metal chair, making its way toward the seat.

"It'll be a cold winter," Father observed. "Look how fat he is."

Even without the papers, they would leave Paris. That evening, after taking a long walk together, Father and Uncle Eugene announced that the family would go to Bordeaux. They would be moving in the right direction, towards Spain, and it should be safer. Someone could come back to Paris, more than once if necessary, to make arrangements and pick up papers. After the encounter with the official, Rachel was relieved. His matter-of-fact warning had, in one short meeting, made Paris seem filled with danger. Even the seemingly ordinary walk through the park hadn't calmed her unease.

She was glad to have spent time in Paris, even in these circumstances. The war changed things, of course, but it was still Paris. But it had never felt like anything more than a way station, and the temporary nature left her restless and eager to go on with the journey.

Alexander had an announcement of his own.

"I won't be going with you. I'm going back to Brussels while I still can." They all stared at him, too startled to say anything for a moment. "I'm going to defend my thesis and get my degree. Wherever we end up, I'll need to have that if I expect to get work as a scientist."

Father answered him immediately, "It makes no sense to go back towards the Germans."

"The Germans are here too, and they'll be in Bordeaux."

"You know what I mean. We've been steadily traveling *away* from them. Everything we hear tells us that the situation in Belgium is getting worse, not better. Why go back when we're closer to escaping?"

"Because it makes no sense to throw away years of study and work.

A Small Door

Why should I let the Germans take away my PhD on top of everything else they've taken?"

"They're not taking away your degree. You'll be able to get a job in America, and after the war, you can finish your degree."

"Not the kind of job I want and have worked for. Not without having defended my thesis. Without that, I have no degree. I can't wait until the war is over, whenever that might be, to finish."

"It's not worth putting yourself in danger."

Mother had been silent up until then, letting Father do the talking. She reached out and encircled Alexander's wrist with her hand. "Don't go," was all she said.

"I have to."

"You don't have to, you want to."

Alexander and Father faced each other across the table, identical blue gray eyes locked. They might have been alone in the room.

Daniel spoke up. "Alexander is right. He should go back."

But his father wouldn't back down. "You want to go back. Universities in America know there's a war. They'll understand that you have everything done for your PhD except the final piece of paper. And we're not without connections in the States."

"The Americans have plenty of their own scientists without taking on faith someone who hasn't defended his thesis. For all they know, I might not be getting through. As for connections, I'll get better connections—names and letters of recommendation—from professors in Brussels. Freddy and his family may have money, but they don't know anyone at the universities."

Father had another weapon. "Are you planning on coming back through Paris?"

"I have to, all the trains come through here."

"Are you going to stop in Paris?"

Alexander hesitated. "Yes, I'm going to try to convince Elise to come with me."

"Insane. She's safe where she is. You're risking yourself for romantic nonsense. This is no time for wild gestures." As soon as the words left his mouth, they all began talking. Mother pleaded with Alexander not to go, not to take the risk. Daniel and Rachel argued with Father. To them, it made sense for Alexander to go to Brussels for his degree. Of course he would stop in Paris on his way south. Elise would be safer with him than staying in occupied Paris. It wasn't romantic nonsense or a wild gesture. Those words from Father were like fuel to the fire for his children. Back and forth went the argument.

"Stop!" Father didn't raise his voice, the apartment walls were too thin for shouting, but his tone silenced them. They rarely argued with him directly. He knew they didn't always do things the way he would have wanted, but Rachel had never outright refused to obey, and she didn't think her brothers had either. This time was different. He could stop the argument, but he couldn't change their minds, or Alexander's decision. Father said, "I know I can't stop you—"

"You can't."

"But I can tell you how wrong I think you are."

"You've made that perfectly clear."

"Don't come back to Paris. It's dangerous," Mother begged.

Rachel wondered, though not aloud, whether the danger in Paris was from the Germans or Elise. They all knew Mamma didn't think Elise was right for Alexander. Too young. The family was all right. After all, Elise's grandfather had been a close friend of Mamma's beloved father, but they weren't observant. Mother wasn't a fool; she knew Alexander wasn't "frum" either. She suspected he did (and ate) things she wouldn't approve of when he was out of the house, but with the right kind of wife ... Not Elise. Not here, not now, in wartime. They couldn't force Alexander to marry someone of their choice, the way they had with Lena. But they wouldn't say any of that, not that it would have made a difference. Alexander was just as sure of his opinions as his father. He would go to Brussels. The rest of them would go to Bordeaux, and he would meet them later.

"I'll leave on the first train tomorrow. I'll write when I get to Belgium. A letter. A telegram is less safe."

"Write in Flemish," Daniel said. Maybe there were fewer Flemish speaking censors, though Alexander would be careful what he wrote. Father nodded at the suggestion, but said nothing.

"Alex," Mamma pleaded.

"I'll be back with you before you know it, Mamma. Don't worry."

"Think about what I said," that was Father.

This time it was Alexander who merely nodded.

He left on the morning train.

8

Alexander ~ November 1940, Brussels

The train was full, most trains were these days, but he managed to get the last seat in a second class compartment. The other passengers were an anxious looking older woman clutching a large bag, a woman and a boy, an older working man, and two young women, about his age, chatting quietly together. The only other sounds were the shouts of the rail workers, the train noises, and the occasional loud voices, in German, of soldiers on the platform and in the corridor.

Almost on time, the train started. He was off.

He was glad to be on his way, back to the university, back to the completion of his work. There wasn't anything left to do except defend his thesis and collect his degree. He could hear his father's voice in his head, "We don't go back, we go away from the Germans." He wouldn't be going back if there was another way, but he wasn't going to take the chance of losing all those years of study and work. He wasn't going to spend any more time than necessary in Belgium.

He wished he had something distracting to read. A newspaper or a novel. But the newspapers were thin and a waste of time, just a few sheets of approved news or propaganda, which was either lies or things that made you angry. And with books—well, you never knew whether what you were reading might draw attention to you, and it was better to blend in with the crowd. His father kept saying that to them, and he was right. Alexander admitted to himself that his father, a reasonable, intelligent man, was right about many things, though not everything. He wasn't planning to live his life the way his father had lived his.

Alexander had never been one to blend in. At home, he was the oldest (Lena was seven years older and out of the house by the time of his bar mitzvah), and at school he was one of the brightest, always sure of himself, always with something to say. He had never been the type to become part of the background. He hadn't ever even thought about it before—how he behaved in a group—he was just himself, Alexander Brody. Now he needed to be anonymous, and it didn't come naturally.

He could take out his notebook and slide rule and review some calculations. They didn't really need review, but it would be something to occupy the time. No, working with a slide rule would draw attention. Just sit and look out the window.

The train made several stops. Before the war, there were trains between Paris and Brussels several times a day, express and local. There were few express trains now. With fewer passenger trains running, the ones that did go had to make more stops. He could see a few people getting off, and many more getting on the train at each station. The compartment door would open, someone would look in, see there were no seats, and let the door slide shut. Halfway through the journey, the corridor began to fill up.

Despite the noise of the train, the journey was strangely quiet. The other passengers in his compartment didn't talk. Even the two girls travelling together and the mother and son didn't converse much. No one took out packages of food; with the ever tightening rationing, even though no one was going hungry, people ate less, or at least ate less publicly.

Just a few hours and he would be back in Belgium, though you never knew how long a wartime journey would take. Travelling from occupied France to occupied Belgium—was that crossing a real border?

There were long, unexplained stops between stations, and times when they waited in a siding for a freight train to pass. In Amiens, some passengers got off and others got on. There seemed to be some delay and all the tickets and identity cards were checked again before the train began moving.

The tracks went through Armentières on the way to Lille. Six months before, there had been smoke, the smell of burning, and the sound of shelling. Now there were just ruined buildings in the wintry dusk.

At Lille, there was another ticket and identity card check. This time, the conductor employed by the railway was accompanied by a German soldier. The soldier scrutinized Alexander's papers, looking from the photograph to his face. A small movement of his head brought a second soldier over.

"Brody, is that a Belgian name?" he asked his colleague in German. The other soldier looked at the papers, then at Alexander.

"Maybe a Jew?"

Without letting on he spoke German, Alexander asked in French, "Is there a problem?" When the soldiers ignored him, he repeated his question in Flemish.

The first soldier asked him, very slowly, in German, what he was going to do in Brussels. Though he understood very well, Alexander looked puzzled. The soldier repeated the question even more slowly.

Alexander answered, still in Flemish, "Student."

After studying his papers again, the soldier nodded and they moved on.

Alexander breathed a silent sigh. His papers had passed muster. They contained only one lie, stating he was born in Antwerp, not London. But what was most dangerous—being British, Jewish, a university student? How many lies could you tell before you got caught out? What part of who you were could land you in trouble?

He arrived in Brussels and got on a tram. The schoolboy sitting beside him was chuckling as he read the comic strips in the newspaper. Seeing Alexander's sidelong glance, the boy passed the paper to him as he got off.

"Tintin ... always good!"

Alexander looked at the strip. Two men, obvious caricatures of Jewish businessmen, were talking about the expected crash of an asteroid on Earth. One of them laughed as he gleefully predicted that the crash would free him of all his debts to suppliers.

He got off the tram to walk the final blocks to the Goossens' house and threw the paper in the nearest rubbish bin.

Lucas wasn't home from the university yet, but Mme. Goossens greeted him warmly.

"Are you planning to go to Antwerp?" she asked after serving him a cup of tea and hearing all his news of the family.

"I should see my grandmother and my aunt." She looked as though she wanted to say something. "What do you hear about things in Antwerp?"

"There's a German appointed council—the Association des Juifs en Belgique—and all Jews are supposed to be registered. For the registered, there's a dusk to dawn curfew, and all Jewish businesses are labeled." He nodded. They had heard the same from friends in France. "I've been to see Mme.

Brody and your aunt. They've not registered and are trying to avoid going out if they can," she hesitated again. "If you go, be very careful," but before she said any more, Lucas came in and greeted him enthusiastically.

Over dinner, Alexander heard about the progress of Lucas' research, which was going too slowly, with several failed experiments and dead ends.

Alexander joked, "I always said I'd finish before you."

Lucas shook his head in mock despair and went on to fill him in on news of their fellow students and the academic gossip of the chemistry and physics departments.

"It's tricky, but the university's pushed back against some of the new German rules. They were told to let go of all the Jewish teachers, but they didn't, though no one knows how long they'll be able to hold out." They were silent for a moment, then Lucas asked, "What are your plans?"

"I've written to Professor Vermeulen, but given him no details about when and if I planned to return." Lucas nodded. It was better to disclose no information in writing that a censor, or even a nosy postal worker or secretary, might see. "I'll go see him tomorrow and find out when my defense can be scheduled. My father and uncle are working on getting the right papers, and it would be better if I could rejoin them as soon as possible."

"Vermeulen should be in tomorrow. I'll go with you."

Luckily, Professor Vermeulen liked to be in the lab early and they were able to enter the building without running into anyone they knew.

"Brody! I was wondering when you'd turn up."

Alexander breathed a sigh of relief. He knew Vermeulen liked him, but he had been wary of counting on too warm a reception. The professor immediately began talking science, further putting Alexander at ease. And he was the one who brought up the subject foremost in Alexander's mind.

"We should schedule your defense soon. I've been thinking about who should be on the committee." He named several professors in the department. One name struck Alexander.

"Professor Renard. I don't think he likes me."

"I know what you're thinking. He definitely leans toward the Germans, and he's an antisemitic bastard, but scientifically, he's fair. He'll recognize the value of your work. And it would be hard not to have him, given how close his field is to yours." Alexander nodded. He trusted Vermeulen. Besides being a solid scientist and a brilliant teacher, he had good political instincts. His PhD students always did well.

Lucas had shut the lab door when they came in and they heard a loud squeak as it opened. Antoine Leclerq, a graduate student about a year behind Alexander, looked surprised to see him.

"Brody! I didn't know you were back."

Professor Vermeulen addressed Leclerq before Alexander could respond. "Our appointment wasn't until later, Leclerq. I have some things to take care of before I can sit down and go through those ideas with you."

"I know. I was in early and thought I'd check if you'd had a chance to go over the paper I gave you. If you haven't, we can change our meeting time. If you have other things to do …"

The professor frowned slightly. "No. I've read the paper. We'll meet at two, as arranged."

"Fine," Leclerq moved toward the door, then stopped. "I can have a word with the janitor about fixing the squeak in the door," and as Vermeulen continued to frown, he added, "if you like."

"Don't bother. I quite enjoy the squeak." Leclerq left and Lucas went to make sure the door was shut before Vermeulen said, "It can be quite useful." He turned back to Alexander. "I should be able to see everyone we've mentioned before next week. I'll try to schedule the first meeting as soon as I can. Then you and I can go over the work to prepare. Where will you be staying?"

"With Goossens. I'll be going to Antwerp, but only briefly."

"Be careful there. From what I hear, the climate is less pleasant than here in Brussels. And I don't have to warn you about keeping a low profile here. Leclerq will of course spread the word that you're back, but I suggest you work here or at Goossens' rather than in more public spaces. No need to flaunt your presence." Alexander tried to thank the professor but Vermeulen cut him off, "Politics notwithstanding, there are standards, both in science and in human morality, that will continue past this war. Now, we just need to arrange to secure your degree."

After the veiled, and more open, warnings from Lucas, Mme. Goossens, and Professor Vermeulen, Alexander didn't know what to expect in Antwerp. It was certainly odd to get on the train with a feeling of apprehension, a train he'd taken almost every weekday for years without being in any way aware of his surroundings. Instead of getting off in Berchem, the suburban stop closest to home, he stayed on till the central station.

There were German soldiers inside the station and on the street outside. As he went towards his aunt's apartment, he was careful to walk with a measured pace, neither rushing nor walking too slowly. He resisted the urge to let his eyes search for familiar faces among the people he passed. He wasn't quite sure what he would do if he did meet someone he knew. Stop and talk in the middle of the street? Share news? He was relieved when he reached his destination without having to answer that question.

He climbed the three flights of stairs to Tante Rosa's apartment and knocked on the door. The door opened slightly and he saw a sliver of his aunt's pale, thin face looking out anxiously. When she recognized him, she pulled him in quickly, shut the door, and enveloped him in a tight embrace. He never remembered his aunt hugging him before.

"Mamma, Mamma," she called, followed by a stream of incomprehensible Hungarian; the only word he recognized was his own name. His grandmother shuffled into the room, looking exactly as she always had, with none of her daughter's effusive excitement. Uncle Itzik followed his mother-in-law, with a smile and a happy greeting for his nephew. They drew him into the dining room. Finally, Tante Rosa stopped fluttering around and sat.

"So, explain," said Uncle Itzik. "Are you alone? Why are you back? Is everyone well?"

Alexander explained. Where the rest of the family was. That they were all well. That he was back to finish his degree and get the formal piece of paper. That he was staying in Brussels to do that, and once he was finished, he would rejoin the family in France.

"I thought you were finished with the university," said his grandmother. "Your parents said you were done." Her voice, as usual, sounded mildly accusatory. He explained again that though the research, writing, and exam taking were over, his thesis had to be accepted by a committee of professors before he could receive his degree. She nodded, but he knew she was only convinced that once again they had not told her the complete story, and that her grandchildren would still most likely disappoint her.

"Did you see many soldiers?" Tante Rosa asked fearfully.

He wasn't sure what to answer. What was many? There were of course more than the last time he had been here, in May 1940 (when there were none), but not more than he expected to see. Antwerp was occupied, just like Brussels and Paris.

"Not too many."

"We try not to go out more than we have to," she said, and Alexander could hear Uncle Itzik's foot tapping nervously on the floor. He looked at his uncle. Never a big man, Uncle Itzik looked as though he had shrunk in the last half year. His shoulders were more hunched, his nose and bushy eyebrows bigger, with his face seeming to take up less space than his most prominent features. Alexander looked at his watch.

"I need to leave to catch the train before it gets dark." The late December dusk came so early.

"Will you come again?" his grandmother asked.

Uncle Itzik shook his head, ever so slightly.

"Be very careful," was his aunt's way of telling him not to come without contradicting her mother.

They walked him to the door. Awkwardly, he kissed each of them on the cheek. He wasn't surprised that his aunt clung to him briefly. But his grandmother held onto him for a moment longer, and whispered in Yiddish, "Be safe."

There were two German soldiers at the end of the street, smoking. He was careful not to pick up his pace. He looked up and one of the soldiers caught his eye and glared at him. He kept on walking. There was a slight queasiness in his stomach, followed by a wave of anger. This was his city! How dare someone make him feel threatened here in his hometown! But he said nothing, just walked to the station and caught the train back to Brussels.

New Year's came and went with more hope than expectation. Maybe 1941 would be better than 1940, but no one was counting on it. The war news (the real war news from the BBC) was not encouraging. Cardiff and Portsmouth were bombed early in January. Right before New Year's, London experienced the worst bombing of the Blitz so far. The Old Bailey, the Guildhall, and several Christopher Wren churches were badly damaged. Alexander hadn't been in London in several years, but as he listened to the BBC with the Goossens, he could picture the familiar landmarks and found it hard to imagine the city without them. But despite the bombing, the British seemed to be holding on. He could imagine his English aunts tidying up the dust after an attack, putting the kettle on for tea and making mild complaints about the inconvenience. It was a warming thought. It didn't seem that the Americans were likely to join the war any time soon. Charles Lindbergh had given a speech before Congress recommending that America negotiate a neutrality pact with Hitler.

There was discouraging news from inside Belgium too. Leon Degrelle, leader of Wallonia's fascists, the Rexist Party, gave a speech in Liege announcing the party's support for Nazism. It wasn't surprising, but it added to the gloom. No Jew who grew up in Belgium was a stranger to antisemitism. There were thugs in Antwerp who called Alexander and his friends names and threw rocks at them. There were students in the high school who avoided having anything to do with Jews, including one who conspicuously brushed invisible dust off his clothes if a Jewish student happened to touch him. And there were teachers who had different, much tougher standards when grading Jewish students' work.

The newspapers of the far right, especially during the Depression years, complained about "Germans," mostly Jewish refugees, "flooding" into the country. Antisemites of the left blamed Jewish capitalists for the country's economic distress, and those of the right blamed Jewish communists.

But they never thought it would be like Germany. They not only heard Hitler's speeches broadcast on the radio, but they heard from the refugees seeking safety in Antwerp what life had become for Jews in Hitler's Germany. Alexander's father had helped many of the refugees, giving them a place to stay, finding work for them and helping them to deal with the authorities, and Alexander had met many of them and heard their stories.

Soon after the turn of the year, Alexander received letters from Daniel and Rachel in Bayonne. Even knowing there might be darker news they weren't writing, the letters cheered him. Clearly they were happier in Bayonne than in Bordeaux, despite the crowded accommodations. Reading Daniel's descriptions of the nighttime "symphony" of snores from Father and Uncle Eugene, and how Maurice's tossing and turning had almost booted him out of the bed on several occasions, made Alexander even more grateful for his narrow cot in Lucas' bedroom.

Rachel was almost lyrical as she described the beach in Biarritz and the small pleasures available to them in the resort town. She didn't complain about the sleeping arrangements—maybe none of his female relatives snored or kicked. Considering the circumstances, they were strange letters. There was barely any mention of the most important things on their minds. They didn't ask about his work—interest was implied. The only mention of the continuing quest for exit papers, visas, or laissez-passers was a brief addition from his father at the end of Rachel's letter: "We expect to hear from our friend in the city soon." Mother didn't write at all, it being thought too dangerous to write in English. Rachel did add a typically "motherish" message—"Mamma says to take care to keep bundled up in the cold, and don't forget to give our deepest thanks to Mme. Goossens."

Despite the paucity of real news, the letters gave Alexander pleasure. He had been so eager to leave and get back to the university, so focused on his "mission," that he didn't realize how much he was missing the family. Rachel and Daniel both wrote well—he could hear their voices as he read their letters.

There was a letter from Elise as well. She told him about her lectures, particularly her chemistry class. In Paris, they had talked about how much chemistry a doctor really needed to know. She didn't enjoy the subject and claimed one could be a perfectly good doctor with less of it. Biology, pathology, anatomy, and physiology—they were important—but chemistry was just an added unpleasant chore.

No, he had argued, everything depended on chemistry and on physics. If a doctor was to be truly modern, and not just a glorified nurse, he or she needed to be a scientist and understand the basic principles that supported all the other subjects. He had gotten rather impassioned and proclaimed, "Chemistry is life!" She had just looked at him and quirked her eyebrow, and he had burst out laughing. She had that ability to bring him back down to earth without totally deflating him.

The letter gave news of her family and of her friends he had met. She told him about the films she had seen and asked if he had gone to the cinema in Brussels. Nothing about the war, rationing, the Germans. It was a good letter.

Alexander was impatiently waiting for news about his defense committee. Everything at the university was moving even more slowly than usual. The Christmas holidays, when professors and staff were harder to reach, had started early and dragged on way into January. Professor Vermeulen and Lucas explained that everyone felt so unsure about the future that they avoided being at the university more than they needed to, using the holidays as an excuse to be less available. If you weren't in your office, no one could involve you in a political conversation or controversy. Fuel shortages meant the buildings were even harder to heat than usual, and the newspaper (the weather statistics were generally believable) said that the winter of 1940–1941 was turning out to be the coldest in many years. When M. Goossens, Lucas' father, read that out to the family one morning at breakfast, Alexander and Lucas looked at each other.

"I guess they can't lie about that," Alexander commented.

All the waiting was difficult. He had gone over his thesis, edited, checked, and recalculated. He read, walked, saw a few safe university friends in Brussels, wrote letters to the family and Elise. He went to the cinema and sat in the dark corners of warm cafes nursing a single cup of ersatz coffee or a glass of beer. Going to Antwerp might put both him and the relatives there in danger, so he didn't go. And to be truthful, facing his aunt's worry, his uncle's restless anxiety, and his grandmother's habitual sour disapproval didn't tempt him. So he waited.

Anxious though he was, he didn't want to pester Professor Vermeulen. He tried to not visit him more than twice a week. But the first week in February, the professor had good news for him.

"I've scraped together enough money to hire you as my temporary assistant." Alexander began to protest but Vermeulen talked over him. "It's not charity. The money is to help prepare some experiments and edit a few papers for publication. It has to be done anyway, and this way you have a reason to be here. I can't hire you to assist in my classes, but you can do this." Though the faculty had managed to hold on to their Jewish instructors despite official pressure, they couldn't hire anyone new. "And this way you won't get into trouble."

"I wasn't planning on getting into trouble."

"Of course not. But too much free time, coupled with your natural impatience and the kind of over enthusiastic policing that goes on now, is a recipe for trouble. I plan to send you back to your family in one piece, with your degree."

"Thank you."

It did help to have employment. He went into the lab regularly, and was able to lose himself in working on experiments and calculations, some were even continuations of his thesis work. He did some editing and spent time talking science with the other graduate students. Most of them avoided politics. It was a sharp contrast to before the war, when the campus was full of political meetings, discussions, and conversations fueled by endless cigarettes and cups of coffee.

One poignant memory was of Andre Hendrickx, whom he had met in the first year chemistry class. Andre was a good student, with the makings of a decent scientist, but he was more interested in politics. A socialist, he kept trying to convince Alexander to come to meetings and lectures with him.

Alexander just laughed him off. "I'm a scientist. Politics aren't for me."

"Sooner or later, politics are for everyone. Even scientists will have to pay attention."

Alexander had smiled. He would stick to the lab, where everything had a logical cause, even if you couldn't see it right away, and if the experiment didn't work out, you tried again, changing one variable at a time until you figured out what the next step in the process was. Andre had gone to Spain in 1937 and not come back.

In March, Alexander got a letter from his father asking him to go to Antwerp and check on the house and the office. "Don't do anything dangerous, but it would be good to know how things stand."

Once again, he took an early train from Brussels, but this time he got off in Berchem, just outside of Antwerp. He walked the familiar streets till he got to the Avenue Elisabeth. Before he even got to the house, he had a surprise—the big old trees that had lined the avenue as long as he remembered had been chopped down. It gave the street a blank, empty look, and shocked him more than the aftermath of bombings he had seen in France. He walked slowly down the street and stopped near the edge of the house next door to home. From the street, everything looked the same, the windows were

A Small Door

clean, the front garden well kept. It was almost as if he could just walk up to the door, take out his key, and walk in to hear his mother greet him. But he couldn't.

The curtains moved slightly and Alexander took a step back and pulled his hat down further. There were people living in the house. He didn't know who they were, and clearly his father knew nothing about them. He turned around and walked back to the station.

He took a tram to the diamond district, where the offices of Brody and Langermann were located. The storefronts, like those in Brussels and Paris, were dingy and half empty. In the windows of some shops were notices saying that it was a Jewish owned business. Some of them were closed and looked as if they would not be reopened. Alexander wondered how long the others would be able to stay in business, and whether there were enough Jews left in Antwerp to support them.

The office was on the second floor; he took the stairs rather than the elevator. He unlocked the door and went in. The normally busy rooms were silent. A film of dust covered the desks and work tables. Alexander went into his father's private office. More dust on the desk, which was cleared of any papers. His father was well organized; his desk was usually neat, but not empty. He sat in his father's chair and opened the top drawer. A bottle of ink, pencils, a couple of old-fashioned nibs, paper clips, blotting paper, and stamps. The left hand drawer held some of the firm's stationery.

He wrote a brief letter to his father, explaining that people were living in the house but he hadn't spoken to them, and that the office was as they had left it. He addressed and sealed the letter.

He decided that going back to his aunt's apartment to see her and his grandmother might be too dangerous—not for him, but for them. Mme. Goossens came to Antwerp to see them regularly, and she said they hardly ever went out now. You never knew who might be watching the building, and receiving a new visitor might set off an alarm of some kind. He posted the letter on his way to the station and was back in Brussels by dinnertime.

In the weeks following, he felt uneasy about not having gone to see his grandmother. He tried to be honest with himself. Yes, his visit, if observed, might have caused some danger. But it was also true that he had no desire to see Bonmama. A sharp, judgmental woman, she rarely had a kind word to say to any of her grandchildren. She complained that her friends could boast about *their* grandchildren, but hers did nothing to crow about. When she had come to stay with them on holidays, Rachel moved out of her bedroom for Bonmama, who criticized everything that Mother did. She rarely if ever smiled, and had long one-sided conversations with Father in Hungarian, which no one else understood. You were supposed to love and honor your elders, but none of them felt either love or respect coming from Bonmama. They were polite to her, that was all. Did politeness demand that he visit? And then there was his aunt. Alexander felt for her, cooped up with his sour grandmother and restless uncle, but she might be more anxious if he came.

As Passover approached, he thought more about going to Antwerp. He admitted to himself that Antwerp under occupation made him more profoundly uncomfortable than Brussels or Paris. The familiarity of the city, contradicted by the presence of the German soldiers (and the absence of familiar faces), was deeply disturbing. Brussels was the university, the Goossens and other friends, all still there. Paris was, well, Paris, and he had no prewar experience of Paris. But Antwerp … Antwerp felt like someone had come into his bedroom at home, put all their personal belongings on top of his, and then told him not to sit down anywhere.

Mme. Goossens asked him what he wanted to do about Passover. Would he go to the local synagogue since it was still open? He supposed he could go and someone would be sure to invite him, a Jew on his own, to a seder. But he didn't want to go to a seder with strangers. He would skip the seder this year. Skip Passover completely. Another reason not to go to Antwerp. They would ask what he did for the holiday. His father would probably not ask him.

About once a week, he bought the Antwerp Flemish newspaper just to read what was happening. It was censored, like all the papers, but some news managed to be reported. The week leading up to Easter, the paper was filled with antisemitic bombast. Fascinated almost against his will, he bought and read some of the more extreme right wing Flemish papers, the ones pushing for more collaboration with the Nazis. The poisonous ranting made him nauseous. It was a modern update of blood libel hysteria. And there was no way to answer back.

On Easter, the Goossens went to church. They weren't particularly religious, but they attended services Christmas and Easter. Mme. Goossens had, like most Belgian housewives that year, saved enough ration coupons to put together a festive meal from whatever was available in the shops and markets. M. Goossens opened two of his remaining bottles of wine and it seemed almost like a normal holiday.

The next morning, Alexander went into the lab to finish some work, even though it was Easter Monday and no one else would be there. On the tram ride back to the house, he thought he heard fellow riders mentioning Antwerp, but he didn't want to ask anyone what had happened. He didn't have to wait long to find out.

Lucas and his mother were waiting for him when he came into the house. He took one look at their faces and asked, "What's happened?"

Lucas glanced briefly at his mother and answered, "There's been a riot in Antwerp."

"What?"

"They say it was the Vlaams Nationaal Verbond (Flemish National Union), De Vlag (The Flag), and the Algemeene SS-Vlaanderen (Germanic SS in Flanders) behind it."

"What did they do?"

"Vandalized two synagogues—in the Van den Nestlei and the Oostenstraat—burned Jewish shops, and attacked the home of the chief rabbi."

Alexander was silent for a moment and then he spoke so quietly it seemed he was talking to himself. "The Oostenstraat is our shul. And Rabbi Rottenberg, I know him. His son was in Daniel's class. I think he's even vaguely related to my brother-in-law." He thought about the shops he had passed in the diamond district, with their signs identifying them as Jewish owned. How many of them were left now? He stood up. "Bonmama, Tante Rosa, and Uncle Itzik!"

Mme. Goossens stood up too, and took his arm. "They'll stay in the apartment. In hiding. We've made plans in case things got worse. The apartment will be closed up, as though no one is living there. We've arranged it with the concierge, a good woman. They'll only use the water at night, and I'll bring them food every week. It's all set."

"But the risk—the risk for you—if anyone finds out!"

"No one will find out. I'll be very careful. Only Lucas, my husband, and the concierge know. And now you."

There was little change at the university through the rest of April. Professor Vermeulen expressed his deep sadness at what was being called, at least by those whose sympathies were against the Germans, the Antwerp Pogrom. Antoine Leclerq, whose pro-Nazi views were becoming more and more open, smiled broadly at him and asked if everyone in his family was all right.

Alexander set his teeth and answered, "Yes."

Leclerq was part of a small but significant group of students and professors who were agitating to get rid of "foreigners" at the university. One day, Alexander overheard Leclerq repeating that and commented, quietly, "Like the Germans?"

Professor Vermeulen took his arm and pulled him into a private room. "You're lucky only I heard that."

Alexander started to speak but Vermeulen cut him off. "You're very smart, Brody, but you'd better start applying that intelligence to something besides science. Yes, you were only saying what many of us think and feel, but it's too dangerous for anyone to say it out loud, especially you. The Germans have all the power right now, and men like Leclerq will always side with those in power, especially when their views coincide with their own petty prejudices and jealousies. We need intelligent ways to fight back, and to continue living and protecting what we think is important. Having you picked up and deported is not going to help anyone. To be blunt, as a British born Jew, you need to keep your mouth shut. I know your papers don't say you were born in Britain, but faked papers are only good as long as no one looks at them carefully. If I know where you were born, so do others. You need to keep your head down until we get you through your degree and back to your family."

"It's going so slowly. I'm ready for the committee, but it's all dragging on. I know you're doing your best—I'm not blaming you."

Vermeulen nodded. "There's talk among the faculty—not Leclerq's crew—of closing down the university rather than cooperate with the Germans." In response to Alexander's look of alarm, he added, "That's another reason I'm trying to get your defense scheduled—before that can happen. I'm just telling you so you realize how much is going on. Closing the university would keep us from having to follow the new regulations, which get more and more onerous and restrictive. But it also will cause great hardship for staff who depend on their salaries, and put on hold the lives of students—not that the war hasn't put many lives on hold already.

"Enough already. Let's go back to the lab."

April turned into May. It was almost a year since the Germans had invaded Belgium. There was an even greater feeling of unease in Brussels. The morning of the tenth, Alexander and Lucas were on the tram to the university when they heard the latest news. It wasn't in any of the newspapers or on the German controlled radio, but people were whispering what they had heard. The workers at the Cockerill Steel Works in Seraing, in the industrial part of the country, had gone on strike.

By the time they got to the university, there was more news. The strike was spreading. Workers all over the provinces of Liege, Hainault, and Limburg were joining in. Alexander heard the whispered conversations but didn't stop. He kept walking towards the lab, determined not to get involved in any discussions.

In the hallway outside Vermeulen's lab, Leclerq and two of his friends were talking. As soon as he saw Alexander, Leclerq and his friends blocked the path to the lab.

"Well, you must be happy, Brody. Your communist friends have convinced the Belgian workers to ruin Belgian industry."

"I'm not a communist."

"That's what you say. But of course you wouldn't admit it."

Before Alexander could say anything more, Lucas grabbed hold of his elbow, pushed past the other men, and pulled him into the lab. Alexander was angry.

"But it's true. I'm not a communist!"

"That's not the point. Leclerq is just trying to rile you."

"Well, he's succeeded. I'm sick of his veiled and not veiled comments."

"I know you are. But you can't answer back!"

"Why not? Should I just be the cowardly, beaten down Jew, bow my head and sidle past him, licking his feet?"

"That's not what I mean and you know it."

"That's what it feels like. Just keep my head down and take the crap they dish out."

Lucas just looked at Alexander. He walked over to the door and listened. Then he opened the door. The corridor was empty. "Let's take a walk."

They left the building and walked toward the park, striding quickly, without talking. They had been walking for more than fifteen minutes when Alexander finally slowed down.

"I feel so useless. I'm just waiting around while everyone else is doing something worthwhile."

"Your degree is worthwhile."

"Of course, but I'm beginning to think my father was right. I am selfish."

"Is that what he said?"

"No ... he said I was being wildly romantic, coming back here for my defense and then going back to Paris to try and convince Elise to come with me."

"Those seem like normal things to want to do."

"But these aren't normal times. I know what you're doing." Lucas raised an eyebrow skeptically. "Well, I don't know exactly what you're doing, aside from your studies. But you're doing *something* for the Resistance, don't bother to deny it. And so is Vermeulen, I'm sure. And your mother is risking herself to help my family in Antwerp. It makes me feel like a selfish jerk."

"You're not a selfish jerk. None of us know what the perfect choices are now. We're all just stumbling along, doing what we can. Even someone like Julien Lahaut, leading the strike in Seraing, or the saboteurs blowing up trains—who's to say if what they're doing will really help win the war or just get more people killed."

"And ..."

"Like Vermeulen said, keep out of trouble, defend your thesis, get Elise, and get out of Europe." Alexander sighed. "Now let's get back before Vermeulen sends out a search party."

They turned and headed back to the university.

The strike was settled after ten days, and the workers got a pay increase. Lahaut, the communist strike leader, was imprisoned, and the authorities (the Germans) clamped down hard on any other possible labor unrest.

In June, there was good news, or what seemed like good news: the Germans invaded Russia, who then joined the Allies. Maybe Hitler could be defeated.

If only the Americans would come into the war! But at the beginning of July, Alexander was feeling more anxious and tense. The war continued and none of the news sounded good. In Antwerp, his grandmother, aunt, and uncle were firmly in hiding. Mme. Goossens went each week to bring them provisions and keep them connected to the outside world. Alexander was impressed and humbled by her unassuming courage. His family would be forever indebted to her.

At the university, tensions continued to rise. The collaborationists became more strident, knowing they had the power of the occupiers behind them. On the other side, Alexander was aware that more students were involved in the Resistance. His own inactivity maddened and shamed him. He knew Lucas was working with the Resistance. There were nights when he came in late, or not at all, and didn't tell Alexander where he had been. "The less you know, the safer you are."

As he watched the people he admired most putting themselves at risk, he thought again of Andre. It seemed that politics *had* caught up with him, and once again he was choosing science over action. But he knew that having come this far to secure his degree, he wasn't going to risk himself in some grand gesture. And his family, especially his father and Daniel, had sacrificed to allow him to study. He owed it to them to not take unnecessary risks. He thought about his brother. He should have been able to go to university; he would make an excellent engineer. He wanted to study, but there was no money. Instead, he learned to be a diamond cutter and did his military service. Daniel didn't complain, didn't express any resentment. But Alexander felt guilty for his own good fortune, and for Daniel's support. When this was all over, he would do what he could to make it up to him.

He was grateful for the support of Professor Vermeulen. The professor was deeply involved in disputes within the university between those who wanted to close as a gesture against tightening official regulations and those who felt that they needed to continue their work. Alexander had no idea what Resistance work Vermeulen might be doing, and he didn't ask. The professors and students involved with the Resistance didn't talk about politics. The Goossens didn't talk about what they were doing either. Alexander wondered if, after the war, people would be able to regain the habit of openness.

Finally, he heard his defense was scheduled for July 28th. He wrote to the family, still in Bayonne. He sent them a brief postcard in Flemish, giving vague news about his plans and telling them that Bonmama, Tante Rosa, and Uncle Itzik were well. In reality, he hadn't been to Antwerp in months, but those details could wait until he saw them in person.

After all the delay, his defense was somewhat of an anti-climax. He knew his work was solid, and he had certainly prepared for any questions they could throw at him. It all went quite smoothly. Even Professor Renard, a well known antisemite, didn't give him a hard time. By the first week in August, it was over, and he had his PhD.

He said his goodbyes to Professor Vermeulen and the Goossens. So much feeling remained below the surface, but he felt sure he would see them when the war was over. He took the tram to the central station one more time and boarded the train for Paris. Paris and Elise, then Spain, and America.

9

Rachel ~ November 1940, Bordeaux

Bordeaux didn't make a positive impression. The city might have been pleasant if the cold and imposing limestone monuments were cleaned and the grass and trees were green. But everything in wartime November Bordeaux was gray or brown—the public buildings, remnants of the city's history as a great port; the Allée de Tourny, with its sad, shuttered carousel and bare trees; the Garonne River, dirty water reflecting the dull gray sky. No one lingered in the big squares patrolled by German soldiers. The low apartment houses on the side streets were dilapidated, the buildings and their iron railings needed cleaning, or a fresh coat of paint.

The only thing new and bright were the posters and official notices. The curfew notice was everywhere. Either the Germans thought the Bordelais were very dim, or it was a way of preventing anyone from forgetting, however briefly, that they were under occupation.

Le Feldkommandatur Communiqué
Il est rappelé à la population que l'heure limité de la circulation
dans la ville est fixée a 22 heures. Toutes personne qui ne sera
pas pourvue d'une AUTORISATION SPÉCIALE deliverée
par le Feldkommandatur lui permettant de circuler après
22 heures, sera immediatement arretés.

(The population is reminded that the curfew hour is 10 p.m. Everyone not having a special authorization from the Feldkommandatur permitting him to move after 10 p.m. will be immediately arrested.)

As in Paris, the announcements had to be read discreetly. Rachel's father said it over and over, "Don't do anything that makes you stand out."

The propaganda posters were worse. Ugly caricatures of Churchill, blaming him and the English for everything the French suffered. "Viktoria" posters proclaiming that the Germans and their allies were fighting a crusade to save Europe from Bolshevism. A brave French farmer and his wife, standing proud and fierce in a sunny yellow map of France beset by rabid dogs labeled "Freemasons," "de Gaulle," and of course, "the Jew." Even Mother, who didn't read French, knew what the signs and posters meant.

Bordeaux was a city more the size of Antwerp than Paris. In Antwerp, Rachel could hardly go a day without meeting someone who knew her or the family. In Paris, she had been able to be anonymous; there were so many different types of people that passersby might not even recognize her as Jewish. But here there were fewer outsiders, and it felt as though their Jewishness, even without a star on their coats, was more obvious.

It reminded Rachel of Mademoiselle Evrard, a particularly antisemitic fifth grade teacher. She never said anything overtly anti-Jewish, it was in the way she said your name and the little digs she gave. "Ra-chelll Brody," she said, sharply drawing out the syllables and trilling the letter r in Brody in a very unfrench way. Or she would mention something happening at a church and say to the Jewish girls in an exaggerated, falsely apologetic voice, "Oh, pardon, Rachel, Esther, Sarah," and you knew she wasn't apologetic at all.

As soon as they found a place to live, Father returned to his wartime "hobby": studying food conditions. Since there was no restaurant in the small private hotel, the landlady agreed to prepare meals if they provided the food. Father had elevated the mundane task of searching for scarce staples, standing in queues, and listening to rumors into a research project. He seemed to be gathering material for an economic study rather than just trying to feed his family. Rationing was less strictly applied in Bordeaux than in Paris, and there were luxuries the family hadn't seen since they'd left home.

On their third day in the new city, Uncle Eugene and Maurice came back to the hotel triumphant, bearing packages.

"Real mayonnaise!" Uncle crowed, as though he had found the holy grail.

"We found a shop that had prepared salads—really nice looking—and ready made fish dishes that looked quite tasty," added Maurice, in a more matter-of-fact tone. "And a notice urging people to use their 'fat' ration for butter."

"Real butter?" Rachel was skeptical. It had been quite a while since they had had anything other than margarine.

"Real butter," Uncle confirmed. "They seem to be trying to discourage the use of oil. There must be more than enough butter. There were canned foods, and we were able to get honey."

"We stopped for a coffee and they gave us milk with it." Everyone was impressed. There had been no milk in Paris for weeks.

"Did you go to the train station?" Father asked Daniel.

Daniel nodded. "No news." No one they knew had come from the north. There had been no express mail delivery of the visas or the laissez-passer papers they were waiting for. Father was silent for a moment before launching back into considering why certain foods were available in Bordeaux and not in Paris, involving a lecture on the transport systems of wartime France.

Rachel listened for a while and then walked to the window. It looked like rain. Again. She was restless. Bored. With the rain and the early darkness, there was less opportunity to walk in Bordeaux. And less to see. The gray river, the gray buildings, the closed faces of the people hurrying to get off the streets, out of the sight of the soldiers.

In Paris, there were the famous streets and buildings, even if she couldn't go inside. There were the Parisian women, stylishly dressed even in wartime. The bouquinistes along the Seine had their wares spread out, and though one had to be very careful with money (and books would be heavy to cart around), the weather had been nice enough to stand by the river and read without buying. There were the Bernheims to visit. People they knew from Antwerp came through, to stay or to move on, and told their stories of escape and close calls and brought news from home and other friends and acquaintances.

In Bordeaux, they had no distraction from what had become the essence of their lives—survival and escape. Shop for food, wait for news, wait for papers. Keep Mother company—she couldn't shop since she didn't speak French; she couldn't cook, since there was no kitchen; and there was no household to run. Talk to each other about the same things—what there was to eat, the war news (and what news could be believed). Don't speculate about the family left behind in Antwerp or the family being bombed in London, don't wonder about how Alexander was doing or when he would join them.

Paris had opened a newer, bigger world to Rachel. Now she felt once more closed in by her parents, without even the freedoms she enjoyed in Antwerp. She wondered what it was going to be like when they left Europe for New York or Cuba, where they had talked of going first.

One day when Daniel and Rachel were out, she brought up the subject. "What do you think it will be like in Cuba?"

"Hot."

"No, I mean, what will we *do* in Cuba."

Daniel was silent, thinking. "I want to rejoin the army, but I'm not sure how."

"But the Belgian army was defeated, demobilized."

"If I can get to England, I can join there."

"How would you get to England?"

"I'll go to the British Consulate in Cuba, or in New York if we get there quickly enough. As a Belgian soldier and a British subject, they'll probably take me."

"Mamma will be upset."

Daniel shrugged. "I'm not going to sit out the rest of the war."

"But what about me?"

"What about you?"

"What can I do in Cuba? Or New York?"

"What can't you do? You'll get a job. You had a job in Antwerp, you can get a job again. The money will be needed."

She thought about that, and when she spoke again, it was as though she was just musing aloud.

"And there'll be lots of different people, not just people who've known all of us forever. Pa won't know everything about everyone I meet—who their parents and grandparents are, whether they're 'our' kind of people ..."

"How observant they are or how much money they have," Daniel added with a smile.

"They won't be able to push me into marrying someone."

"Leaving Antwerp will let us escape more than just the Germans."

"Do you really think so?"

"Whatever Cuba or New York is like, it will be different. And different is good. The Antwerp rules won't work there."

Every few days, there were new posters, warnings, and instructions glaring out from walls and kiosks. Acts of sabotage against German military installations were announced with the warning that there would be "group reprisals." Male relatives of troublemakers and saboteurs would be shot; female relatives would be condemned to forced labor; children below the age of seventeen would be sent to "une maison d'éducation surveillée," a place one could only imagine.

One day, when Rachel was reading the latest warning, she noticed a young mother holding the hand of a girl about five years old, a pretty child with pigtails and bright dark eyes.

"What does it say, Maman?" the child asked.

"Shh … it's not for children," the mother answered.

Rachel looked around. In the knot of people, ranging from young people like her to an older man with a cane, no one smiled at the curious child. No one even looked at her or her mother. In fact, it seemed as though everyone carefully avoided looking at anyone else. They read the sign and walked quickly away. Rachel realized she had been standing there too long and did the same.

That evening, Rachel looked at her mother, who was sitting across the table, barely eating. She looked thinner, they all did, but also smaller. Mother was short, barely five feet tall, and Rachel was maybe an inch taller. They were small people. That sentence echoed in her mind: they were small people.

There were times she wished she were even smaller, small enough to be unnoticeable. Their Belgian accents marked them as outsiders. There were shops that didn't have the goods that had been advertised once they got to the head of the queue. Or cafes where they were asked, in a tone that didn't imply a choice, to move to another table, near the rubbish or in a dark corner. There were the looks, and whispers too soft for the words to be distinguished, though the meaning was clear.

One day, Beatrice, Louise, and Rachel were in a queue that snaked out the door of a shop and into the street.

"I don't see why good French butter should go to foreigners." The voice came from behind them; Rachel resisted the urge to turn her head, though Louise didn't.

"If they want butter, they should go back where they come from," another voice answered.

"That is, if they come from anywhere. They have no real place. Leeches, living off good French Catholics."

"Well, maybe the Marshal will be able to do something about them, now that he's in charge. He saved us at Verdun, he should be able to get rid of a few Jews."

Louise turned around, but before she could say anything, Rachel stepped on her foot, hard. Louise gasped, glared at her cousin, but held her tongue. Beatrice stood stiffly, silent. When they got to the counter, Bea handed over the ration tickets and money, took the butter, and they walked out of the shop at a deliberate pace, not looking at the women still waiting in the queue.

"Old cows," Louise said as soon as they were beyond any listeners.

"Cows waiting for butter," Rachel answered, and they began to laugh. They couldn't stop laughing, despite the disapproving looks from an elderly couple taking their constitutional down the avenue. But when they got back to the lodgings, they didn't tell anyone about the conversation in the shop.

The best thing to happen in Bordeaux was the book. Rachel found it when she moved the bed to reach a handkerchief that had fallen. It was a paperback that had been left by some previous occupant of the room, nothing valuable, except that it was in English! Even if they could have found English books in Bordeaux, they wouldn't call attention to themselves by buying one, but this book had just appeared! A green Penguin, which meant a detective story. She rushed to show her find to the others.

"Look what I found on the floor under my bed!" She held up the book in triumph. "*The Mysterious Affair at Styles*, by Agatha Christie," she announced.

Maurice reached for the book, "Let me see."

She held the book away from him. "I found it. I get it first."

"Maybe not everyone wants to read it?" Rachel looked around at the others hopefully. Everyone wanted a chance to escape into a cozy English country house and solve a problem that didn't have anything to do with their situation.

Louise suggested, "How about we go from youngest to oldest?"

Rachel's father smiled at her. "I think oldest to youngest would be better."

Louise flushed and said, "Then who reads the fastest? That person can go first."

"Daniel should go last. I'm sure he's the slowest."

Daniel glared at Maurice. "What makes you think I read slowly?"

"You're always the last one to finish eating."

"Just because I don't gobble my food, doesn't mean I don't read quickly. That's ridiculous."

Before the conversation could deteriorate further, Beatrice suggested, "What if we take turns reading it aloud? That way, no one has to wait and we'll all get to enjoy the story. Reading aloud takes a bit longer, so that'll give us more time with it."

"Like a family in Dickens!" Louise was all enthusiasm.

They agreed and decided to begin that night, after supper. Not more than one or two chapters would be read a night, to make the treat last longer. Between readings, the book would live under Mother's pillow so no one would be tempted to read ahead.

Since she had found the book, Rachel had the honor of reading the first chapter. Mother and Beatrice were mending, Louise drew, and Daniel doodled as the story unfolded.

As soon as she closed the book, Beatrice started, "So who do you think will be killed? And who's likely to be the killer?"

"The old lady with the money will be the victim, of course," her brother answered. "For the murderer, there are as usual too many suspects."

"The younger son with the strange expression on his face and no money," was Father's suggestion.

"Maybe the beautiful young wife is having an affair and the mother will threaten to expose her, so she's killed," Mother put in.

"Of course, it can't be the odd younger husband whom nobody trusts; that would be too obvious."

"Except if he has a watertight alibi—then he must have done it."

"What about the London specialist who's an expert on poisons? Who'll back him for the murderer?"

"And his name is Dr. Bauerstein. He's probably Jewish, which makes him automatically guilty," Maurice put in.

There was a brief, uncomfortable pause before Beatrice said, "It must be the least likely character—either the young orphan girl or the narrator's friend, the older son."

"The young orphan is totally dependent on the old woman. Maybe she's sick of being bossed around and kills her to escape her control."

The next night, Mother read.

Several pages in, Maurice broke in, "Cynthia works in a hospital dispensing poisons! I knew she was too sweet to be true. Either she's the murderer or an accomplice."

"Too obvious," Daniel answered. Mother continued reading, and after a few more pages, the "famous detective Hercule Poirot" entered the scene.

"Why is the only Belgian such a clown?" Louise asked.

"He's not just a figure of fun," Uncle answered. "He's also a brilliant detective."

"And what's a Belgian detective doing wandering around the English countryside?"

"He's a war refugee. Like some other people you might know," her brother said, sweeping his arm past the older members of the family.

"Oh, the war. I forgot about the war. Their war."

They were silent for a moment, reflecting on a story where it was possible to forget a war.

The third chapter began with a plan of the bedroom floor of the house. They passed the book around so everyone could study the diagram before Beatrice started reading.

"Eleven bedrooms and only one bathroom. They must have to wait forever." That was Louise.

"Four of the bedrooms are empty," answered Daniel, "so there are only seven of them using the bathroom."

"And maybe they have basins in their rooms so they can brush their teeth and shave without going to the bathroom." Mother was the practical one.

"Or even washstands with pitchers and bowls."

"And chamber pots under the beds."

Father interrupted before anyone could respond to Maurice's last comment. "How about we leave off discussing the sanitary arrangements and let Bea read?"

As soon as it happened, Louise interjected, "I knew Mrs. Inglethorp would be murdered!"

A Small Door

Beatrice continued reading. When she finished the chapter, almost everyone had something to say.

"It must be the husband," Bea said. "He's disappeared."

"Too obvious," put in Daniel. "He'll turn out to be innocent and someone who looks completely fine, like Cynthia, will be the real villain."

"I don't trust Mary Cavendish. She's up to something," Mother said.

"She's up to something, but it doesn't have to be murder," contributed Uncle Eugene.

"If she's having an affair with Dr. Bauerstein, she either isn't the murderer or he isn't in on it since he asked for the post-mortem." That was Father.

"He had to ask for the post-mortem since the other doctor wanted one. Wait … it was Dr. Bauerstein who was suspicious about the death first. So he must be innocent."

Maurice put in, "Not necessarily. He could be playing a very deep game. And if he thought it would have to come out eventually about the poison, he couldn't not notice something odd. After all, he's an expert on poisons."

"They say that poison's a woman's weapon."

Everyone laughed as Daniel said, "You've read too many mysteries."

The next night, Daniel read.

"So many clues! I can never keep track of them—coffee spilled, a bit of fabric, candle grease, how do we know what's important?"

Louise was impatient. "Can't we just read on?"

Daniel struck a pose, laid his finger alongside his nose, and said in a thick accent, "That is why you are not the detective, ma petite. Leave it to Monsieur Poirot."

"We could make a list of all the clues—a chart to fill out as we go on," Beatrice suggested.

They made an elaborate chart to keep track of the clues as the older generation watched with amusement.

Uncle Eugene declined to read, so Father took the next chapter. Halfway through, Louise interrupted, "They're going to meet the lawyer/coroner, and Poirot is worried that Cynthia doesn't take sugar in her coffee! What's going on in his head?"

Rachel wondered, "Why is anyone taking sugar? Pa, was sugar rationed in England during the Great War?"

The cousins all waited to hear the answer. No one put sugar in tea or coffee anymore.

"It was rationed. But some people probably used their ration in coffee." He went on reading the long chapter.

The next morning, Daniel and Rachel were walking to the market.

"I expect you've figured out who the murderer is by now. You're always so good at puzzles."

"There's no point in trying to figure it out. The enjoyment is in suspending belief and letting the story carry us along. Once we know who did it, the magic will be gone and we'll have to leave Styles."

It was Maurice's turn to read the next chapter, a short one. He tried to make it more amusing by using different voices and hamming it up. He was a good reader but a terrible actor and halfway through the chapter they were all ready to take the book away from him if he didn't stop the performance.

"All right, all right, I'll just read," he laughed, and finished the chapter.

The next two chapters were more exciting. Maurice was convinced he knew who the murderer was.

"I still think it's the husband," Rachel said. "I know he's the obvious suspect and it's never the obvious suspect, but he has the best motive. And now we have the stupid policeman coming in to muck everything up. Inspector Japp. Why is the policeman always so wrong and stupid?"

"And they're not even Germans," Maurice added.

"The Germans aren't necessarily stupid and wrong," Uncle Eugene put in. "They don't care whether they have the right person or not—they just shoot them or put them in prison or deport them, and if it turns out they have the wrong person, well too bad, they pick up someone else."

Everyone was silent for a moment.

"How about another chapter?" suggested Mother, "I'll read it."

No one complained when she took up the book and began reading chapter eight. Partway through the chapter, she read about the extensive news coverage of the murder and how it upset the oh so proper residents of Styles manor. She continued, "'It was a slack time. The war was momentarily inactive, and the newspapers seized with avidity on this crime in fashionable life.'"

"Momentarily inactive," Beatrice repeated in an undertone, and then Mother went on with the story.

The next awkward part was the argument between two of the characters about Dr. Bauerstein, the "Polish Jew." Why, even in the middle of a meaningless mystery, a bit of fluff they were sharing to help escape reality, did it have to be thrown back at them? After a momentary hitch in her voice, Mother went on reading.

Two nights later, it was Beatrice's turn.

"Dr. Bauerstein arrested! But why would he murder the old lady?" Louise expressed what they all thought.

"Because he's a Jew, of course. Jews don't need reasons to commit crimes," Maurice said bitterly.

"But in England!" Mother exclaimed. She was silent when they all looked at her. Rachel was terribly disappointed and didn't want to hear the rest of the story. It had been spoiled for her. But Daniel had taken the book from Beatrice and was leafing through it.

"There are three more good sized chapters. He can't be the real murderer. It's just another red herring. Go on, Bea."

She continued to read. The doctor wasn't taken up for murder, but for spying.

"Is that any better?" asked Louise.

"Of course it is," answered Daniel. "He's from Germany. He's a patriot. Poirot says so. And it's the Great War. Those Germans weren't like these, even if they were the enemy."

They knew what he meant, but Rachel grumbled, "Still, why can't the Jew be the hero and solve the mystery?"

"That'll have to wait until *you* write the book," her father said, smiling.

"I thought they said he was a Polish Jew. Now you're saying he's German." That was Louise.

Maurice answered her, "Polish, German, it doesn't matter. He's Jewish. Don't you know all Jews are alike?" He gestured with his hands, caricaturing a big nose and a greedy leer. His attempt at humor fell flat.

They continued with the book until the murderer was revealed and Poirot explained his cleverness to all. But pleasure in the diversion had been marred. Too much reality had intruded on the idyllic English countryside of Styles.

The days ran together, always the same. Besides going to the shops and the market for food, there were two important daily events. First, waiting for the Paris train. Someone they knew might arrive in Bordeaux with a package or news, either from Paris or Antwerp. A little later came the post.

Father had arranged from Paris, via telegraph to Madrid, for the Spanish transit permit, the last official piece of paper they needed to cross the border out of France. He had been told it would take less than a week, but the weeks piled up, and the express letters from his contacts in Paris came regularly saying that the Spanish papers had not arrived.

When the Spanish visas finally did arrive, Father's contact took the papers to the German authorities to get the permis de sortie.

Despite her reluctance to get her hopes up, Rachel began to look at Bordeaux differently. They'd be leaving very soon, and then leaving France. After that, leaving Europe, maybe forever. She didn't know where they were going. The visas said Congo, but they wouldn't go there, not with Lena in New York and the family in England.

When would Alexander join them? He had written from Brussels that he was staying with his university friend Lucas and making the final preparations for his thesis defense. He didn't go to Antwerp often, it was too risky, but Lucas' mother had been going there regularly, checking on Bonmama and Tante Rosa. His letter was cheerful and short; you had to know Alexander well and read carefully between the lines to get any information out of it. Of course, the censors had read it.

A letter came from the Paris contact. There were "delays." No further explanation. Father kept looking at the letter, as if hoping some more information would emerge. He hated not knowing what was really happening, and not being able to do something about it.

"Maybe the delay is a blessing in disguise. Alexander will be back by the time the passports come through," Mother said cheerfully.

Father hesitated, and then said, "You're probably right, Freda. It will all work out for the best."

Rachel wasn't sure that was true; she didn't think Father thought it either. Alone with Daniel or the cousins, she might share her real thoughts, but not with the adults, especially not Mother.

It was raining again when M. Jacobowitz arrived. It was Maurice's turn to meet the Paris train, and the weather was so miserable no one volunteered to go with him. They could hear him talking as he tramped up the stairs—the low tuneless rumble of his voice was unmistakable.

Mother put down her mending, she was always mending now, and looked hopefully at the door. They all did.

Maurice came in, leaving his wet umbrella outside.

"Dad, Uncle Ernest, M. Jacobowitz is here."

They could see from M. Jacobowitz's face that the news was not good. He went straight to Father and handed him a package. "I'm afraid I couldn't get the permis de sortie. There's been a change of staff in the office, and then the Christmas holidays are coming …" his voice trailed off.

Father frowned slightly, but Mother jumped in, "Rachel, put the kettle on. M. Jacobowitz is wet and tired. I'm sure he could do with a cup of tea."

Despite his disappointment, Father remembered his manners, took the guest's coat and led him to a chair. M. Jacobowitz had been a small-time importer of kitchenware from Czechoslovakia in Antwerp. Mother knew him because her father had been in the same business in London, though on a much larger scale. When Germany occupied the Sudetenland in 1938, M. Jacobowitz had seen the writing on the wall and gone to Paris, where his wife had family. He was the kind of man who always seemed to "know someone," and he had been helping them try to get the right papers. He was making plans for his family to leave Paris and stay in the countryside.

"How is your wife? And the little ones? Alain must be getting big by now."

"Yvonne is doing well, and the children also. Even with all the rationing, they grow like weeds."

"You must take some things back to Paris with you. The fruit and vegetables here are wonderful."

Rachel brought over a cup of tea. "Do you take milk? We have some."

"No, thank you," M. Jacobowitz smiled. There was silence as he drank his tea. Finally, he spoke again. "I don't think you'll be able to get the permis. It's the Congo visas. None of the German officers dare approve them. But," he hesitated, looking around, "there are other possibilities."

"Right now we'll consider everything," Father voiced what they were all thinking.

"I can try to get you visas to some other country, far away, not some place you really want to go, but some place both outlandish and innocuous enough that another application for a permis, at the same office, would be successful. Or, I know someone who can take the passports to Brussels, where the Kommandatur will grant the permis de sortie even with the Congo destination. Of course, that will be much more expensive."

"How much more?" Uncle Eugene asked.

M. Jacobowitz named a huge sum.

They were all silent.

Finally, he spoke. "We could smuggle you over the border into Vichy, and try from there to get out of France."

"That means starting all over!" The words were out of Rachel's mouth before she thought.

"Yes," Father said, "but we might have a better chance of success."

"I think going back to the same officials in Paris who refused us once is a waste of time. Either we pay the price to try Brussels or we go over to Vichy," Uncle Eugene stated.

"So much money!" Mother put in.

"If it gets us out, it's worth it." Daniel sounded very decided. Everyone looked at Father and Uncle Eugene, waiting for them to make a decision. The two men looked at each other.

Father turned to the family and said, "Let's hear everyone's opinion. Which choice should we take?"

Rachel was more than startled. They were never consulted about significant decisions. Alexander, Daniel, and Rachel often disagreed with Father, and sometimes even told him so, but he never asked them before he made up his mind.

Daniel repeated his belief that they should send to Brussels. Everyone agreed with Uncle Eugene that there was no point in returning to the Paris office—that seemed to offer little chance of success. Father favored crossing to Vichy, but the others wanted to make one last huge effort and try to get the papers in Brussels. Maurice suggested that maybe Alexander, who was in Brussels already, could try. But M. Jacobowitz's contact had better connections. Better to use the strongest route.

After more discussion, the decision was made. M. Jacobowitz would use his connections to try Brussels. After accepting a food package for his fam-

A Small Door

ily, Father and Uncle Eugene saw him to the train station, where he caught the late train back to Paris.

The waiting began again.

Daniel and Rachel were coming back from the market, when she asked, "What if we can't get out of France?"

Daniel didn't answer right away. "We'd have to stay here, or probably go somewhere else in France, somewhere safer."

"But where is safer?"

"I don't know. Maybe Vichy; it's not under the direct control of the Germans, but that means getting over the demarcation line."

"Some people are going to the countryside."

"That only makes sense if you know someone who will protect or hide you. Otherwise we'd be even more conspicuous in the country than here."

"We left Paris because it was too dangerous; we can't go back there."

"And then there's the question of money."

"I have no idea how much money there is."

"Well, think about it—no one is working or doing business. In Antwerp, you and I and Bea had jobs, the business was finally bringing in money again. Now, nothing. Eight people need some income to live on."

"So what are we living on now?"

"Savings, as much as they had. And I'm sure they have unsold diamonds with them, and jewelry."

"Who will buy diamonds during a war?"

"There will always be rich people, people with money who want to get a bargain buying from someone who's desperate to sell."

"We're not desperate."

"Not yet."

Soon, the real war came back. Not the everyday war of frightening posters and rationing, but bombing. They had heard bombing before in Bordeaux, but it had been at distant military targets, not in the city itself. But on December 8th, at dusk, the distant rumble of planes came closer and what seemed like huge numbers of aircraft flew in from the sea over the tidal basin and the Garonne River. Along with everyone else in the hotel, they came down from their rooms to see what was happening.

It was a beautifully clear winter night. Despite the danger, Rachel felt cheered to see the British airplanes wheeling in over the city. There was a huge explosion in the harbor, and they huddled closer together. They couldn't see the harbor, they could only hear the roar of the planes, the whistling of the bombs, and the explosions that followed.

Suddenly, flames shot up into the sky from the harbor, illuminating the night and the dark airplanes.

"They must have hit a tanker, good for them."

There were more explosions, closer.

A man came running down the street, shouting, "To the shelters! They're coming closer!"

They followed the concierge down into the shelter, a small damp room in the cellar of the house. There were a few chairs and benches along one side of the room. Mother got a chair, the rest squeezed onto the benches. Rachel looked at her mother, sitting straight with her back barely touching the chair, and then at her father, who looked as comfortable on the bench as he would on the best upholstered armchair.

Rachel got up, walked over to the concierge, and asked a question, quietly. The woman explained that one had to go up to the lobby floor for a toilet. Rachel looked at her mother and raised her eyes. Mother nodded. The two of them shared the "blessing" of easily stressed intestines. It was Rachel's task to ask for the location of the facilities so Mother would not endanger them through her lack of French.

Everyone was quiet. What was there to talk about? Everyone had been through bombings before and knew what *could* happen. What small talk could you make in a situation like this? Rachel noticed the older man sitting across the room—what was his name? It was a very ordinary French name. M. Allard, that was it. He was completely bald but had enormously bushy eyebrows and a luxurious mustache. Her eyes became fixed on his mustache and she realized that he had equally thick untrimmed nose hairs that seemed to cascade from his prominent nostrils like a waterfall joining the stream of his mustache. She forced herself to look away before he caught her rudely staring.

She wished for a book, even a boring one. One of those old-fashioned advice books—it could be called *Polite Conversation in a Bomb Shelter*. Maybe that would be just one chapter in Etiquette for *Civilians in Wartime*. She began to make up more chapter titles. "Rules for Standing in Queues," "How to Pretend Not to Hear Offensive Remarks and Languages You Aren't Supposed to Know," "How to Present an Appropriate Level of Concern When Reading Notices Posted By the Occupation Forces." An especially loud explosion startled her. She was pleased to realize that almost a half an hour had passed.

Mother had her eyes closed and Father was talking quietly to the manager of the hotel. Daniel was writing in a small notebook (how clever of him to have a notebook!). Louise was leaning against Beatrice's shoulder, and Maurice was talking to Daniel, who wasn't listening.

Another explosion. Were they coming closer? Daniel would know. She thought back to the first bombing, on May 10, in Antwerp. Then the exploding airplane at De Panne on the French border. The ditch near the farm. The two days of shelling in Carly. Watching Boulogne burn.

Remembering other bombings was not helping her feel calm or pass the time. She should go back to her imaginary etiquette book. Her mind was blank and all she could do was wait for the next explosion. Daniel slid into the seat next to her.

"Have you noticed M. Allard's nose hairs?" he asked very quietly, in Flemish.

"Where do the nose hairs end and the mustache hairs begin?" They began laughing.

M. Allard glared, which only made them laugh harder.

Daniel asked the group, in French, "Who knows a good story?" They passed the night telling stories and were able to return to bed at dawn.

There was a huge British air raid in the middle of one night. Rachel sat up in bed. Beatrice and Louise were lying with their eyes wide open, listening. Rachel pulled on her dressing gown and opened the hallway door. Hotel guests were pulling on coats and running for the nearest shelter. Father came up to her.

"Go back to bed. They don't mean us this time. Go back to bed," he repeated. "They've come at last."

Confused, but obedient, she crawled back into bed next to Louise.

"What's happening?" Louise asked.

"Air raid. Pa said to stay in bed." They lay in bed listening to the anti-air-craft guns, trying to hear the bomb explosions through all the other noise. "Pa said," she started, and hesitated before going on, "Pa said that they've come at last, but not for us."

After a few moments, Beatrice said, "The British are bombing the Germans, not us. They're coming to save us."

In the morning, they took the usual walk to meet the train from Paris. The train station had clearly been targeted, but the bomb had missed its mark by a few meters and demolished the house next to it. Another must have fallen in the goods yard or on the shunting tracks. Gangs of workmen were busy clearing the debris. Rachel looked at the ruins of the bombed house and wondered what had happened to the people who lived there. Had they gotten out in time? Or did they, like her family, stay in their beds, certain the bombs were not for them? After years of living with the dirt, noise, and inconvenience of being next to the railroad station, they were now subjected to the final blow of having their house bombed.

No news on the morning train (which arrived only a quarter of an hour late) and nothing in the post. The German controlled newspapers said nothing about the raid. In the bakery queue, they heard the most reliable source of wartime news—rumor and gossip.

The queue was long, whether because everyone needed bread or wanted news.

"My cousin came in from _____ this morning. He said they hit Merignac."

Rachel whispered to Louise, "To the south, I think. A small village."

"Why would they bomb a village? It must have been a mistake."

The man behind them heard her and said, "German airfield."

"Oh."

A few days later, another order was posted on lampposts and kiosks forbidding civilians to be within three hundred meters of the neighborhood where the airfield had been, confirming that the British raid had been successful.

The next raid began in the evening, a few hours after dusk, at eight o'clock. This time, the river port in the center of Bordeaux was the target and the attack lasted several hours. Once again, the air raid sirens called people to go into the shelters, but the huge spectacle was too much to resist. Rachel's parents' room had a small balcony and they all crowded onto it.

Searchlights from the ground swept the sky, and their eyes followed the beams of light, looking for the incoming British bombers. The anti-aircraft shells burst with quick flashes high up between the lines of light, with their familiar sound. Suddenly, every other sight was wiped away by a sharp, vivid light, very white, and stronger than daylight. Then debris floated down gently like burnt out fireworks.

For a few minutes it was quiet, oppressively quiet. Then they could hear the hard metallic zoom of the planes coming nearer. After that, was the ominous whistling of the bombs, followed almost immediately by the crashing explosions. Then the furious barking of the anti-aircraft guns started again.

Rachel happened to look at her father's face, illuminated by the glare of the explosions, and was startled to see he was smiling, no, grinning almost, with exultation. She looked around at the others and saw a similar expression mirrored, to a greater or lesser extent, on everyone's faces, and recognized the same emotion within herself. It was joy, a strange new kind of joy. Maybe it was wicked to feel joy at a time when innocent people were being killed, but there it was.

In the morning, they joined the crowds of people streaming to view the damage.

"It looks like ..." Louise began, her eyes scanning the quiet crowd around them.

"A town after an air raid," finished Daniel.

One of the beautiful rococo buildings near the waterfront, the Bourse, had been hit, and several houses near it were destroyed. The Bourse was still burning, and it was impossible to get close enough to see the damage. The fire brigade was working to put out the flames.

They followed the crowd down to the waterfront. Two ships had been hit and were partly sunk, sticking halfway out of the water. The Baudoinville, a ship Rachel had seen in the Antwerp harbor before the war, was intact. Had it been a target?

During the following days, there were more raids, many at an area of the docks where, rumor had it, German and Italian submarines were kept. Once again, an order went out that no civilian was to come within three hundred meters of the area. There were several more air raids, and after each one, the restrictions around certain neighborhoods were tightened. The rumors in the market and shops were that the British were very successful in hitting important targets, and the Germans were going to retaliate, not just against the British, but against the people living in the neighborhoods, who were suspected of funneling information to the British.

But since they had no idea who was sending the information, the Germans decided, as they usually did, to punish the easiest targets. The French police served a notice to every household in a "suspicious" neighborhood with refugees who had arrived at the beginning of the war from other parts of France. They were told to come to the railway station three days later, whole families, at a certain time. Each person was permitted to bring fifty pounds of luggage. Even the sick and very old were required to go. They were taken to Tours, in the heart of France, where they could not do any more "mischief."

The bombing raids went on. One morning, Daniel came back from the market with the local newspaper. It was useless for finding out the news, the Germans controlled the flow of information and every paper in France printed the same misleading news. But general orders to the local population were printed there, and it could be dangerous to miss one.

Daniel handed the paper, folded open, to Father. "Read this."

Father quickly scanned the page as everyone watched and waited. "This is not surprising."

"What?" Uncle Eugene held out his hand for the paper, and Father gave it to him as he spoke to them all.

"Every foreigner, whether a resident of Bordeaux or a temporary visitor, has to present himself at the office of the prefet de police with his identity papers and all documents justifying his presence in the city. There is a list of days and times to report—it goes in alphabetical order."

"But we registered when we first came, didn't we?" Beatrice asked.

Daniel explained, "We did, but since we thought we would be leaving soon, we never bothered to find out if there was something else we needed to do. We've been here much longer than expected, waiting for all the papers.

And this new order, following all the bombing and restrictions, is more serious."

Mother turned to Father, "What should we do?"

Uncle Eugene answered, "I don't think we should go to the police. Our papers are in order, but I don't like the idea of the Germans knowing any more information about who and where we are."

"I agree, but if we don't go to the police, we could be in serious trouble."

They were all silent for a few moments until Uncle Eugene said, "Then we need to leave here."

"But our papers, and ... Alexander," Mother's voice quivered slightly.

"We'll write to M. Jacobowitz and to Alexander. They will be able to reach us. And further south, we'll be closer to Spain. We may be able to make useful connections."

Once again, they packed their bags. Uncle paid the last hotel bill, and early on the misty, chilly morning of December 24, they took the streetcar to the train station for the last time. They boarded the southbound train from Paris, the same one that had brought them to Bordeaux six weeks earlier. Three and a half hours later, they were in Bayonne.

10

Rachel ~ December 1940, Bayonne

The Bayonne train station looked like all the other stations they had been through. They wheeled their luggage to the cloak room.

"We'll only be here a few days. Only take what you need for now."

On the big open plaza in front of the station were the usual assortment of cafes and hotels, as well as waiting streetcars. They had a recommendation for a hotel just a little way into town.

Louise spoke up. "We've been sitting so long. Can we walk to the hotel?"

Tired of the journey's inactivity, they set off. The sun was shining as they crossed the square, turned to the right, and began walking across a bridge. Halfway across, they stopped and looked around.

"Oh!" sighed Beatrice, echoing what they all felt. After the dreariness of Bordeaux, Bayonne looked wonderful. The bridge over the Adour River led to a second bridge crossing the Nive as it came to join the Adour. Three old sailing vessels were docked on the far side of the river. A row of picturesque houses flanked the banks of the Nive and were reflected in the water. Beyond them were the stately buildings of the city, and further away, a range of mountains, the Pyrenees.

The hotel was on a wide tree-lined avenue. Inside, there were already several people they recognized from the train—French people coming from Bordeaux to escape the bombing.

Uncle Eugene went up to the reception desk, requested rooms, and after listening to the answer, came back.

"They only have two rooms available."

Father was inclined to take them, but he looked at Mother.

"It's only for a few nights, until Alexander and the papers come," she said. It would be a tight squeeze for eight people, the four men in one room, Freda and the girls in the other, but everyone was happy to be away from Bordeaux. It was for just a few days.

They were on their way up to the rooms when an air raid siren went off. The source of the siren must have been very close to the hotel; they could feel the air vibrating from the noise. The guests began to panic—why had they left Bordeaux if only to run straight into an air raid?

The landlady quickly explained, "It is nothing, only practice. They do it every Tuesday at noon."

Moments after she finished speaking, the all clear sounded.

Father said, "A happy place, where they just *practice* for air raids."

They spent the afternoon exploring the town and getting their bearings; they liked everything they saw. One thing they couldn't find—Chanuka candles. It was the first night of the holiday. The Chanuka candle holder had been left in Antwerp, but they would make do.

"We could use oil instead of candles," Rachel suggested, "Like back in Maccabee times." But oil wasn't that easy to get on Christmas Eve with wartime rationing. Many shops only sold to their regular customers and closed early for the holiday.

"We should get as much oil as we can. Who knows how long the shops will be closed," Father said.

They separated into groups to look. Rachel and her father had gone to two shops without luck when they came to a small grocer in a side street. There were few things on the shelves, and what was on display was not what most customers would want. A young woman was behind the counter. Father asked for oil.

"What kind of oil?" That was a good sign. At least she didn't immediately deny having any oil at all.

"What do you have?" If you asked for something specific, like olive oil, and they had only rapeseed oil, they might just say no and end the conversation. They had become skilled in the nuances of wartime shopping.

"Some vegetable oil," the shopgirl answered vaguely.

"We'll take it."

"How much?"

Father took out the ration tickets and counted out the ones for fat. The girl looked at them, nodded, and went into the back of the store. While they waited, they looked around. There was a second opening leading to the rear of the shop, closed almost entirely by a curtain that seemed to move slightly.

When the clerk returned with the oil, she was followed by an older man, balding and stooped. He said nothing, but watched closely as Father paid for the oil and handed over the ration tickets. Then he spoke.

"Gut yontiff," he murmured.

Father repeated, "Gut yontiff. Is this your shop?"

"It was. Now it belongs to my friends—Mademoiselle's family." He inclined his head toward the young woman. When the occupiers ruled that Jews could no longer own businesses, the owners who could had sold to friends who would give the profits to the Jewish former proprietors.

"Keep well."

"You too. Come back if you need more oil. Maybe it will last for eight days." He gave a fleeting smile before disappearing behind his curtain.

That night, back at the hotel, they contrived a small lamp out of two tin lids and wicks of ripped rags. Gathered together in one of the bedrooms, they lit the wicks and sang the traditional blessings and holiday songs. In Hebrew, they thanked God for the miracles he had performed for their ancestors in "those days and these times." For now they were safe, even without miracles.

The next day was Christmas, and everything in Bayonne was closed. Beatrice had an idea.

"Let's go to the beach!"

"The beach in December?" her father said skeptically.

"Yes, in December," she answered. "We're not in Belgium, this is the South of France."

Rachel took up the argument. "The tram in front of the hotel goes to Biarritz."

Biarritz! A glamorous luxury resort! Homeless refugees in the middle of a war, and Biarritz was only a tram ride away! It was irresistible.

When they arrived, it didn't look very glamorous. All the larger hotels had been taken over by the Germans as command posts, offices, or hospitals. Even the casino was being used as a "Kommandatur." Many of the luxury shops, branches of the famous Paris fashion houses, were shut down, and the few that seemed to still be in business looked sad and dowdy. The crowds on the streets and beach were mainly German soldiers, with a few leftover Americans in the mix.

But there was the sea and the rocks, and the waves breaking against the

"Rocher de la Vierge," splashing and foaming. And the wonderful view to the south with the whole range of Spanish mountains at the base of the Bay of Biscay, and you could see, in the clear December light, far out into the ocean. Not the cold gray North Sea of the Belgian coast, but the seemingly endless Atlantic, which on its farthest shores touched America.

The girls quickly took off their shoes and ran onto the sand, followed by Daniel and Maurice. They played in the shallows like they had done as children. They had lunch in a cafe near the beach and took the tram back to Bayonne just before dusk, ready to face what the next stage would bring. And the oil they had bought did last them through the eight nights of Chanuka, though that seemed a pretty minor miracle, if a miracle at all.

In Bayonne, just as in Bordeaux, Paris, and Lille, they quickly settled into a routine. There was no way to cook in their cramped, stuffy rooms. Restaurants were restricted in what and how much they could serve, and gave preference to their regular customers. On an early foraging expedition, Father found a small restaurant several streets away that was willing to accept them as "regulars" for the midday meal.

"But not meat, monsieur, I can't give you meat. Fish and omelettes, but no meat," the manager told him, and he agreed immediately, not letting on that he wouldn't have eaten the nonkosher meat anyway.

The next day, they arrived at the restaurant and were greeted like old customers, seated at what would become "their" table. The food was simple but well cooked, with soup and plenty of fresh vegetables. With it came bottles of the local red wine.

Father poured wine for everyone. He had always followed the religious rules about food quite strictly. But what was simple when one lived in a city with Jewish grocers and butchers was much more difficult now. He ate no meat, but insisted that Rachel, even more painfully thin than usual, do so. He didn't ask where the food came from, and ignored the fact that the fish and vegetables he ate might well be cooked in the same pots as nonkosher meat, even pork.

At home, he never would buy or drink wine that wasn't kosher, but he relished trying the different vintages as they traveled. He always said the same thing, as if to fend off any criticism, "We need the vitamins." It was a joke, but he also felt that they needed all the nourishment they could get.

Morning and evening meals were monotonously similar. The first morning, they had eaten the hotel breakfast. The dining room was pleasant enough, and they sat at two tables right next to each other. The waiter put a basket of bread on the table. No butter, no margarine, and a pot of jam so small it would only provide each of them with a thin scrape on a slice of bread. Father looked at the waiter, one questioning eyebrow raised. The waiter shrugged and walked away.

"I suppose this is it," Eugene declared as he reached for the bread. It was dry and sour, and the jam couldn't disguise its inadequacy. The waiter came back with a coffee pot and poured the liquid into their cups. It was black and of the consistency of coffee, but the taste was vile. There was saccharine on the table, no sugar, and of course no milk. That was the first and last day they ate breakfast in the hotel dining room.

The day after Christmas, they began exploring, partly with the eyes of tourists, but more with the intent of foragers. The girls found a bakery that would take their ration tickets and make sure they always had bread. They found butter the first few weeks, and then it completely disappeared. Once in a while, they could find some jam or marmalade. Cheese, luckily, was easy to get, and in reasonable quantities. Most of the other food in the shops was useless without a stove or hot plate. The mainstay of their morning and evening meals, besides bread, was canned tuna and sardines, which came from a nearby town. Breakfast and supper were bread and tuna or sardines, followed by bread and cheese or marmalade, accompanied, thankfully, by fresh fruit.

The hardest was not being able to make a hot drink in their rooms. One dull evening, Daniel announced, "True civilization means being able to have a cup of tea or coffee whenever one wants it."

"I think even savages have hot drinks. You don't need civilization for that," Uncle Eugene answered.

"Right now, I would settle for it being a luxury," Mother sighed. The hotel coffee was undrinkable, so if they wanted to finish a meal with tea or coffee they had to go out to a cafe, and even there, real unadulterated coffee was unavailable. What was sold on the coffee ration was called "national coffee," made up of sixty grams of coffee mixed with one hundred and fifty grams of roasted barley. It was passable, but the monthly ration was only two hundred and fifty grams per person, and that ration usually arrived at least a month late. Some shops sold what they called "a different kind of coffee." It was not rationed, but no one knew what was in it and it tasted awful.

One day Maurice came back from a walk with a triumphant air.

"I found coffee," he announced, like a gold prospector who had found the mother lode, "in a cafe only six streets away."

"Real coffee?" Rachel asked doubtfully.

"Real coffee," he assured her.

They all followed Maurice to sample the treasure. It was a shade less terrible than what they had in other places, but Maurice always insisted that it was real coffee.

Every day at eleven thirty, they went to the train station to meet the Paris train. Sometimes they were really expecting someone, M. Jacobowitz with the passports, friends or acquaintances from Antwerp, but sometimes they went because there was nothing else to do.

Before the new year, another letter arrived from Alexander. He was still in Belgium, waiting for the granting of his PhD. He asked them to excuse his handwriting, which was even more difficult to read than usual.

"I am writing in an unheated room (the norm here), wearing my winter coat and gloves. Everyone talks more about being cold than food rationing, though I'm sure less food makes people feel colder. From what I hear, Paris is even worse. Our friends there, with their grand apartment of seven rooms, spend most of their time in the smallest one, huddled around an electric heater. The Levys, on the other hand, stay in bed until noon to keep warm, and then go out to find one of the few heated cafes."

Bayonne, being in the south, was warmer than Paris or Brussels. Still, the winter was cold. Luckily, the radiators in their two rooms were always warm and there was always hot water for washing.

Most of the rooms in the hotel were occupied by German officers. When they passed them in the hallways or the lobby, they were polite. The officers spoke little or no French, and the family were careful to act as though they understood no German, speaking only French in public places. Mother, of course, spoke not at all.

Soon after they arrived in Bayonne, Father and Daniel were headed out in the early morning when they saw a German lorry pull up in front of the hotel. Several soldiers jumped off and began unloading coal and bringing it into the cellar.

"So that's why we always have heat and hot water! We're lucky to be living with German officers!" When they had moved further out of earshot, Daniel continued, "Do you have a special brucha (blessing) for German soldiers providing heat?"

Father answered, "We'll just use an all purpose brucha."

There was another advantage to sharing the hotel with Germans. The officers living in the room next to theirs had a radio, and every day at the same time, they tuned into the BBC. If they opened the closet door and stood near it, they could hear the broadcast as clearly as if they were in the same room. Listening to the Germans' radio became part of the daily routine. Though communicating directly with the outside was very difficult, they could at least find out what was happening in the rest of the world.

Father and Uncle had friends, the Fishbeins, who managed to make it to Lisbon. Before they left Bordeaux, Gustav Fishbein had promised to do what he could in Lisbon to arrange papers for the family. But there was no normal mail service from the occupied zone to the outside world. Mail was smuggled either across to Vichy France or Spain before being sent on, and then any return mail had to take the same route. Correspondence could take weeks, and when you didn't get an answer, there was no way of knowing whether your letter or the answer had gotten lost. They managed to get some mail from Alexander with a bit of news about the family left in Antwerp, and from the Bernheims in Paris, but since they had left home, almost eight months earlier, they had no news from Lena in America or from the family in England.

They had no reason to worry about Lena, safe in America, but they knew she must be terribly worried about them. Mother was one of a large, close family based in London, and they had always written frequent letters and spent vacations together. Many of her nephews were probably in the army. Where were they? London had been bombed so much—what had happened to the family? How were they managing? The little news they got from England, either from the censored French papers or the BBC, was fright-

A Small Door

ening. They had no way of knowing how the Blitz had affected the family. They tried not to talk about it, but it was a constant source of anxiety.

It was clear to the Bayonne natives that they weren't from the area. Many times when they were waiting in queues, their neighbors in line would ask them, "Are you Luxembourgers?" It was an odd question, and they didn't understand what prompted it.

Father was at the train station with Daniel and Rachel waiting for the Paris train to come in when they heard two men speaking what sounded like a German dialect. They weren't soldiers, and were speaking quite softly.

Father turned to the men. "Are you from Luxembourg?" Ernest asked in French.

The men nodded.

"We're Belgian."

One of the men asked, in Yiddish, "And what are you doing so far from home?"

"Probably the same as you."

"I doubt it."

Daniel broke in, "We keep getting asked if we are Luxembourgers, since we clearly aren't from here. Are there many of you here in Bayonne?"

At that moment, the train came in and everyone busied themselves checking whether there was any news or parcels for them. When the train left, the five of them walked over to a cafe and introduced themselves.

"Our story is, unfortunately, sadly similar to many these days," began Josef Gutman, a man in his forties. "When the Germans took over, the small Jewish community in Luxembourg was forced to leave. They wanted to get us out quickly, so our way was smoothed. Our businesses were bought up, at bargain prices, and we were given visas for somewhere in South America, I'm not at liberty to tell you where. We were put on a special train, accompanied by the Gestapo, through France to the Spanish border. The Gestapo took us over the French-Spanish border and travelled with us to the Spanish-Portuguese border. Up until then, everything went smoothly, if not pleasantly. But the Portuguese wouldn't let us in."

"Why not?"

Gutman shrugged. "No one told us. But we couldn't get off the train.

For ten days, the train stayed in the station, with all of us on it. Even though there were old people and women with babies and young children, we weren't allowed to go into the village to shop, and we didn't have enough food or water. You can imagine what it was like." He paused for a moment and drank some of his coffee. "Finally, we were sent back to France. But not to freedom. We are in a large shed on the edge of Bayonne. We are about three hundred people, and are cared for by the French Red Cross."

"And what will they do with you? Are you supposed to stay there until the war is over?" asked Daniel.

"No. We are expected to arrange to leave Europe, getting visas and permissions through friends or relatives abroad."

"Just what we are trying to do. But how do they expect you to do that stuck in a camp?"

"Since the Germans want us to leave, they're helping us, believe it or not."

"I'd believe almost anything of the Germans. But how are they helping you?"

"The Germans required us to elect two 'Obmann,' or chiefs. I am one. Every two or three days, I make a journey, with my Gestapo escort, to Irun, the first village on the Spanish side of the border. I take the letters and cables for overseas and pick up the incoming mail. Now, tell us how you landed in lovely Bayonne."

Father explained their situation, ending with, "My daughter and son-in-law in New York would help us, but unlike you, we have no way of getting in touch with them."

"Maybe we can help."

"How?"

"If you give me letters or cables to your children, I'll send them on when I go to Irun. No one examines who we are writing to."

"I don't know how to thank you. It's not just that we need their help; we know they must be sick with worry not knowing where or how we are."

"We understand completely."

Before they parted, Gutman arranged a meeting with Father before his next trip to Irun.

The rest of the family was overjoyed when they heard the news. They all talked at once. Mother began to cry. It had been one of their many unspoken worries, the inability to tell Lena in New York and the family in London that they were well and safe. Poor Mother, who was unable to speak in public without giving away her Britishness. She had no one to talk to but her family, and yet to share her worries about Alexander, about her sisters and brothers in London besieged by the Blitz, about Lena and her children far away in New York, knowing nothing about where they were, to share those worries would somehow make them more real, so she was uncharacteristically silent much of the time.

With the help of the Luxembourger Obmann, they could not only communicate with New York and, through Lena, with London, they could reach the Fishbeins in Lisbon. They began to feel there was some substance to the hope they had been feeling since arriving in Bayonne.

One of the first things Father and Uncle Eugene had done in Bayonne was find the synagogue. There was a very old Jewish community that was well integrated into the life of the city. The first Jews had come to Bayonne from Spain and Portugal at the time of the Inquisition. Their services were in the Sephardic style and some of the prayers were in Spanish, Portuguese, or Ladino. Though the melodies were unfamiliar, the community was welcoming. Going regularly to services, they got to know and be accepted by members of the community. They met the owner of the shop where they had bought the oil they used on Chanuka.

One shabbos morning, they were approached by one of the prominent members of the congregation, M. Lopez.

"M. Brody, M. Langermann, my family and I would be honored if you and your family would join us for dinner tonight."

They accepted immediately.

The home was outside the city, and as they were walking there, Uncle Eugene told the others what he knew about the family.

"M. Lopez's father was a general in the Great War. The general is dead but his widow, the matriarch, is always addressed as 'Mme. la Generale.' Their business, one of the biggest importing firms in Bayonne, has been put in the hands of an Aryan 'liquidator,' but it's someone they've known for years and they expect he'll take good care of the business, as much as is possible in these times."

They approached the house through the beautiful orchard. Between the fruit trees and the house were extensive flower gardens. Behind the house, they could see the large kitchen garden and enclosures and outbuildings for cows, horses, and poultry.

They were welcomed by M. Lopez himself and introduced to his mother, wife, and two daughters. The house was clearly old and a bit shabby, but carefully maintained.

Beatrice complimented Mme. la Generale. "What a beautiful home you have, madame."

The old lady smiled and told them some of the house's history. "It was built a little more than two hundred years ago. During the time of my husband's grandfather, there was a big battle near Bayonne. It was in 1814, when Wellington's army had come to invade France from Spain. Wellington himself set up his headquarters here and stayed in the house."

They were suitably impressed and enjoyed the dinner, which because of the family's large garden and livestock, was much more luxurious than the usual wartime fare.

Walking back to the hotel, Daniel asked his father, "So, Pa. What was your great grandfather doing in 1814 while Wellington was lodging with the Lopezes?"

"Studying Talmud and barely eking out a living in Hungary, far away from Napoleon. And your mother's great grandfather was doing the same thing, hoping the Russians, the French, and the Austrians would stay far away from their corner of Poland. "

Beatrice spoke up with a surprising contribution. "We could use a new Wellington now."

Father befriended M. Silva, who had lived in Bayonne all his life. He offered to take him to where serious black market business was done. Rachel went along.

M. Silva warned them, "You must buy something. Otherwise they will think we're spying for some authority."

It would have been easy to overlook the nondescript shop in a small side street. They went in and looked around. Like most shops in Bayonne (and all over wartime France), the shelves were mostly empty. Some dusty cans of tomatoes, beans, and sardines, a few tired looking vegetables, mostly turnips and rutabagas that before the war had only been used as animal fodder, and signs indicating what had been sold in better times.

But surprisingly, there were several customers already in the shop waiting to be served. The two women behind the counter seemed to be doing quite a good amount of business. As they watched, the first customer made her request, in a voice too quiet to be overheard. The shopkeeper answered, equally quiet, and the customer nodded and reached for her purse. She counted out a large number of coins and, from beneath the counter, the owner brought out two dozen eggs.

Rachel almost gasped aloud. Eggs had been unavailable for at least two weeks. The satisfied customer put the eggs in her satchel and left the store. The next customer had a similarly whispered conversation and, in exchange for money, was given a bottle of cooking oil, another scarce commodity. No tickets were exchanged, despite the fact that both eggs and oil were rationed.

When it was their turn, Father asked if they had any cheese.

"Non, monsieur," the thin, red haired woman answered sadly, "We haven't been able to get any cheese this week."

M. Silva came up and said quietly, "Monsieur is a friend of mine. I hope you can help him."

The woman looked at M. Silva, and then at Father. "I'll check in the back. We might have something." She returned moments later with a small package. "You're in luck, monsieur. I had overlooked this piece."

Father glanced at M. Silva and asked, "How much?"

The shopkeeper whispered a price that seemed astronomical. When he hesitated, the woman added in a whisper, "Fifty-five percent fat." The legally permissible level was forty percent fat. He counted out the money and the cheese was handed over. No ration tickets were requested.

As they were leaving the shop, two German officers came in and went straight to the counter in front of the other customers. They were greeted with smiles by the two shopkeepers.

When they reached the end of the street, Father remarked, "Well, that was interesting."

M. Silva smiled. "The husbands of the shop owners are prisoners of war in Germany. They each have several children still at home, and one of them is supporting her elderly grandmother."

"People do what they can to survive in these times."

"Still, most people I know go to them rarely because they're uncomfortable with the nature of the business. Their most regular customers are the Germans."

When they had parted from M. Silva, Father turned to Rachel.

"What do you think?"

"I'm not sure what to think. They're breaking the law, but is the law fair?"

"Do you mean the laws that govern rationing and set prices?"

Rachel nodded.

"We complain about it, but the purpose of those rules is to ensure that food is fairly distributed and that not only the rich get to eat."

"And so food can be sent to Germany to feed their people and their soldiers. You've told us that before."

"That's true. But without rationing or price controls, many people wouldn't be able to buy any food."

"What about how much business they do with the Germans?"

"If they refused to sell to the Germans, do you think they could stay in business?"

"How can they feel easy in themselves, catering to the enemy?"

"They're taking care of their families. That's the first priority for most, if not all, people."

"It's very complicated."

"Most important things are. Even more so in wartime."

They had been in Bayonne for six weeks and there was no news about their visas. They were safe for now, but who knew what might happen? Despite the temporary feeling of comfort, they had to get out of Europe. That was the only *real* safety. They decided that Daniel would go to Paris and try to find more information.

He left the next day, with many instructions and whatever food gifts they could gather for the Bernheims, including some from the "black" women, as they had taken to calling the owners of the black market shop.

Beatrice turned to her father and uncle. "Before the war, did you ever imagine you'd be involved in smuggling?"

Surprisingly, the older generation all smiled.

Uncle Eugene answered, "Whenever there are unreasonable laws or life-threatening situations, smuggling becomes a way to survive. And in some places, the borders have changed so frequently and so arbitrarily that smuggling is the only way to do business."

Father added, "Did you ever hear the story about Shmiel Kessler?"

"Not that old story!" Mother broke in.

"Is he a relative?" Rachel asked. Her mother's maiden name was Kessler.

"Distantly."

He told them the story. "Shmiel was a hassid, with a full beard, payis, big black hat and traditional clothes. He was also a smuggler. During the very last months of the Great War, he was arrested for smuggling by the Germans and jailed in Brussels. He happened to be in the same cell as the mayor of one of the municipal divisions of Brussels, who was there for political reasons. They got to be friendly—there isn't much choice when you're locked up with someone, and Shmiel was quite gregarious.

"When the war was over and the mayor was liberated, he didn't forget his cellmate Shmiel Kessler. The smuggling charges brought by the Germans were forgotten, and Shmiel, who was born in a tiny shtetl in Poland, was made a Belgian citizen."

"What a great story!" enthused Louise.

"Wait, there's more. Shmiel continued doing business, some legitimate, some less so."

"You mean smuggling," put in Louise.

"He traveled quite a bit, especially to Germany. He was in a cafe somewhere in Germany in the early thirties. At the next table was a group of brownshirts, drinking. They noticed the hassid sitting nearby and started to taunt him, calling out all kinds of antisemitic slurs. Shmiel was quiet for a while, drinking his coffee, but finally he turned to face them and said, 'Haven't you ever seen a real Belgian before?'"

They all laughed.

"So there's a fine tradition of smuggling and heroism in our family," said Maurice.

"Don't say that," Mother said, clearly embarrassed.

"He was a hero, Mamma," Rachel protested.

"I wouldn't go that far," Uncle said, "From what I remember, he was a bit of a jokester."

"Jokester, hero, smuggler—a well-rounded individual," said Maurice.

Father smiled and added, "The way I remember him, he certainly was well rounded," and he held out his arms in front of him to indicate a large belly.

They all laughed, even Mother, but Rachel asked a more serious question. "Where is he now?" She looked at her mother.

"I don't know. Maybe still in Antwerp."

Rachel said quietly, "Where being a 'real' Belgian won't help much."

They had arrived at the beginning of Chanuka, in December. Now it was almost April and Passover was approaching.

Daniel returned with news of their friends in Paris and a few vague promises from officials, but nothing concrete in hand. The day after his return, there was a postcard for him. He read it to himself and frowned.

"It's from Marcel, Marcel Olshansky." Marcel was a school friend of Daniel's. He had a difficult home life and had often spent time at the Brodys'. The family were all fond of him. "He's in the concentration camp in Gurs, he is ill and has very little food." They had all heard of Gurs. It was not far over the demarcation line, in Vichy-controlled territory, and was known to be a miserable place.

"We have to help him!" Rachel said immediately.

Beatrice asked, "But how?"

Mother looked at Father. "Can we at least send him a food parcel?"

Father nodded and stood. "Daniel and I will find out how to do that. The girls can put the parcel together."

Father went to see M. Silva, who seemed to know what was possible and how to accomplish it in wartime Bayonne. After Daniel had recounted Marcel's situation, M. Silva explained the difficulties.

"As you know, Gurs is in Vichy territory and we can't send anything directly there. You will have to take the parcel to St-Palais, a small town near the demarcation line. I know someone there who will smuggle it over the line, where it can be sent either by parcel post or by messenger to your friend in Gurs. It's not without danger, and by no means foolproof, but it's the only possibility I know of."

Daniel looked at his father. "Marcel is alone. His family is still in Antwerp, and even if they weren't ..." Marcel, even when he lived at home, often had to fend for himself or count on his friends to help him out.

Rachel and Beatrice went to a shop that had a sideline in making up parcels to send to prisoners. So many French families were sending packages to men in German prisoner of war camps. To the standard parcel, they added a couple of cans of condensed milk and a packet of chocolate they had been saving.

Though St-Palais was not far from Bayonne by road, the train connections were bad and it would take a whole day to get there. Daniel left the next morning and was gone for two days.

Late in the evening of the second day, he returned to the hotel room, still carrying the parcel. He sat down heavily and began to tell his tale.

"I got to St-Palais easily enough, despite the wretched train connections and some unexplained delays. It's a small enough place and I had no trouble finding the cafe where our man has his 'headquarters.' But when I got there and recognized which man he was, he was sitting at a table with a French gendarme."

"Oh no!"

"Yes. Well, I waited for the gendarme to leave, went up to the man, introduced myself and explained what I needed. He said he was sorry but he couldn't do anything for me. 'I've just been interrogated by that gendarme. Someone must have denounced me and I'll have to lie low,' he told me."

"So there's no way to get the parcel to Marcel?" Rachel asked.

Her brother answered, "That's not the end of the story. The gendarme came back into the cafe and saw me talking to the man. He pulled me aside and asked to see my papers. He looked at them and asked me what I was doing in St-Palais. I didn't have a good excuse, so I told the truth—that I was looking for a way to send a parcel to a sick prisoner in Gurs. Of course, I didn't tell him about the other letters I was carrying to be mailed in Vichy, and I just hoped he wouldn't search me. As you can imagine, I was pretty nervous. The gendarme wrote down what I said in his notebook, hesitated, and then let me go. I didn't waste any time lingering in St-Palais, and I don't know what will happen to the man who was going to help me."

Less than a week after Passover, they got bad news. Their application for transit visas through Portugal had been denied. They would have to find another way out.

There was more bad news to come. They had already noticed that fewer refugees were arriving in Bayonne; they rarely saw any on their daily walks to the train station. Many of their Antwerp friends and acquaintances had left after brief stays, but they had been in Bayonne for four months.

Beatrice came back from picking up their mail with one last letter from the Fishbeins in Lisbon.

"We board the boat tomorrow. We're so sorry that we couldn't be of more help to you. But we have received word that there is a message for you at Cook's Travel Agency in Lyon from your children in America."

Mother was excited and relieved.

"Help from Freddy and Lena!"

Uncle Eugene broke in with a dose of reality. "But in Lyon! In Vichy. They might as well have sent it to Berlin."

A few days later, they got a message from Cook's that there were instructions to provide passage to New York waiting for them in Nice, which was also in Vichy. It was wonderful that Lena and Freddy knew where they were and were trying to help them, but maddening that the help was just out of their reach. Another door closed.

The next week, the bellboy knocked on their door one afternoon. "Someone to see you in the lobby, monsieur," the boy said to Father.

The young man came up to him immediately when he entered the lobby. "Monsieur Brody?"

"Yes, I'm Ernest Brody."

"I come from the Cook's office in Biarritz with a message from our representative in Irun, in Spain. Our Madrid office has money waiting for you for your passage and expenses. You can pick it up there."

Madrid! How were they to cross into Spain?

Mother said it aloud, "And how are we to get to Madrid?"

Their permits to leave the country—"Passir scheine" in German (which could only be used with the right visas and other permissions)—were due to expire. It had always been possible to extend them, but now the German authorities had announced that there would be no more permits given, and expired ones would not be prolonged.

Maurice stated the obvious. "We're stuck."

"Those permits were very expensive, and now they're useless," Beatrice, who had been involved in purchasing the permits, added.

"How expensive?" asked Louise, despite her father's frown.

Father answered, "Forty thousand francs per family." An enormous amount of money, and all for nothing.

"It's the Congo visas that are the problem, isn't it?" asked Beatrice. She still felt responsible for that mistaken decision.

Her father answered, "You did what you could. There's no point going back over that now."

"We need to figure out what our next step will be. We need new visas, if possible, and the permits to leave France. From what we are hearing, it's now easier to get those permits in the free zone than here. So we have to cross to Vichy. Permission to cross is now under the control of the Germans, not the local French authorities, so we can't expect to get it. We'll have to cross illegally, which is dangerous, or stay here under the Germans."

Daniel spoke first. "All along, you've told us that we need to get away from the Germans. If we stay here in Bayonne, we might just as well have stayed in Paris or gone back to Antwerp. We've come this far, we should go on."

Rachel agreed. "I don't think staying here makes any sense. It isn't really safe."

The others agreed.

Only Mother was reluctant. "But what about Alexander?"

Father had known she would voice that concern, and he had worried about it as well. He was gentle but decided in his answer. "Alexander will follow us. The children are right. We aren't safe here."

Daniel explained what he had learned about crossing to Vichy from his adventure with the parcel. "The demarcation line is being guarded by new troops brought from Austria. They have lots of experience with smugglers. They also have police dogs and motorbikes. In many places, patrols pass every few minutes. If they catch you, you're sent to Gurs or another concentration camp.

"If you manage to get across, you have to avoid the French gendarmes. If they stop you without a sauf-conduit, they either turn you back over to the

Germans or send you to prison and then the concentration camp."

No one said anything. There were no easy choices, but they had to leave France.

In May, there had been a big changeover in the occupying forces. The rumors floating around town were that the Germans were preparing to invade Spain. The well-trained and professional soldiers who had been in Bayonne were replaced by older troops with drab uniforms. Some of the motorized transport was replaced by horse drawn vehicles. It was all very mysterious and no one knew which rumors were more likely to be true.

There had been one positive effect of the shift in German troops. There were a few days between when the "old" troops left and their replacements arrived. With better rooms open, the hotel manager offered them new accommodations. Rachel, Beatrice, and Louise got a much bigger room for themselves, and Ernest and Freda moved into a room of their own.

"I'd much rather you have these rooms than 'them,'" the manager said.

It was now the middle of June. Finally, the rumors were replaced by real news. On June 22, Hitler's army attacked the Soviet Union.

"Is that good or bad?" asked Louise.

Maurice answered, "It could be very good. Part of Hitler's army will be busy fighting the Russians, which means fewer soldiers to fight the British. And the Russians will now come into the war on the side of the Allies. The more countries helping the Allies, the better."

"But will it make any difference *here*, in France?"

"Probably not."

Rachel disagreed. "It already has. We have better rooms because they sent those better German troops to fight the Russians. Now we know why they changed the soldiers."

"Better rooms doesn't help win the war," Maurice came back.

"No, but it makes our life pleasanter. I don't hear you complaining about not hearing Pa snoring."

It was impossible to tell from the censored French news what was really happening in the war, and in their new rooms, they had no access to a radio broadcasting the BBC.

Father decided to go to Paris. They had to have visas to a neutral country or they wouldn't be able to get permission to leave France even once they had crossed into Vichy.

He had no luck with visas and returned to Bayonne. They would continue to write letters and use their contacts, both in Bayonne and in Paris, in the hope that something would come through.

The next day was Saturday and, as usual, the men went to the synagogue. They spoke to their "local" friends, M. Silva and M. Lopez, after services and shared their lack of success.

M. Lopez offered his advice. "Maybe you should give up the plans to leave France, since they seem pretty hopeless anyway.".

M. Silva added, "Can you really get to someplace that would be better? Vichy is not an improvement. As long-time residents, we have many connections at the prefecture. We can use our influence to regularize your position with the authorities, so we wouldn't have to worry about being 'illegal.'"

Father answered for the family. "We are very grateful for your offer, but we're determined to leave. We'll find a way."

Two days later, a letter arrived from the Brazilian consul in Bordeaux, very official looking with a fancy seal. Everyone gathered around while Father opened it (since it was addressed to him). He read it once silently, and then again, still silent.

Finally, Rachel couldn't wait. "Well? What does it say?"

"It says the consul has received instructions from his legation in Vichy to give me and my family immigration visas for Brazil. He requests that I call at his office with my papers."

Everyone was talking at once, laughing, almost crying, and hugging each other.

Mother said, "This must be because of Freddy and Lena. Freddy must have managed it."

Father agreed.

"Now what?" Louise asked when they had all settled down.

"Tomorrow morning, Eugene and I go to Bordeaux to get the visas. Then we can apply for the transit visas from the Spanish consul so we can travel to Bilbao."

The trip to Bordeaux was simple, and they returned with the Brazilian visas in their passports. With those visas, the Spanish consul in Bayonne gave them the transit visas. They were ready to leave.

Rachel looked at the neat piles of belongings on her bed. They would fit easily into her suitcase. A year ago, she had been packing in Antwerp, trying to decide whether she should take her galoshes or not. She had been frightened and, to be honest, a bit excited. She had worried about Daniel, about to go into combat with the army. It was a long time ago.

Louise came in to pack. "It's strange. We're packing; we're leaving; we're not leaving."

"I know. Now that the fathers have decided we're smuggling across the line, it feels like we should just leave."

"Uncle Ernest said we had to wait for the signal. I guess it's the signal from our 'guide' or our people smuggler, but how will they decide when to give the signal?"

"When it seems safe to cross, or more safe than not safe, since it's never really safe."

"Are you scared?"

"A bit. Aren't you?"

"Yes."

"We'd be idiots if we weren't scared. But after all this time feeling like we're in limbo, it's great to be moving."

"Wherever we're going."

"Hopefully not Brazil, though anywhere without Germans would be an improvement. But I'd love to be in New York with Lena."

Louise finished her packing and the two went next door to the "parents' room."

Maurice was asking his father a question. "I understand that we can't carry the luggage with us. Aside from the physical awkwardness, we can't look as though we're traveling or call attention to ourselves. But if we take the luggage to the railway station, send it across the demarcation line to Pau, come back here and check out of the hotel, and then leave pretending we're just going for an evening stroll, won't that draw attention to us?"

Daniel put in, "Well, you know we Jews are known to be strange."

Louise giggled until her father gave her a stern look before answering Maurice. "Anything we do is going to be different from our usual routine."

"We've lost so many clothes along the way, now that we finally have some bits and pieces, it would be a shame to have to leave everything here," added Mother.

"To say nothing of the expense of having to once again buy everyone a new wardrobe," put in Beatrice.

Two days later, they were just finishing breakfast when M. Silva came to see them. It was amazing how much useful information seemed to come his way, and this time was no exception.

"I've heard something which might be of great use to you. No, thank you, I've eaten," he said to Freda as she offered him food. He continued, "It seems under certain conditions it is again possible to get the Passir scheine to leave the country from the Kommandatur in St-Jean-de-Luz."

They thanked M. Silva profusely for his information. When he left, everyone started talking at once. Finally, Ernest put up his hands for quiet.

Beatrice wondered, "What conditions? That sounds vague."

"We won't know the conditions until we ask."

Freda was nervous. "Even asking could be dangerous."

Daniel thought of another problem. "But what if the signal from our smuggler comes before we've arranged for the Passir scheine? We don't want to be left with no arrangements."

"We'll have to put off the smuggler."

"But how? We can't just say, 'Today's not convenient, we'd rather leave next Tuesday.'"

"No, of course not, don't be silly. But we have to try at St-Jean-de-Luz. If that works out, we wouldn't have to risk the illegal crossing, we could take all our luggage, and we'd just have an hour to Hendaye, across to Irun, and then a train to Bilbao. Eugene and I will go to St-Jean-de-Luz tomorrow morning." Ernest turned to Daniel. "If the messenger comes, tell him we can't leave, that one of the girls has a high fever." He turned to Rachel, Beatrice, and Louise. "You girls stay in your room for now; that will make it more believable."

Everything went smoothly. They met the conditions, which still hadn't been spelled out for them. The Kommandatur agreed to issue the needed permits, which would arrive by post in a few days. Since they no longer had to send the luggage separately, they could shop for the transatlantic journey before they left Bayonne. A year of living under wartime scarcity and rationing had taught them a new survival strategy—buy what you can afford that's available, take what you can carry. It was much simpler.

Regulations governing the shops seemed to be changing every day. There were rumors that items that had been off ration were going to be rationed, and shoppers were trying to buy what they could in advance of the change. Then all shopkeepers were told not to sell anything, but to do an inventory of all their goods and send it to the authorities, who would then decide on new rationing guidelines. The already sparsely stocked shelves were emptied. Luckily, the Brodys had made friends among the shopkeepers. Before taking their inventories, their friends set aside some things for them to purchase, with or without ration tickets.

Other rumors were more worrisome. They heard that an old lady was kept back at the frontier, despite the fact that she had a regular Passir scheine, and taken to Gestapo headquarters. She was questioned there for hours during the night. The border police were willing to let her cross, but the Gestapo had veto power, and after sending her back and forth between the two authorities several times, she wasn't allowed to leave France.

The next rumor was that the Kommandatur in St-Jean-de-Luz had been denounced and was under suspicion. The Gestapo would no longer recognize permits signed by him. Of course, no one could go to the Kommandatur and ask if the permits he had issued were still valid. They were not supposed to know about any of the rumors.

"We'll leave on July 10, just as planned," said Father.

11

Rachel ~ July 10, 1941, Bayonne

Rachel was once again standing on a railroad platform waiting for Father and Uncle to buy tickets, only in Bayonne instead of Antwerp. Mother, Beatrice, Louise, and Maurice were there, and Daniel instead of Alexander. They boarded the Paris express to Hendaye. There was a festive feeling as the Silvas and some of the Lopez family went along to see them off at the Spanish border. The excitement, plus the relief that they were finally on their way, was a heady mix.

As they pulled into the station at Hendaye, Maurice remarked, "Look, they're celebrating our departure." The border station was decorated with large flags, both Nazi and Spanish ones.

M. Silva spoke to one of the guards, and came back to explain, "It's a send off for some Spanish officers who are leaving to fight with the Germans at the Russian front."

Daniel said, "They don't realize the honor of having us among them. If they did, there'd be a band as well as the flags."

They said goodbye to their Bayonne friends and entered an official waiting room, where they passed through a barrier to the examination area, a smaller section furnished with a few wooden folding chairs and a table for the officials. Photographs of Petain, Hitler, and General Franco hung on the wall.

There were just a few other people waiting. Two officials came in and sat down at the table. A couple speaking Spanish approached them first. As soon as they were finished, Father walked up to the table and everyone followed. He handed the documents to the officials. They just glanced at them and put them aside.

"You must get new Passir scheine," one of them said quietly, "These are no good anymore."

Uncle began arguing. The officials were quiet and polite, but firm. "We have new instructions. You must go to Bordeaux and ask for the red permits; these are blue and no longer valid."

It was all over.

They turned around and went back through the barrier. Stunned, they looked at each other, all the nervous elation of just a few minutes before gone. No one knew quite what to do or say, they just stood there.

Minutes later, the officials came out of the waiting room and into the entrance hall.

Mother went up to them, abandoning her usual silence and speaking in English. "Please. We've been trying for so long. Isn't there anything you can do to help us?"

The two men, young enough to be her sons, looked sympathetically at the anxious woman pleading with them.

"We're sorry, but we have orders. We can't disobey. Why didn't you leave earlier?"

Always polite, Mother thanked them and walked back to her family.

The train back to Bayonne left an hour later. There were festivities on the platform as the German officers celebrated with their Spanish comrades leaving for the Russian front. But this time, even Maurice and Daniel didn't joke.

Since they had paid for an extra two days at the hotel, just in case something went wrong, they were able to get the same rooms. They put down their luggage and everyone turned to Father and Uncle Eugene. They looked at each other.

Uncle spoke. "We go back to the previous plan."

"Not to Bordeaux for new permits?" Maurice asked.

"No. That seems like a fool's errand. We can't wait around hoping that the official situation will get better; it just gets worse. I'll take the bus to Bouliac this afternoon. I'll find M. Arpin and tell him we want to renew the arrangements we made before. The sooner we can cross into the free zone, the better. No more waiting—we need to leave as soon as we can. I'll be back tomorrow morning."

Though all they had done was take two relatively short train rides that day, they were drained. Mother went to lie down, exhausted. They were tired, but restless. Despite the midsummer heat, they walked down to the river and watched the boats in the port. No one said anything, but all had the same thoughts, wishing they could board a ship and sail away, far away.

Uncle Eugene came back from Bouliac, all the arrangements made.

"'Madame' will be our guide across the demarcation line. And no, I don't know her name. In these situations, the less we know, the better. When the messenger contacts us, we take the bus to Orthez; we get off outside of town, so fewer people see us. Madame will meet us there."

More waiting.

At ten the next morning, the messenger burst into the room.

"We leave today. Conditions are favorable. After today, Madame is not sure when there will be a suitable opportunity. She is making the final arrangements and the first bus leaves in an hour, the second in the afternoon."

They would go across in two groups. First the Langermanns, then the Brodys.

Everything moved quickly after that. They would have liked to repack the luggage but there was no time. They took it to the train station, put it in the cloakroom, and left the claim tickets with M. Silva. He would send the bags on to Pau. There was just enough time to take care of the baggage, check out of the hotel, and get to the bus.

There were two buses a day between Bayonne and Orthez. Uncle Eugene, Beatrice, Maurice, and Louise went on the first bus. Rachel hugged Beatrice and Louise. If all went well, they would be together that evening in "Free France."

Rachel and her family ate their last meal in Bayonne at noon at a cafe near the train station. Rachel was too keyed up to eat much and they were all quiet.

Their bus was scheduled to leave mid-afternoon, but they arrived at the departure point early, with nothing else to do. The other passengers arrived laden with assorted packages; no one seemed to travel unencumbered now. Most seemed to be people from the surrounding countryside who had come to Bayonne to shop, on business, or to see family. The Brodys managed to find seats. Rachel was squeezed in between Daniel and the window.

The road went across the countryside. There were frequent stops, with people getting off in villages whose unfamiliar names Rachel said to herself, as though she needed to memorize every fact about the journey. Saint-Pierre-d'Irube, Guiche, Sames, Leren, Bellocq, Berenx, Baigts-de-Bearn, Salles-Montgiscard. A few passengers got on to ride to Orthez. Outside of Orthez, the stops were more frequent as people got off closer to their homes.

Just before the bus was to make its last turn into town, Father stood up and walked to the door. The family followed him.

It was early evening and there were people out for a stroll. A group of strangers getting off the bus was an unusual sight and they caught people's attention. Rachel stayed close to Daniel and tried to look nonchalant. She was sure all the onlookers knew what they were there for. Three girls walking arm in arm called out, "Bonne chance!"

Father caught sight of Madame coming toward them, sauntering along as though she had no destination in mind. She nodded her head and they followed her to a car and piled in. They drove through the town and then out again on the other side. Rachel realized she was trying not to look out the windows, as though if she didn't see the people outside, they wouldn't see her. She relaxed slightly when the paved streets gave way to rougher country roads.

Madame told them about the group she had taken earlier in the afternoon. Just when they were almost over, one of the young men had lost his nerve and started shouting that he heard a motorbike.

"I had a terrible fright," she said. "Most of them were already over the line, but one girl was still in the car. I took off with the car, hoping to lose the motorbike. It turned out to be a false alarm. I came back a little later and got the girl over too.

"Here we are. You'll follow me. When I tell you to run, you run. Once you're across, you'll see a lane to the right. Go down the lane."

She parked by a house near the gate and they followed her out of the car. Mother shook her stiff legs. They walked down a country lane, Madame in the lead. She signaled with her hand when she wanted them to slow down or walk faster. At the bottom of the lane, they saw a main road—the demarcation line.

Madame signaled to stop. She spoke to someone inside a garden; they couldn't see who it was. Then she signaled—fast, run, fast. As they passed her, she pointed to the road and said, "Run across—fast—fast!"

A Small Door

On the other side, they saw the lane to the right and plunged onward. It was steeply uphill, not really a road, but a stony, muddy track. Mother stumbled and Father and Daniel pulled her up, practically dragging her along. They kept running until they were out of breath and had to slow down to keep together. Though the path was shady and cool, they were drenched with sweat. Someone called out to them and they began to run faster again.

An elderly peasant, puffing and panting, caught up. "You don't need to run so fast anymore; the worst of the danger is over. I'm to show you where to go." He let them stop for a few minutes, then led them to another path.

Now they were at the edge of a field, next to a hedge. "Stay close to the hedge, and don't lift your head above it," he warned. "Otherwise they can see us from the Kommandatur over there." He pointed to a white building on a slightly elevated spot.

They walked single file, hugging the hedge, without speaking a word. Rachel could feel a small stone in her shoe but didn't dare stop.

They reached another road. The guide stopped for a brief rest and Rachel quickly emptied the pebble out of her shoe.

The old man turned around and said to Father, "You are in France now." He pointed back where they had come from. "Over there, that is Germany—here is France."

Daniel looked at his sister and raised an eyebrow.

About a half a mile along the road was a barrier and a guardhouse with French gendarmes. They asked the old man, "Is this the second lot?" They took the passports, looked them over and made some notes. Just as Uncle Eugene had explained in Bayonne, the gendarmes told them that in the morning someone would go to town with the group, since they were only a frontier post and could make no official decisions. One of the gendarmes led them to a farmhouse inn where the Langermanns were waiting. The cousins fell into each other's arms as though it had been weeks rather than hours since they had parted.

After a meal of real eggs and fried potatoes, they went outside. It was a lovely mild summer evening in the country, very dark and quiet. There was no moon, but the clear night was filled with stars. Rachel looked up at the sky. She knew it was the same sky they had seen the night before in Bayonne, but it was different. Her body felt light, and spent, as though a great physical pain had ended.

They were up early in the morning, waiting for the bus to take them and one of the gendarmes into Oloron-Sainte-Marie. The bus was an hour late, and the gendarme arrived just before it was ready to leave.

When they arrived in the town, the gendarme gave a slight indication with his head and they followed him to the local police headquarters. It was an ordinary looking building with a small office in the front room. A few officials were working, filling in papers and answering the phone, and the police chief was sitting at his desk underneath the portrait of Marshal Petain. The gendarme handed the chief the passports and whispered a short report.

No sooner had the chief put down the passports, than he began shouting, "What are you doing here? You have no right to be here! I should send you right back to the Germans!"

Beatrice, Louise, and Rachel all moved closer together. Mother's knuckles were white as she clutched her bag even more tightly than before.

At last, the chief stopped shouting. "I will give you a sauf-conduit valid for one day so you can travel straight to the border at Canfranc. That is all I can do."

Rachel could hardly believe Father didn't just say thank you and back out of the office. Instead, he said, "All of our luggage was sent to Pau. If we could just go there, wait for our things, and then go right to the border ..."

The official didn't even let him finish. "Either you accept what I offer you, or—the car is waiting outside, in a quarter of an hour, you can be back with the Germans."

Of course, they accepted his offer. But he wasn't finished. "You will have to leave tomorrow on the five a.m. bus. No hanging around to wait for the afternoon bus. You can telegraph from Canfranc to have your luggage sent on."

Father tried one more time. "But we only have French money; we can't take it out of the country and we have no Spanish money. Can we stay long enough to change money?"

"No. You'll have to make arrangements at the border." He turned to the man at the nearest desk. "Prepare the necessary forms," and then in an

A Small Door

undertone, "Make them valid for two days."

No one said a word.

It took an hour for the forms to be finished. They left the gendarmerie with the papers in their pockets.

No one slept much that night. They were waiting for the bus well before the scheduled departure time, and again, the bus was late. It was a three-hour journey to the Canfranc train. The bus was crowded and the men had to stand. Most of the trip was uphill through the mountains. The heavy old vehicle seemed to be panting and there was a smell of burning rubber. Nearly at the top of the steepest gradient, the bus paused and some of the men got out and helped to push it. Rachel looked out the window, thinking to herself, *We are leaving France*. She dozed, woke, and fell asleep again. At last, they reached the train station.

Just after they boarded, French officials came through to check everyone's papers. There were two of them, middle-aged men with almost identical mustaches, except that one was darker than the other. They seemed to be taking a long time looking at the papers. The one with the lighter mustache handed the sauf-conduits back to Father and asked to see the passports again. They moved out of the compartment and conferred in the passageway, looking at the passports. Rachel looked at her father, who was watching the officials.

Finally, they came back into the compartment. "Everyone can go except these two." Holding on to two of the passports, darker mustache read out the names, "Daniel Brody and Maurice Langermann—British subjects, military age. I can't let you cross."

Daniel answered, "But we have a sauf-conduit from the gendarmerie in Oloron."

"Not good enough. You'll have to see the chief in Pau. But the rest of you can continue."

Daniel picked up his bag.

"We'll go to Pau." He turned to his father. "We will meet you in Bilbao. I'll write to you Poste Restante there."

Mother took Daniel's hand and held it tightly, looking at Father, who nodded at his son. Uncle Eugene took money out of his wallet and gave it to Maurice; Father did the same for Daniel.

"But Ernest—" Mother started.

"It will be alright, Freda," he answered, "Daniel knows what to do. We'll see the boys soon."

She was silent. She hugged Daniel tightly as he and Maurice said good-bye.

Daniel and Maurice stood on the platform as the train pulled out. Rachel watched them until they were out of sight.

The train, like the old bus, was climbing into the mountains. Rachel had never seen mountains like these—one magnificent vista after another—as they traveled through the stark and beautiful Pyrenees.

Suddenly, the train plunged into a tunnel. There was only a dim light inside the train. The tunnel seemed to go on forever. Rachel felt a rising panic—what if they weren't going toward Spain, but to some horrible prison camp deep in the earth? Louise held her hand tightly. She looked across at her father, trying to make out his expression in the near dark. After what seemed like forever, the train left the tunnel and pulled into a station. Canfranc.

Surrounded by the mountains, the Canfranc train station was huge and imposing. It would not have looked out of place in Paris or London rather than in a tiny mountain village with only one street. Grand waiting rooms, a cavernous main hall, and rows of platforms and tracks. And people! Mostly men in business suits, workman's clothes, or German and Spanish uniforms, but some families as well, refugees like them, many looking as bewildered as Rachel felt.

They followed the signs to the Spanish border control. A French official took their French money, leaving them five hundred francs, and returned with a receipt. Then the Spanish officials took their passports. Customs officials looked over their paltry luggage. Finally, the Spanish officials stamped their passports and gave them back.

"Do you have money to continue your journey?" the official asked. Father showed them the francs. "No French francs accepted. Dollars, pounds, pesetas, or Swiss francs." Father turned to Mother and whispered something. She reached into her pocket and handed him a gold bracelet. He handed it to the official, who gave him a hundred Spanish pesetas and a piece of paper with his name and address.

Their first night in Spain was in the town of San Sebastian, about half-way to Bilbao. Rachel was so tired, both physically and emotionally, that she noticed nothing about the place itself. They found a hotel, ate a little, and fell exhausted into bed.

Rachel woke suddenly out of a deep, dreamless sleep. Sirens!

"The Germans are here too!"

Beatrice, Louise, and Rachel stared in terror at each other. At least one of them must have screamed because Father and Uncle rushed into their room.

"It's the factory sirens calling people to work."

The train to Bilbao took only a few hours, but it could have been minutes or days. They were out of France, out of the reach of the Germans. Still traveling, still homeless, but it felt different. Rachel tried to explain *how* it felt different, but she stumbled over her words.

Her father put it in a familiar context. "We are out of Egypt but still wandering in the desert." That seemed about right.

The train stopped often, and not always at a town or a station. Another passenger explained, "Many of the tracks were damaged in the war." Rachel was puzzled at first—the war? There was no war here. But then she realized he meant the Civil War, over not three years before.

By the time they reached Bilbao, they were hungry and lost no time finding a place to eat, and then lodgings in a hotel, where they settled into a new routine of waiting. Waiting for Daniel and Maurice. Waiting to leave Europe.

It was strange and wonderful to be in a city not at war. They walked around Bilbao. There was destruction left from the Civil War of 1937, but no current danger. Bomb-destroyed buildings were not a new sight for them, it was almost commonplace. They tried, often successfully, to decipher the Spanish signs, and were baffled by the few in the Basque language.

Underneath everything was anxiety. They talked about their worries for Daniel and Maurice. Daniel wrote good-humored letters from Pau. He and Maurice were bored; there was nothing to do but wait and go swimming in the public pool. They had bought themselves native flutes and were attempting to play—a painful exercise since Maurice was tone deaf. Their room was barely adequate and filled with insect life, but Daniel was sure they would be in Spain soon.

They knew that Daniel and Maurice were relatively safe in Pau and would probably be reunited with them soon. The deeper anxiety was for Alexander, still back in Belgium. Any letters they had received from him were so vague (because of censorship) that they gave little comfort. It took so long for the mail that all one could deduce was that the writer had been able to write "then," several weeks or even months before.

Just a few days before the scheduled sailing date, a postcard arrived from Alexander, postmarked Antwerp. He assured them that all was well and he would see them soon. But how much could he write on a postcard from occupied territory?

As the day they were to sail approached, everyone became, if possible, even more anxious. Where were Daniel and Maurice? They had heard nothing further. When the day finally came, Mother was ready to stay in Spain. She could not envision leaving without either of her sons. While Father was trying to calm her, the luggage they had sent from Bayonne to Pau finally caught up with them. Father convinced Mother that they had to go down to the dock.

As they approached the dock, Rachel saw two familiar figures—Daniel and Maurice. She ran to her brother. Though they were not usually a demonstrative family, Mother clung to Daniel, unaware of the tears on her cheeks. They had just arrived from Pau, via Canfranc.

They all boarded the ship to Cuba and sailed away from Europe that afternoon. Rachel stood on the deck with her family and watched as the shoreline disappeared. She could hardly believe that they were finally leaving. Less than two years earlier, she had been in London, anxious to get back to Belgium before Lena made this same voyage. In that time, she had left her home, experienced war and occupation, and lived in conditions she had previously only read about. Two years ago, if you had asked her what her future held, she would have shrugged and said that she would probably work until she got married and had a family. It had all seemed mundane and expected. Now she was going to cross the ocean and had no idea what was going to come next. After all the fear and anxiety, she felt as though a door had opened in front of her.

"If only Alexander were with us," Mother said softly.

12

Rachel ~ July 1941, Leaving Bilbao

The tickets, one for each family, booked in Bayonne and paid for by Lena's husband Freddy in New York, had been picked up in Bilbao. The words "Segunda Clase" had been crossed out and "Turista B" was written in, but they were so happy to be leaving Europe they would have settled for steerage if that was available.

The cabins were small and stuffy, the bunks were cramped, and nobody cared. It was only temporary. Rachel wondered when that phrase "it's only temporary" would stop being part of her everyday life.

Even after the coast of Spain, and Europe, had disappeared, Rachel, Daniel, and their cousins stayed on deck, as did most of the other young passengers.

When the first meal was served, Father looked at it carefully before he said to Rachel, "It's only until we get to Cuba; you don't have to eat the meat." She was surprised. Because she was so painfully thin, Father had insisted that she eat the nonkosher meat (when it was available) in France. But now, so close to safety and freedom, adherence to the religious rules seemed possible again. Rachel did as he said and Mother looked relieved. Not following the laws of kashrut had made her very uncomfortable.

They talked about what they would do when they got to Cuba.

"Will Lena be able to come to Havana?" Rachel asked.

Father nodded. "I hope so."

"We'll be able to write to the family in London," Mother said.

"You can start before we land. That way, you can put the letters in the post as soon as we get there."

"I wonder what Cuba will be like," mused Louise.

"Hot!" answered Maurice and Daniel in unison, and they all laughed.

It was already hot, so hot that all the young people brought their mattresses up on deck to sleep in the open air, where they could feel the sea breezes.

They were not the only Jews on board, or the only Belgians. The population on the boat was a grab bag of displaced Europeans. Poles, Czechs, Hungarians, Rumanians, Austrians, and Germans. Between their knowledge of German and Yiddish, they could speak to many of the other refugees, and of course there was no trouble communicating with the Belgian, Dutch, and French passengers. Most were hoping that their stay in Cuba would be short—they really wanted to go to the United States. When their fellow travelers found out that the Brodys and Langermanns spoke English, they were in high demand.

It was hard to keep a straight face as passenger after passenger tried to start a stilted English conversation with one of them to practice their minimal language skills. Rachel found herself explaining elements of her mother tongue that she had never thought about.

"No, English has no genders."

"The adjective goes before the nouns."

"I know it doesn't look like that, but that's how it's pronounced."

One evening, Louise said, "I'm glad I don't have to learn English."

Her uncle said, "Maybe we should be learning Spanish."

Maurice put in, "Why bother? We'll be going to America soon enough."

Father didn't answer, but he raised one eyebrow, his expression skeptical.

Later on, Rachel asked Daniel, "Why does Pa think we should learn Spanish?"

"Maybe he thinks we shouldn't count on getting into the States quickly."

"Why shouldn't we? Lena and Freddy are there."

"They're not citizens. And it's wartime. You never know."

"I don't think we'll have to wait too long."

So they didn't bother learning Spanish, except for two phrases. They could say to the sailors on the Spanish ship, "mucho calor," very hot. To which the sailors would answer, "manana mas," more tomorrow. And sure enough, the next day was even hotter.

Aside from the heat, the two-week trip wasn't bad. Rachel spent the time with all the other young people, laughing, talking, playing cards, and giving impromptu English lessons.

The ship docked in the early morning, and by noon they were off the boat. Rachel put down her bags and looked around. It was hot, the sun was beating down and everything was bright and loud. There was a rickety wooden barrier separating the new arrivals from the crowd on the pier. And what a crowd! People of all ages, and carts, stands, and peddlers, with the smell of food wafting over and everyone talking, shouting, buying, selling, strolling, and rushing. And the people looked different. In Belgium and France, Rachel had seen Africans from the Congo or French colonies and Arabs from Morocco or Algeria. Not many, but some. But here, the crowd was made up of men, women, and children of all shades, from the deepest black to a light cafe au lait. Before she had a chance to take any of it in, they were led onto a bus and driven away from the port.

"Where are we going?" Everyone had the same question, but no one knew the answer. Rachel and her cousins were glued to the windows—taking in the white and brightly colored buildings, the palm trees, the brilliant tropical flowers, and the brilliant tropical people. Soon they arrived at a group of buildings surrounded by a high fence. The bus was let through a gate and a young man in uniform boarded.

He made the same announcement in four languages—Spanish, English, French, and German. "You are at the refugee camp of Tiscornia. You will be examined and interviewed before being free to leave for the city of Havana."

When they got off the bus, they were shown to their rooms and given piles of forms to fill out. The lodgings were simple, with iron cots and thin mattresses, but they were clean. There were shelves and dressers for their belongings and tables and chairs where they could sit and write. No sooner had they reached the rooms, than the sky opened up and a torrential rain began to fall. In less than half an hour it stopped and the heat of the sun dried up the puddles. So different from the constant drizzle of Northern Europe.

Father and Uncle Eugene began filling out the forms, and Daniel was sent to see if he could telegram their arrival to Lena in New York. Dinner was served in a big tent at long tables. The food was plain but edible, with more fresh fruit and vegetables than they had seen since leaving Europe.

The three days they spent in Tiscornia were a blur to Rachel. She helped her mother wash out their clothes, sat waiting to be interviewed by the officials, and chatted with her cousins and the other young people.

Uncle Eugene had been very active in the Zionist movement in Antwerp, and he was able to contact their Cuban branch in Havana. Someone from the office came out to see him and assured him they would do whatever they could to get U.S. visas for his family. Father didn't have those kinds of connections, but he and Mother were sure that Lena and Freddy would be able to help. A representative from the Jewish community came to Tiscornia and talked to Father about finding an apartment. By the time they left the camp with official permission to stay in Cuba, they had a place to live.

Just before they boarded the bus from Tiscornia to Havana, Father received a message. He waved it excitedly.

"Lena's arriving this afternoon! We can go straight to the hotel to meet them!"

Rachel could barely sit still on the bus ride. She was so excited, and she knew her parents and Daniel felt the same.

They reached the hotel and were shown to a table on the veranda to wait. It was all so wonderful and strange—the starched white tablecloths, sumptuous flower arrangements, relaxed groups of people talking and laughing. In other words, a normal peacetime atmosphere that seemed to come from another lifetime.

And then Lena was there. Mamma practically threw herself into her daughter's arms, weeping, and even Father was wiping his eyes. Freddy hugged Rachel tightly before passing her to Lena. Rachel could hardly believe she was really seeing her dear older sister. Like her mother, she kept touching Lena's hand to make sure she was real. After two years, the children, Lillie and Bernard, were shy, but they soon warmed up.

The visit was all too short.

"But you'll be with us soon," Lena promised before she left to return to New York.

Soon after Lena left, the Langermanns received permission to enter the United States. Uncle Eugene's Zionist contacts had been able to smooth the family's way. After all they had been through, Rachel found it hard to part with her cousins, but she was sure they would soon be reunited in New York.

Rachel and her family moved into their new apartment. The American Jewish Joint Distribution Committee offered Rachel a job as a receptionist. Speaking English, French, German, Flemish, and Yiddish, she would be able to help many of the Jewish refugees coming to Havana. Mother joined the local chapter of WIZO, the Women's International Zionist Organization, and found women she could talk to in English and Yiddish. Father had a hard time finding work; the displaced Antwerp diamond industry was beginning to set up factories and do business, but he had little capital and not many stones left from the supply he had taken with him from Belgium. But food and rent were cheap, Rachel was earning, and Freddy sent money from New York.

As soon as they were settled, Daniel went to the Belgian consulate. He wasn't interested in trying to get to New York.

"I'll see New York when the war is over," he said, "But we haven't won yet, and I need to be in it."

Mamma put down her cutlery with a clatter. "You would go back to Europe? We finally got out!"

"Back to the army. They're assembling a company of Belgian soldiers to be part of the British army. I'll join them."

"They'll send you to England?"

"To Canada first, and then to England."

Father said nothing.

Rachel asked, "When do you leave?"

"In two weeks."

Mother was upset that he was leaving so soon, but there was nothing she or Father could say. It wasn't like Alexander going back for his degree—Daniel was a soldier and the war was still going on.

The next day, Daniel and Rachel went for a walk. He tried to explain that he knew how his decision would affect her.

"I'm sorry this is going to be hard for you—leaving the parents for you to take care of."

She half-smiled. "You're not really sorry, you're glad to go."

"I am. It's complicated. We, the Belgians, were hammered in May '40. And since then, we've been running. I know we had no choice but to run, but now I have a choice. I can stay here and be safe, or go back and help finish the fight. And yes, taking care of the parents seems less appealing than going back to the army. That sounds horrible of me, and I wouldn't say it to anybody but you, but it's true."

"I'll miss you."

"I'll miss you too. But we can write. Write down all your complaints—how they're driving you nuts. And hopefully soon you'll be in New York and have Lena."

He left for Canada, as scheduled, two weeks later. And he did write and send photographs of training in the snow and cold. But it wasn't the same as having him there to share her burdens.

13

Alexander ~ August 1941, Paris

A lexander wasted no time when his train arrived at the Gare du Nord. He went directly to the hotel where he had been told he could get a cheap room for a short-term stay with no questions asked. It wasn't by far the best part of town, the room was tiny, and he hoped rather than believed that the bed was bug free. But he didn't have to register with the authorities or say anything about how long he would be in Paris.

He locked the door to his room and set off to walk to the Bernheims'. He had telephoned from the station and been immediately invited for the evening meal. Eating during his stay was going to be tricky. He had no French ration tickets, and he didn't want to impose on the Bernheims too often. Everyone was struggling to get enough food; though they would never turn him away, he knew they didn't have the provisions to feed an extra adult. Luckily, the friend who had told him where to get lodgings had also given him the names of a few cafes where he could get meals without tickets.

Elise met him at the door and seemed as pleased to see him as he was to see her. She brought him into the salon, where he was warmly greeted by the rest of the family.

"Congratulations on your doctorate!" said M. Bernheim as he took Alexander's hand. "Since your parents aren't here to celebrate, we'll have to do it instead."

Alexander was touched as each member of the family shook his hand or kissed him on both cheeks, giving him their praise and congratulations. Elise must have said something to her family because they seemed to take it for granted that he would sit with her.

"Have you heard anything from your parents?" Mme. Bernheim asked.

"Daniel sent me a postcard when he and Maurice arrived in Bilbao. They made it in time to board the ship. I assume they're all in Cuba by now. I have no idea how long it will take to get a letter from Cuba here, or if it's even possible."

"Will they go to New York from Cuba?"

"That's the plan. It might take a while to get all the paperwork in order, though I know my brother-in-law Freddy is working on it at his end. And Uncle Eugene has lots of contacts in the Zionist organization who can help. Maybe Lena will at least be able to travel to Cuba to see them."

"That would be wonderful. I know your parents have missed her. And she must have worried terribly."

M. Bernheim broke in, "And what are your plans?"

"I need to get a new visa and a laissez-passer. I'm not sure whether it will help or not that the rest of my family is already in Cuba. I'll ask around and use my father's contacts, if they're still in Paris, to figure out the best approach."

"We have a couple of acquaintances you might talk to. And you might check with the chemistry professors at the Sorbonne you spoke with before. They might have some useful ideas."

"Thank you. I'll do that."

"And your papers, what is the situation with them? I know there was some concern about that."

"The papers say I'm a Belgian. Which I am, since my father is. They don't say I was born in London, but otherwise they are correct. Since Daniel, Maurice, and Beatrice are in the same situation and they were all right, I expect I will be too."

M. and Mme. Bernheim exchanged a glance.

"Be careful. Don't stay in Paris too long. Things are getting more dangerous—especially for foreigners and Jews. And as a Belgian, you're a foreigner."

"I will be careful."

They went into dinner, which was a more spare meal than in times past, but well cooked and tasty. They peppered Alexander with questions and he told them about the situation in Brussels and Antwerp, about the university and his defense, and his visit with his grandmother, aunt, and uncle.

All of a sudden, Elise said, "The curfew!" Civilians were forbidden to be out on the street from dark to five in the morning, and it was past dusk.

"Don't worry. I can slip past," said Alexander.

M. Bernheim disagreed. "Don't be silly. You just promised us you'd be careful. That means not taking unnecessary risks. You'll stay here tonight. You can sleep in my study. Elise will make up the sofa for you."

Alexander and Elise sat up late talking. He longed to kiss her, but didn't. Her parents were being so generous, and they trusted him.

He left right after breakfast, making arrangements to meet Elise later in the day. She was still going to lectures at the university, though her official enrollment, as a Jew, was tenuous. Nothing official had been done to terminate the status of Jewish students, though, like in Brussels, Jewish teachers and lecturers had been let go. Whether Jewish students would be allowed to take exams was unclear, and Jewish doctors were no longer allowed to practice, but as long as students could still attend lectures, Elise could study.

Alexander walked to the cafe that had been recommended to him. The late August day was warm and sunny, but the city seemed dull. The road traffic was unusual. There were German army cars and lorries, of course, but no civilian cars. Several vehicles had strange contraptions attached to their roofs, which he realized with surprise were boilers burning wood or coal rather than the unavailable petrol.

The faces of passersby looked closed and pinched. They rarely made eye contact and seemed to hold themselves more rigidly, without the usual grace and swing. Only the women walking with German officers had the usual Parisian elan.

The cafe was half full. Alexander sat at an empty table and ordered coffee. It was tasteless but gave him a reason to be there. He opened the newspaper to read the usual propaganda—he had heard the real news on the BBC the night before. While he was reading, his attention was on the people around him. There was the quiet buzz of conversation, some of it totally mundane (or so it seemed to him). He was listening for hints of someone, or something, which might be of use to him—a contact for obtaining a visa.

All of a sudden, the talk inside dropped to an indistinguishable hum, and German voices, punctuated by booted footsteps, could be heard outside the cafe. Conversation didn't stop completely; it was as though the French was an undertone, a kind of drone beneath the percussive German that dominated. Once the soldiers had passed, the French talk became louder and clearer, as though someone had adjusted the controls on a radio.

A man came over to Alexander's table. He gestured at the empty chair and asked, "Si je peux …" Alexander nodded in assent. He was a bit older than Alexander, with untidy dark hair and a bushy mustache. The conversation started with a few remarks about the weather and other general and innocuous topics, though many previously innocuous topics had become less so. Then came the real talk.

"Do you need a guide over the line?"

"No. A visa and exit papers."

"Trickier. And more expensive."

"Can you help?"

"Maybe. Where do you want to go? For the visa."

"Anywhere I can get to. My family is already in Cuba and my sister is in America." Alexander waited for the man to ask why he was here if they had managed to get out, but he didn't.

"Do you need papers?"

"No."

"Are you French?"

"Belgian."

The man was silent, considering. "Come back in two days. I'll see what I can do."

"How do I know I can trust you?"

"Do you have a choice?"

Alexander looked around the cafe. "It looks like I might have many choices."

The man grinned.

"My name is Armand. Ask anyone here if I'm on the level."

Alexander nodded and smiled back, offering his hand, "Alexander Brody."

"I'll see you in two days, Alexander Brody." And with that, Armand got up and left.

Alexander left soon after to meet with Elise near the Sorbonne. As he walked, he wondered what it would be like to be in Paris in "normal" times. Shop windows filled with new and appealing goods. No lines snaking around the block leading to boulangeries or grocers. People strolling along, standing straight, not all rushing to be off the streets. No soldiers. No signs in German. No loud German voices. No signs on businesses saying the shop had been "Aryanized," purged of its Jewish contagion. Only his eagerness to see Elise kept his spirits up.

She was waiting for him at a table in the corner of the cafe, reading what looked like a textbook. He slid into the chair beside her and put his arm around her, startling her.

"That book must be fascinating," he teased. He half-closed it to look at the cover. "*Human Anatomy*. I'd like to teach you some anatomy. Let's start with ... lips."

She pushed him away, playfully. "I'm working on the digestive system."

"Doesn't it start with the mouth? In order to be digested, the food has to pass your lips. I'll show you how to use them."

She smiled as she asked him, "How did your day go? Did you find any useful contacts?"

"Why do I feel you're trying to distract me? Yes, I did meet someone. He thinks he might be able to help me. I have to meet him again in two days. Now tell me about your day, lovely student of human anatomy."

While she talked, he held her hand, drawing tiny circles with his thumb. He noticed another couple kissing at a nearby table. Elise noticed him watching the other couple and stopped talking. He looked back at her and smiled slightly. She didn't smile, but her eyes were fixed on his and he knew she was giving him permission. The kiss was just as he had remembered it all those weeks in Brussels, but better.

At last, she put her hand against his mouth. "People are looking at us."

"You should have picked a table with less light."

"But then I couldn't read."

"Don't read, just kiss."

She laughed and kissed him quickly. "Let's walk."

They left the cafe and walked along the river, stopping to hold each other like all the other lovers in Paris. Even in wartime, Paris was full of lovers. They walked and talked and kissed until she had to go home, and he found someplace to eat and went back to his room.

The lodger in the next room was also a Jew, a man in his early thirties, from Austria originally. He had been in France since the Anschluss in 1938 and spoke fluent, though accented, French. His name was Willy, and he and Alexander became friendly. Alexander saw him when he was coming out of his room.

"Did you hear the news?" Willy asked.

"What news?"

"They've closed off the 11th arrondissement." No need to ask who "they" was. And the 11th arrondissement was a Jewish neighborhood. "Be careful."

"You too." He stayed away from the whole area.

When he met Elise, she had heard more news. "They're checking every-one's papers as they leave the metro. And they're raiding apartments all over the 11th, arresting every Jewish man between eighteen and fifty." Her voice became higher as she spoke. "You have to leave Paris. It's not safe."

"I'll stay away from that neighborhood. I can't leave yet, I don't have the papers. And besides, I don't want to leave without you." It was the first time he had said it aloud. She was silent, so he pressed on. "It's dangerous for any Jew. When it comes to the Germans, you're no safer than I am. Come with me."

"I can't. You know I can't. You shouldn't ask." He was glad she said "I can't," rather than "I won't."

"I don't see why you can't."

"I can't leave my parents. My sisters. My studies."

"Your parents will want you to be safe. You'd be safer outside of France, out of Europe. No Jew is really safe here. Look at what's happening in the 11th."

"I can't."

"Just saying I can't over and over isn't an argument. Why can't you?"

"You don't understand."

"So explain it to me. Or is it that you don't want to go with me?"

"It's not that."

"So explain. I'm not asking you to marry me. I wouldn't press you on that. I know you're not ready, we're not ready. I'm asking you to leave France, to go away from the Germans, from the war. Don't you want to get away from all this and just live?"

"You don't understand, I can't explain." She was close to tears, and he realized he couldn't push her further right now. He took her arm, gently.

"I'll walk you home." They walked silently, almost peacefully, despite all the unsaid words hanging between them. At last, they reached her parents' building.

"Won't you come in?"

"No, I don't think so. Not tonight." He didn't want to impose on their rationed food budget too often. And besides, he was too full of thoughts and feelings to be with them tonight. If he couldn't be with just Elise, he would rather be alone. He kissed her goodnight and began walking toward his lodgings.

Even walking, which usually cleared his mind, didn't help. He wished Lucas was there, or Daniel or Rachel. For the first time since he had left Paris the previous November, he missed, really missed, his brother and sister.

He stopped at a cafe and ordered something to eat, more out of habit than because he was hungry. When the food came, he picked at it but was unable to eat much. He looked around at the other customers. Most of them were men, sitting alone or in pairs. People without wives or mothers to cook for them, without homes and cooking arrangements, paperless wanderers, refugees like him, waiting to leave, trying to leave. There were a few couples or family groups, families on the move like his had been the year before. He wondered how many of these people had legal, up-to-date identity papers with them. If the police had an arrest quota, all they had to do was come into a cafe like this and check everyone's papers. They could sweep them all up. He couldn't eat anymore. He paid his bill and left.

No sooner had he put his key into the lock of his door than Willy came out into the hall. He followed Alexander into his room.

"They're moving into the neighboring arrondissements." *They* again. Alexander nodded. "They're arresting all the men. Men like us."

"I heard."

"I'm leaving."

Alexander wasn't surprised that Willy was frightened and wanted to leave, but he didn't think he had his papers arranged yet.

"Where will you go?"

"I don't know. But Paris is getting too dangerous. Maybe I can get over the line. It might be easier to get out of France from the other zone."

Alexander thought of all the options his father had explored, and of the journey Beatrice and Duvcha had taken the previous autumn.

"I thought you had a good lead on an exit visa."

"Yes. But it will take a while longer. I'm not sure it makes sense to wait.

We're sitting ducks, waiting for the police to find us and pick us off."

Alexander remembered his thoughts in the cafe. He pushed them down. He would not give in.

"We're safer than you think. We speak French, we blend in, we have friends and connections in Paris. They're probably picking up the obvious targets—Jews who look like foreigners, don't speak French, have no money or means of support." When Willy looked unconvinced, Alexander went on, "It's dangerous to go on with no plan and no papers to give us legitimacy. I'm sure I'll have everything I need in a couple of weeks." At the back of his mind was the thought that in that time he would also be able to convince Elise to come with him.

"Maybe you're right. I'm meeting with Georges, the one with the cousin in the prefecture, tomorrow. I'll decide then."

"Good. How about a game of chess?"

Willy had a travel chess set and they played until late, trying not to think of anything except the next moves.

The next day, Alexander went back to the cafe where he had met Armand. Since they hadn't set a specific time to meet, he arrived early and settled in with a cup of coffee, or what passed for coffee, and a book. He looked around at the other patrons. It was easy to tell the difference between the two types. There were the anxious supplicants, nervously waiting for a rendezvous, hoping for some pathway out of the limbo that Paris had become. And there were the "connected"—the people who knew someone who knew someone else who had power, or who knew a guide into a (hopefully) better situation. The members of that second group had the confidence of those who had something to sell and knew it was a sellers' market. Alexander wondered sardonically whether this was what was meant when the books talked about "cafe society."

Armand didn't come, but he sent a message that he would be there the next day, after ten o'clock. Alexander went back to his room, wondering whether Willy had had better luck.

Willy's room was empty, but he had left a note under Alexander's door. It read, "See you in New York." Maybe it was a good omen that things had turned out well for Willy. *What's happening to me*, he thought. *Omens! I'm sound-*

ing like my mother! He laughed and settled down to wait for tomorrow.

He was back at the cafe the next day. He hoped Armand would come— he was feeling uncomfortable being in the same place day after day. As a student in Brussels, it was nice to have a "regular" cafe where they knew him and he could relax, have a drink, meet friends, read or study. Someplace between home and a truly public space. But now there was a danger in predictability.

He had only waited an hour before Armand showed up, looking pleased.

"I've got what you need. A laissez-passer to Spain, via Hendaye, and the promise of a visa to Argentina. And another name can be added if you want."

A huge sense of relief washed over Alexander. He could leave, and if he could convince her, he could take Elise with him.

"What will it cost?"

Armand named what sounded like a huge sum, but not more than what Alexander expected. He could pay that much.

He left the cafe with a promise to bring the money to Armand the next day in exchange for the papers. Now he needed to talk to Elise.

He was too restless to sit and talk in the Latin Quarter cafe where they met. He pulled her up from her seat and said, "Let's go to the river. I have news."

They walked quickly, arm in arm, the few streets to the quai. Leaning on the stone barrier overlooking the water, Alexander told her about his meeting with Armand.

"Tomorrow I'll have all the papers. I just have to get the money and bring it to the cafe." Alexander had left his money in the Bernheims' safe.

Elise's expression was a mixture of relief and sadness. He knew what she was feeling. She was pleased he had gotten the papers—she had been so afraid for him. But it also meant that he would leave, and there was no way of knowing when they would meet again. They walked along the river to a more secluded spot. Alexander pulled her into the shadows and took her into his arms. He traced the shape of her lips with his finger and then kissed her.

"Come with me. I can add your name to the papers. We'll go to America together."

"Alexander ..." She sighed.

He kissed her again, more urgently.

"You can study medicine in America. I'll find a job and you can study."

"My parents ..."

"Your parents want the best for you."

She smiled, a little half-smile.

"And you're the best for me?"

"The best for you is to be safe. To be out of Paris, out of France, out of Europe."

She shook her head again and said nothing. Then she lifted her face and kissed him, and suddenly they were kissing passionately, clinging to each other. He pressed her against him. He wanted her, but he also wanted to bind her to him, to make her feel she *had* to be with him. Finally, she broke away.

"I need to think. Come back to dinner. You have to get the money anyway."

"Elise ..."

"I need to think," she repeated. "Let's talk about something else."

So he told her about Willy as they walked to her parents' apartment.

The Bernheims were happy with Alexander's news. They genuinely liked him, beyond just the family connections between the Bernheims and the Brodys. They weren't sure about his relationship with Elise. She was young, their youngest. Neither Alexander nor Elise said anything to them about the possibility of her leaving with him. They could see that Elise was somewhat downcast, but they attributed that to Alexander's impending departure. After the meal, M. Bernheim took Alexander into his study and opened the safe. Alexander counted out the money he needed to pay Armand and gave the rest back.

"I'll get the rest of the money when I'm ready to leave. It's safer here."

Elise walked him to the door. They stood facing each other, hands clasped.

"Think about it," he said softly.

"I will. I won't be able to think about anything else."

He leaned in and touched his forehead to hers. "I love you."

It was the first time he had said the words.

"I love you too," she whispered, so quietly he just barely heard. "Be safe."

He kissed her gently and left.

He was tempted to go to the cafe as soon as he woke up, either that or go to Elise. But he took his time, having breakfast at a busy enough cafe where he had never been before. "Be inconspicuous," he could hear his father saying. By ten, he couldn't wait, and went to meet Armand. He nodded to an old man, a "regular" he had seen before, and sat down at an empty table. He ordered his coffee and looked around. Armand wasn't in yet, but he saw other men he recognized. Not more than a quarter hour passed before Armand came in and sat down across from him. Alexander didn't say anything; he just raised an eyebrow in inquiry.

Before Armand could say anything, someone hissed, "Police!"

Three French policemen came in the front door. Alexander glanced toward the back exit. More policemen. Another policeman came and stood at the door to the kitchen. There was no way out.

"Everybody stay where you are. We're checking your papers." They took their time examining documents, asking questions. Alexander looked out the window. There was a police wagon parked at the curb. They had come prepared to take people away.

"A Pole!" said the policeman at a nearby table. "You'll come with us."

"But I have a resident permit!" the man objected.

"Yes, and 'Juif' stamped on your identity card. We'll sort it out at the station."

Alexander breathed a bit easier. He had no stamp on his papers. They came to his table. Armand presented his papers and the policeman examined them carefully.

"Looks all right." He gave Armand a suspicious look. "Take off your jacket." After a momentary hesitation, Armand did as he was told. The policeman rifled through the pockets. "What's this?" He took out a long thin envelope, opened it and studied the contents. Alexander couldn't look at Armand. It must be the papers for him. "Interesting. We'll take this, and you can explain it to the captain at the station. Now let's see about your friend." He turned to Alexander, who handed him his identity papers. "A Belgian." He looked at Alexander. "No stamp, but I bet you're a Jewish Belgian." Alexander opened his mouth, but before he could speak, the policeman did. "We'll settle the question down at the station. All we have to do is pull down your pants." When Alexander was silent, he said, "Just what I thought."

They were led into the police wagon. The cafe, which had been full shortly before, was now half empty.

14

Alexander ~ September 1941, Paris

They were crowded into the back of the police wagon. One man was shouting, "This is all a mistake. My papers are all in order." He kept shouting even after the doors were closed and they began moving.

Finally, someone said, "They can't hear you. Save your voice for the police station."

The man settled back onto the bench, his face pinched and anxious.

"I shouldn't be here. This must be some kind of mistake."

Someone laughed humorlessly.

"None of us should be here. But it's not a mistake."

The shouter looked puzzled and said, "But my papers are in order!" No one answered and he stopped addressing them, only occasionally muttering, almost to himself, "My papers are in order."

Armand spoke to Alexander quietly. "I know a good lawyer—Etienne DuJardin, not Jewish."

Alexander reached into his pocket for a pencil and his notebook. He tore out a piece of paper and wrote a quick note to Elise and the Bernheims, telling them he had been arrested and asking them to contact DuJardin. He put away the notebook and pencil and folded up the note.

When they arrived at the police station, they were shuffled out of the van and into a dark hallway.

"Have your papers ready!" shouted the policemen who were corralling them into a line.

Armand nodded, just slightly, at one of the gendarmes. He came a bit closer and Alexander could see Armand pass him a folded slip of paper. Alexander did the same with his note. The man moved away from the line.

As they got closer to the front, Alexander could see an official sitting at a desk, examining the papers that were handed to him. He had several policemen behind and beside him and after he looked at each man's papers, he announced, "Thirty days."

No one was let go. No one got a longer or shorter sentence. After the sentence was pronounced, the prisoner was told to empty his pockets. The possessions were put in a large envelope, which was then labeled, Alexander assumed, with the man's name. Then he was led away.

The man who had shouted in the van had reached the desk and was trying to explain, "My papers are in order. This is all a mistake. I shouldn't be here!" He tried to point to something on the forms. "See, it says here I have official permission."

The official answered, "Keep your hands at your sides. I can read it for myself."

"You can see that I shouldn't be here."

"We'll see about that. Thirty days." His possessions were collected. The official gave a nod, and the man was led away, continuing his protest.

Then it was Alexander's turn. He handed his papers to the official, who glanced at them and then up at him.

"Belgian, eh?"

Alexander nodded and said yes.

"Not much good, the Belgians." The policeman standing next to the official snickered. "Brody. Not a Belgian name. Probably false." Alexander wanted to say that if he had faked his papers he would have been smart enough to choose a name that was unimpeachably Belgian, but he didn't. He was realizing that it didn't matter what he said, or what his papers read. If they wanted to arrest him or, rather, if they wanted to arrest a certain number of men in that particular cafe on that morning, they would, no matter what the facts.

"Thirty days. Empty your pockets." He put down his wallet, a handkerchief, his little notebook, a pencil and his pen, and some change. One of the policemen carefully counted all the money and wrote the sum, along with his name and a list of his other possessions, on the outside of an envelope.

"Can I keep the notebook and pencil?"

The official looked up for a moment and said, "No." Then they led him away.

He just had to hope that the Bernheims would get the note and be able to locate the lawyer and he would be able to help him get out. A lot of ifs and woulds.

The walls of the cell were lined with double-decker cots with thin straw mattresses and thin blankets. It was about the size of his bedroom in Antwerp, with beds for twelve men and a toilet in the corner. There were no lower beds left, so he pulled himself onto an upper one. He looked around. Armand was in the cell, and so was the protester from the van, who soon began to repeat his complaints.

"I don't know why I'm here. My papers are all in order. I have all the right stamps on them."

Another man said to him, "Why do you think the rest of us are here?"

"Wha-at?"

"Why do you think we're here?" The protester didn't answer. "Do you think we're criminals? Lawbreakers? Saboteurs? Spies?" Still no answer. "We're just like you, men who were in a certain place when the police decided to fill out their quota for the Germans."

Another man spoke. "We're not all the same. They're looking for foreigners or Jews or, better yet, foreign Jews."

"But I'm French! I was born here!"

"But where were your parents born?"

Silence.

Later, a meal was brought. A policeman led a prisoner pushing a metal cart that held metal trays. Each tray had a bowl of soup, a small hunk of bread, and a tin cup of water.

"What, no wine?" asked one man.

The policeman answered, "Haven't you heard there's a war on?" and left.

Alexander ate and drank, not because he was hungry, but because there was nothing else to do.

The man whose papers were in order, whom they had since learned was named Felix Shapiro, complained as soon as the policeman had left, "This food is terrible. How are we supposed to eat this?"

Of course, someone had to say, "With a spoon."

It was like being back in school. There was the complainer, the joker, the smart aleck, and Alexander was sure that over the next thirty days other characters would appear, including the bully and the teacher's pet. *And which one am I?* he wondered.

Some hours later, another meal was brought in, the same as the first.

And soon after that, the single light bulb in the middle of the cell was turned off and it was dark. Alexander lay awake listening to the breathing of the other men, and then some snores. Finally, he fell asleep.

The succeeding days were much the same, except that in the mornings instead of soup they were given a hot liquid that was supposed to be coffee and then they were taken out to the courtyard for exercise.

Armand quickly found a sympathetic gendarme and they were able to get brief messages out. M. Bernheim sent word that he was working on getting a lawyer. Just hearing that lifted Alexander's spirits. Some of the other prisoners complained constantly. And there was plenty to complain about. The food, both the taste and the inadequate amount, the smell, both from the toilet in the corner of the cell and the lack of clean clothes (though once a week, they were herded into a cement room with taps on poles for a cold shower, no privacy), and finally, the boredom.

Alexander tried many strategies to pass the time and alleviate boredom. He designed chemical experiments, did mental math problems, wrote letters (in his head) to Daniel, Rachel, and Elise (those were written at night, where darkness gave a semblance of privacy). Two men in the cell played mental chess. Though Alexander was an adequate chess player, he wasn't up to their standard. No one discussed politics—you never knew exactly who might be a conduit to the authorities—but they could discuss and dispute many other topics and issues: football teams; the last Tour de France; where the best bakeries were in each neighborhood; which films they had seen; who was the greatest French writer of the past; whether Racine or Corneille were greater than Shakespeare. The range of topics reflected the range of class and education among the cellmates.

The conversations helped to pass the time—the more spirited the dispute (however trivial the topic), the faster time passed. In his imagined letters, Alexander described his cellmates as cast members in a play or characters in a novel. There was Felix Shapiro, the protester, who, contrary to his name, was never remotely happy about anything. Nicolas was the joker, who not only entertained his cellmates with his humor, but had challenged himself to get at least a smile out of every one of the French guards. He was steadily wearing them down and winning at least a smile from all but the most dour. Bertrand and Lucien were the chess players; Bertrand was a tailor and Lucien a doctor. Lucien was very well read and often engaged in literary conversations with Sylvain, who had been a French teacher at a lycee. Alexander wasn't surprised to find out that Armand had been a grocery wholesale broker, a kind of middleman between the food cooperatives in the country and the small food shops in Paris.

Those were the ones who had been born or raised and schooled in France and spoke fluent French. The poorer, foreign born men spoke less, not just because their French was less good, but also because they were more wary of giving away anything about themselves, even to men in the same situation. Alexander knew that Jakub was from Poland and sold secondhand clothes and shoes. Hershel was also Polish and a cobbler.

They were almost all interested in the fact that Alexander was a chemist, and Nicolas even joked that maybe he could figure out how to create an explosion that would break open the jail. Armand told him sternly that joking about explosions was a stupid idea, and even Nicolas was chastened, though not for long.

Even without paper and pencil, Alexander kept track of the date and the days of the week. They all did; not only did it help make the end of their sentence seem ever closer, it tied them to the outside world, where the days varied, unlike the ones in the jail. Eight days after his arrest was September 12, Alexander's twenty-sixth birthday. He had been in Paris for his twenty-fifth birthday too, with the family. Mamma had managed to make a special dinner and they had all given him small presents—paperback books, socks, a jar of his favorite jam. He had appreciated the effort but he had been restless, wanting to be back in Brussels, frustrated that he didn't have his degree yet. And now, a year later, he had his PhD and was sitting in a French jail with no real contact with the outside world. He didn't bother to tell anyone it was his birthday.

Several of the prisoners were observant enough to be keeping track of the Jewish calendar. The twenty-second of September was Rosh Hashanah, the beginning of the new year. It was another marker of how much time had passed, and, like his birthday, how little his life resembled what he would have expected. Though Alexander didn't particularly miss attending services, he missed the family, the gathering, the feeling of new beginnings. If he was at the beginning of something, it was not an auspicious beginning.

The year was 5702, supposedly counted from the creation by God of the world. In his view, God had quite a few mistakes to correct in his creation.

Ten days later, on October first, was Yom Kippur, the Day of Atonement. Had there been no war, he would have spent the day in synagogue, fasting. In the past, he had fasted because there was no way not to fast, surrounded by family (especially his parents) and the Antwerp Jewish community. Here, no one cared or would be shocked if he didn't fast, and the prison diet was meager enough to make fasting rather pointless.

But listening to his pious cellmates murmuring and chanting their way through the traditional prayers, he thought a great deal about Yom Kippur. He had always appreciated the idea that one had to ask one's fellow humans for forgiveness before asking God for His forgiveness. The ritual of men going around the synagogue asking each other for forgiveness had a certain beauty, if you didn't think about which men would go back to trying to cheat and lie and smear their neighbors within days of the holiday. But this year it seemed hollow. Should he ask for forgiveness from his fellow Jews locked up with him in this cell? Or from the French gendarmes guarding them? And what about the French officials and the German occupiers? What had he done that they might forgive him for?

And what about atoning for his sins before God? It was a long time since Alexander had been a believer. His father prayed every morning at home and went to synagogue on the Sabbath and holidays. Father never went to work or wrote or rode a train or streetcar on those days, and no cooking was done or electric lights turned on. Their home was strictly kosher and even under wartime rationing he ate no pork or meat that had not been ritually slaughtered. But what did Father really believe? He was a modern, intelligent, rational man. He couldn't truly think that God created the world in six days and gave Moses the Torah on Mount Sinai. Did he follow the rules because, like many other things in his life, "that's what people like us do"?

Alexander was a scientist, both by training and by temperament. Whether there was a God or not didn't really interest him, and if there was a God, what the hell was he up to right now?

About a week before the thirty days were up, Alexander got another message from M. Bernheim, explaining that the lawyer had been away and was just now returning to Paris. Alexander was less worried since his sentence was almost up and he expected to be released soon. When he said as much to Armand, the only response was a shrug.

"What? You don't think they'll let us out? They said thirty days!"

"And what made them decide to pick us up in the first place? Is there a logic to the system? Why were we all given the same sentence? Had we all done the same thing? Did we all have the same mistakes in our papers?"

"What are you implying?"

"Don't flap your wings until there's no ceiling above your head." Alexander looked annoyed, but didn't answer. "What, you don't like my brand new old saying? My grandmother would have said that if she had thought of it!"

Alexander couldn't help a small smile, but he was more cautious about getting his hopes up.

The night before the thirty days were up, the mood in the cell was both anxious and expectant. No one slept much that night. As Alexander tossed and turned on his bunk, he could hear the same sounds from the other beds. There was less snoring than usual. They had been taken in groups of four to wash up, and though no one had clean clothes since they had not been allowed to get packages from outside, they attempted to make themselves as presentable as possible.

Finally, the cell door was opened and they were instructed to form a line. But instead of being given their possessions and set free on the streets of Paris, they were led to a bus that was already half full with other men from the jail and a few guards. As soon as the bus was full, it set off.

"Where are we going? came the querulous voice of Felix.

"Drancy," answered the driver.

Armand had been right.

15

Alexander ~ October 1941, Drancy

There was no sign at the entrance. The bus driver didn't announce the name. He didn't need to. They had all heard rumors of Drancy. It was a prison camp on the outskirts of Paris, and though they had heard whispers about people who had been taken there, Alexander had never heard of anyone who had returned.

As soon as they left the bus, they were herded into a courtyard and lined up in rows. The buildings formed a u-shape around the open space. There were windows, but most of them were painted over with dark blue paint. At one end was a long brick structure.

He had no time to notice anything else. A policeman with a clipboard stood in front of them and called out names, quickly, and looked angry with the men who took too long to answer. Then they were led to their rooms.

Alexander had thought the Paris cell was crowded, but he had not imagined how crowded a "living space" could be until he arrived at Drancy. The room was so filled with men that it was hard to perceive its true dimensions. He had a wooden bed, again a top bunk, no mattress, pillow, or blanket. *At least I was wearing a jacket when they arrested me*, he thought as he folded it up to use as a pillow. He remembered his mother looking for a chair to put her jacket and hat on in the Calais barracks. How primitive those accommodations had seemed then! He couldn't imagine his mother in this place. Better not to think about her.

Before he could further examine his new surroundings, a gendarme came in to address the new internees. All eyes turned to him.

"There will be roll calls in the courtyard twice a day, morning and evening. You will proceed to roll call in an orderly fashion, silently, and form three lines. Meals will be distributed at 11:30 and 16:45. There will be one hour of supervised exercise per day. Other than that, you are to remain in your room except to visit the sanitary facilities. Books and playing cards are forbidden. There is to be no contact between prisoners and gendarmes. No correspondence or parcels allowed. No smoking."

When the gendarme left, Alexander looked around the room. There was no furniture except for the wooden bed frames. At the end of the room was a metal pipe above what looked like a wooden trough, the pipe had seven taps attached to it. He tried to count—there seemed to be about fifty men housed in the room.

Men began to speak again. Not the new ones, like him. They were just sitting on their bunks, looking around, dazed or blank, their gaze turned inward. *This* was prison.

Everything up until now was a kind of game; no, not a game, but a trial, where like all the other tests in his life he assumed he would be able to pass with ease. The journey with the family from Antwerp—there was danger, of course. Bombings along the coast, combat around the farm, searching for food and safety. Dangerous, but also exciting, like the survival games they played at Zionist youth movement campouts. The train to Lille through the destroyed countryside, the ride in the German lorry to Paris, they were like being in a movie about war, even while he knew they were real.

Avoiding the Germans and the police in Brussels, in Antwerp, in Paris, that was real too, but it also was like being in a game where he had to outwit his opponent. Even the jail in Paris. It was crowded and uncomfortable and the food was awful, but his sentence was for thirty days, and then he expected he'd be out, ready for the next act, the next challenge in the obstacle course he was running.

But now he realized it was no obstacle course, no game, no movie. *You idiot*, he thought, *they want to crush us. They want us to die. They want me to die.* He looked across and saw Felix, who until they got here had continued to protest that it was all a mistake, that they shouldn't have arrested him. Felix was curled into himself on his wooden bed, silent for once. Even *he* realized that there was no complaining his way out of this.

Alexander sat on his bed, unmoving. He had never been this still, this empty of movement or thought, in all his twenty-six years. No one spoke to him; or if they did, he didn't hear. He had no idea how much time passed before there was a clattering at the door and food was brought in.

The man on the bed next to him gave him a gentle poke. "We have to share. There are no bowls. Or spoons."

Someone put a small piece of stale bread in his lap and handed him a metal container. "Drink some soup and then pass it on. You can take about half of what's in there."

It was thin and gray, barely deserving of the name soup. He didn't want it, but he had been told to drink, so he did. It had barely any taste. The bread was hard, but he ate it.

The meal went quickly. The containers were passed from man to man, the bread disappeared, and the bowls were taken away. They were herded out of the room, back into the courtyard. Lined up in three rows, the roll was called. The men called before him said, "Ici," so Alexander did the same when his name was shouted. They filed back up the stairs, back into the room, back to the bare wooden bunks. Alexander lay down. He stared ahead without seeing until his eyes closed and he fell asleep.

He awoke with a crick in his neck and a desperate need to pee. For a moment, he was disoriented, the way one always is waking in a new place. It came back to him as he heard a voice, "Is there a latrine anywhere here or do we just hold on until the war is over?" Nicolas was back in form.

"I'll show you," said an unfamiliar voice.

Alexander slid off his bunk and said, "I'm coming too."

He followed Nicolas and the stranger out the door to the staircase and down the steps. A gendarme stopped them.

"Red castle," said their guide.

"Is that the secret password?" asked Nicolas. The gendarme glared at him and their guide gestured for them to follow him. They walked to the open end of the courtyard, where there was a low brick building whose function was announced by its powerful smell.

The leader inclined his head and said, "The red castle—men on this side, women on the other."

Alexander tried not to breathe through his nose and did what he came for. The gendarme at the bottom of their staircase glared at them again as they passed him. Nicolas didn't try to make him smile.

Once they were inside the room again, the man turned to them, "Albert Buchalter." They introduced themselves and went back to their bunks.

That first day, Alexander felt numb. He was aware of physical discomfort—the stiffness from having slept on wood, being unwashed, hungry and thirsty, but his mind was numb. After his realization of the night before, he could think no further. He followed the new routine—they received their stale bread and so-called soup twice a day, went down to the courtyard three times, twice for roll call and once for "exercise," where they milled around in a barbed wire enclosure in the center of the courtyard. He heard other men talking and introducing themselves to each other. He responded when spoken to, but didn't start any conversations. In between, he lay on the bunk and stared at the uninteresting ceiling, the blank cement serving as a wall against thought. His sleep was full of dreams, but when he awoke he could recall none of them.

Strangely, it was Felix who brought him back to normal consciousness. The first day at Drancy, Felix had been like Alexander, shocked into silence. But by the next day, he had revived somewhat. When the gendarme came to call them down for the morning roll call, Felix walked up to him and said, "I need to speak to someone in charge."

The gendarme looked past him and announced, "Roll call."

Felix opened his mouth to speak again but someone reached out and pulled him away from the door, to the back of the crowd of men moving to the exit. Alexander was near the end of the line, right behind Felix and the man who had grabbed him.

"I need to speak to someone. There's been a mistake; my papers are in order."

"If you talk to the guards, they'll take you away to the dungeon."

Felix looked skeptical but didn't try to talk to the gendarme again.

Once they were back in the room, Felix began his litany of excuses and complaints again, the same as in the Paris jail. Instead of trying to shut him out, Alexander looked at the man and listened to his monologue.

Maybe he was right. In one way, he was obviously right—none of them should be here. It had nothing to do with whether their papers were in order or not; it was clear they were here because they were Jewish, or because they seemed Jewish, even if their papers had no official stamp. And in a sane world, no one would be in such a place just because they were Jewish. But it clearly wasn't a sane world. And Alexander had been thinking and planning as though the world were sane—as though there was something he could do, some way he could act, that would get him out of the insanity in which he found himself. And what Felix was doing was exactly the same—he was protesting as though he was in a normal situation. But nothing here was normal, and normal reactions weren't going to get any results.

But would anything get results? Maybe if the Bernheims could find and hire the lawyer Armand had told him about, maybe the lawyer could get him out. But he, Alexander, could do nothing.

No, that wasn't true. He couldn't get himself out, but he could survive until he got out. He wasn't sure what surviving involved, other than the obvious of eating the food, no matter how horrible, and doing what he could to keep clean and healthy, but he would do it.

Just like on the "outside," the inmates represented the spectrum of Jewish life. There were men who had never given a thought to being Jewish. They spoke no Yiddish or Hebrew and had no idea *what* the Jewish holidays were, let alone when they were. The Greek alphabet might be familiar to them, the Hebrew one not at all. Lucien, the doctor, and Sylvain, the French professor, who had both been in the Paris cell with him, were very secular. As was Albert Buchalter, who had been a journalist before his paper had been closed down and he was blacklisted, unable to get published under his own name.

Then there were those who thought of themselves as Jewish since they came from Germany or Austria or Poland, where they had been barred from aspects of civic life because of their name or origins, but that was as far as it went for them. Some of them had been politically active—either as secular Zionists who looked to Palestine and a possible Jewish state, or as socialists and communists who hoped to change European society so that being Jewish would be irrelevant. Lev Bestermann was from Poland and, like Alexander, was a scientist, a biologist, and had been doing a postgraduate stint in Paris when the war broke out. His family had told him to stay in France. He hadn't heard from them in months.

There were some like Alexander, not religious, but coming from religious backgrounds. They might not be especially observant themselves, but they were well aware of their difference from the general population. They had both secular and Jewish educations, and though they thought of themselves as modern secular men, their Jewishness was ingrained and inseparable from who they were.

And there were the believers, the observant Jews, who ranged from the secularly educated "Westernized" Jews like his father and Bertrand, the tailor from the Paris cell, to the recently arrived from the East who spoke only Yiddish, dressed as though they still lived in the seventeenth century, and interacted with goyim only when they couldn't avoid it.

He overheard two from the last category talking in Yiddish about Sukkos and how they were going to manage to observe it. From their conversation, Alexander realized the holiday had started the day before. Sukkos commemorated the wandering of the Hebrews in the desert; observant Jews built structures, little huts open to the sky, and ate in them for eight days. The holiday ended with Simchas Torah—the reading of the last part of the Torah and, amid dancing and celebration, beginning again from the story of Creation in Genesis.

At home in Antwerp, they built the sukkah in the back garden and decorated it with leaves, branches, paper chains, and fruits of the season. They ate in it every night, joined by the Langermanns, Bonmama, and occasionally other family members. On one night of the holiday, Mamma made stuffed cabbage, a traditional Sukkos dish in her family. It was often quite chilly on Sukkos. They sat at the table in their coats and the food was brought out at the last minute so it wouldn't get cold.

There would be no Sukkos for him this year. He looked around at the ceiling. There might easily be a hole, or several. Would that qualify as being open to the sky? And it was possible that the soup they were given to eat might contain cabbage.

The observant Jews managed to say the appropriate holiday prayers, even if they had none of the usual items and surroundings. It was useful that so many prayers were repeated—memory could be relied on when prayer books were absent. The discomfort of the surroundings, though cold, could easily remind one of wandering in the desert, but without the welcoming manna from heaven, which would have been much appreciated.

One morning, they were hustled out of their rooms a second time after the usual roll call. Prisoners from the whole camp were lined up in the courtyard. Gendarmes could be seen entering the staircases into the rooms.

"Maybe it's the cleaning crew," quipped Nicolas.

When the gendarmes came back out, it was clear they *had* been the cleaning crew, but not in the way Nicolas implied. They were carrying books, decks of cards, checkers, dominoes, anything the prisoners had managed to collect to help pass the time and retain some semblance of normalcy. The prisoners watched in silence. When they were led back into their rooms, there were frantic searches of the hiding places and relief that not everything had been found.

A little over a week after Alexander arrived, conditions improved slightly. There had been a food riot the day after Yom Kippur, before Alexander had arrived. Apparently the ritual fast had made it even clearer to many how close to fasting they were on every other day. In response to the protests, each prisoner was issued his own bowl or billy can and spoon. The soup, though still vile, was thicker, with some recognizable ingredients.

"I see a piece of onion!" someone remarked.

"Yesterday I recognized a shred of cabbage."

"That's nothing. I actually had a carrot."

"A carrot?"

"Not a whole carrot, or even a whole slice. But it was orange!" No one wanted to speculate about what else might be in the soup, but it did seem a bit more nourishing.

Several men from their room, because of their "good behavior," were put on kitchen duty. They were much envied, both because the duty gave them a chance to do something during the endless hours and, more importantly, it held the possibility to steal a bit of food. One of them came back from the kitchen saying, "We've been threatened with the dungeon or worse if we eat any of the raw vegetables."

"Why is that? Do they count the carrot splinters?"

"No, if people eat raw vegetables they might get too healthy," offered someone else.

"It's actually the opposite," said the kitchen worker, "We're so unused to eating anything but soup and stale bread that when the men eat raw food they get terrible diarrhea."

"Oh, I see, they don't even want us to have too much shit."

"Only the shit they give us. They don't want us to produce too much of our own."

A Small Door

Everyone was cold and hungry. Alexander had lost weight and his nose dripped incessantly. Many of the men were gaunt and had hacking coughs. The worst off were of course the ones who had been in poor condition or ill when they were arrested. Not only were they without adequate food, they had no medicine. Several men who had already been at Drancy when Alexander arrived were unable to get out of bed by themselves. Their roommates half-carried them down for roll call and at exercise time put them down on the ground and walked around them to shield them from the gendarmes. Lucien tried to help them, but without any medicines he could do little. Finally, a doctor from the local prefecture came to examine them, and five men were taken away to the infirmary.

"That's all we have room for," answered the doctor when Lucien pointed out that there were others in equally poor condition.

The change in food seemed to signal an improvement in conditions. Instead of gathering the men in the courtyard, morning roll call was done in the rooms because of the foul November weather.

"How kind of them to let us sleep late," one man offered.

"Well, they already serve us breakfast in bed," answered another.

At the end of October, they were each issued a straw mattress. They were thin, and no one examined them too closely, but it was more comfortable than sleeping on bare boards.

On the first of November came even more welcome news. The gendarme who did the morning roll call announced, "From now on, correspondence and parcels from the outside will be permitted. Each prisoner may send two postcards per month and receive the same number. Prisoners may also receive one food parcel of under three kilos per week, and one linen parcel every fifteen days, at which time dirty linen may be sent back to be washed. Tobacco, alcohol, medications, and writing paper are forbidden. Linen parcels may contain books, with the exception of prohibited publications and anything related to politics."

The men were cheered by the announcement. Postcards and pencils were provided and Alexander immediately wrote to the Bernheims, saying he was well and letting them know that he could receive parcels. There was a great deal of discussion among the prisoners about how and what to write on the postcards.

"Don't write anything about the conditions here. They won't allow it."

"They might not even cross it off or tell you to take something out. They might just throw out the card and never send it."

"I don't want my mother or wife to know what it's like in here anyway."

They agreed that they should ask for different books. That way, they could pass them around and have a wider variety of reading material.

The weather was getting colder. It was often raining and windy when they were taken out to exercise, the cold spitting rain of late autumn. The dust rising from the pebbles in the courtyard settled and turned to black mud. Alexander found it more and more difficult to sleep. Without enough food, no warm clothes or bedding, he was too cold to get comfortable. He thought about the wonderful new warm coat he had bought the previous year in Paris to replace the one left behind at home. He supposed the landlord of his lodging had taken it to use or sell.

Then the heat came on in the rooms—not enough to be really warm, but it was a bit more comfortable. And the first packages arrived. The prisoner in charge of mail distribution arrived in the room, accompanied by a gendarme, of course. Everyone stood by his bed, waiting for his name to be called. Alexander could see that the packages had been opened and then clumsily rewrapped. When his name was called, he went forward and took his parcel. He recognized Elise's handwriting on the paper. He hesitated before opening the parcel, holding on to the pleasure of seeing his name in her writing the way he remembered drawing out the pleasure of opening birthday presents as a child.

The contents had clearly been inspected—more than inspected. A small container of raspberry jam had been punctured with a knife. The loaf of bread had been broken into pieces. All that remained of a small, precious square of chocolate was the wrapper. The gendarme who had taken it decided to taunt him with the empty paper. But it was food, decent food, and it had been packed by her hands. Though some of the men wolfed down the contents of their parcels, many did what Alexander did and savored it slowly over several days, prolonging the pleasure. It wasn't enough to really relieve their hunger, but it made them feel less abandoned.

Some men received no parcels. Either they had no one on the outside to send one to them or their families were too destitute to buy anything. There were only a few of them, and the other men offered to share their provisions. Most of the parcelless refused the charity, knowing how little everyone had.

With the improvement in their situation, came a lifting of everyone's spirits. Most of their early conversations, beyond complaints and the information about the camp given to new arrivals, were extended introductions. Names, professions, where they had lived, whether they were married or had children. As men discovered connections—who had lived in the same neighborhood, had gone to the same school, had personal or professional acquaintances in common—conversations expanded. It passed the endless expanses of time and distracted them from the discomfort. Lev and Alexander discussed science, books and literature were debated, and, as in the Paris jail, mental chess was played.

And then there were those who made up "projects" for themselves. Two cycling fans were planning a massive cycling tour from one end of Europe to another, to begin as soon as possible after the war ended. Since they had no maps, their discussions of possible routes could go on endlessly. Lev was doing a survey of insect species in the room. He wondered, since there was so little food around and it was chilly, whether that would influence the number and species of insects. He counted the insects and drew a map on the wall with tally marks indicating how many of each species he found in different parts of the room. Alexander teased that he didn't think there was a Nobel prize for insect studies. Lev answered that he was jealous that he, Lev, could do *his* science, while Alexander had no chemical lab to work in.

Alexander and Sylvain were discussing whether Belgium had any literature that could be considered separate from "French" literature as a whole when they heard one of the gendarmes coming up the stairs. They had already been out for their walk, and it wasn't time for a meal or roll call. Everyone looked to the door.

The gendarme was followed by two men with Red Cross armbands. They walked around the room, looking at everything and everyone and asking a few questions. The gendarme watched and listened as the prisoners answered. Then they left without saying a word. The men wanted to be hopeful, but they had learned not to expect improvements.

"Just because they let them in, doesn't mean they'll listen to what they say," said Armand, ever the realist.

"Then why let them in at all?"

"So they can say they allowed the Red Cross to inspect the camp. They won't let them say anything publicly."

"Can they censor the Red Cross?"

"They can censor their own mothers if they want to." The Red Cross visit had one positive consequence. The sickest men, those who were so weak they couldn't sit or stand or had bodies swollen with malnutrition, were released.

As November wore on, new rumors traveled through the camp. The "news" was disseminated through the "Outhouse Radio." The only place prisoners from different areas of the camp could see and talk to each other inconspicuously was at the red castle, the latrine at the end of the courtyard. Outhouse radio said that the whole camp was scheduled to be closed on November 25.

In Alexander's room, the men fiercely debated whether the news was true, and what would likely happen to them if the camp closed.

"They're not going to just let us out."

"Maybe they'll release some of us. After all, they did it with the sick men."

"Don't get your hopes up. They'll probably just send us to another camp."

"There are camps at Le Vernet and Saint-Cyprien. And probably others."

"Or they could send us to Germany."

That suggestion stopped the discussion. No one wanted to consider that possibility.

On November 23, the prisoners were ordered down to the courtyard ten at a time. The yard was filled with piles of thin feather mattresses, one for each prisoner. With the feather mattress added to the straw one, the bed was almost comfortable. As they had with each improvement to their situation, the prisoners tried to figure out what might be behind the change.

"If they're going to close the camp in the next few days, why would they give us new mattresses? It must mean the camp will stay open," said Bertrand.

"That's assuming there's any logic to what they do," grumbled Guy, the resident cynic.

"Oh, there's logic in what they do, it's just not always the kind of logic we would use," added Armand. "But I agree, they probably wouldn't give us mattresses if they were going to close down the camp."

"Maybe the mattresses are infected and we'll all die before they close the camp." Felix had gone from protesting to paranoia in the six weeks at Drancy. Since they didn't look at his papers and release him when he didn't belong there, they were obviously trying to kill him. He couldn't decide whether he shouldn't eat his soup because they were probably trying to poison him, or whether they wanted him to be suspicious and die of starvation as a result. Though many of them had tried, it was hard to talk Felix out of his paranoia, since in many ways it made sense to the others.

"The mattresses won't kill us, Felix," reassured Lev, "They don't want us to die that quickly. They're enjoying the process too much."

Alexander had wondered about that. What was the real purpose behind their imprisonment and poor treatment? Restricting the lives of Jews made sense if they wanted them out of the country, out of Europe. Make it difficult to impossible for them to get an education or earn a living, burden every aspect of their lives with regulations, and they would leave. But why keep them in prison? However poorly they were housed and fed, it still cost the authorities to do so. And who was really in charge? Were the Germans telling the French authorities what to do? Or were the French taking the initiative in the hope that that would please the German occupiers? The result was the same, but Alexander wanted to understand why it was happening.

The guards who worked at Drancy (at least the ones he came in contact with) were French, not German. Did they all hate Jews? Or were they just used to doing what they were told, being gendarmes and part of a semi-military structure. Alexander knew that everyone was having a hard time getting by in wartime France. If your job was as a gendarme and you had a family to support, how much choice did you have?

Policemen were used to dealing with criminals, wrongdoers. What did they think when they looked at the prisoners they were guarding now? Were they so antisemitic they thought of all Jews as criminals, they way the propaganda portrayed them? As the prisoners got thinner, sicker, dirtier, did that just arouse disgust rather than pity or compassion? Alexander wondered what his father would say.

November 25 came and went, and the camp didn't close. The days were shorter, darker, and colder.

The first week in December, electricity was wired to the rooms—a few single bulbs hanging from the ceiling for fifty men.

The evening of December 11, an announcement was made—the Americans had entered the war on the side of the Allies. It was hard for the prisoners to hide their excitement from their jailers—the war could be won.

They had finished their evening soup and Alexander could hear the final murmurings of the grace after meals coming from his orthodox neighbor when a gendarme entered the room.

"Gather all your belongings and report to the courtyard. Immediately!"

"What?"

"No questions! Hurry!"

The prisoners complied, whispering, speculating among themselves.

"Maybe they are closing the camp."

"But where are they sending us?"

No one dared hope they would be released. No one voiced the fear they would be deported to Germany.

They filed down and lined up. Searchlights illuminated the courtyard filled with prisoners, men on one side, women and children on the other. The gendarmes seemed almost as nervous as their charges, pushing the slower or panicky prisoners with their fists and feet, creating more chaos. Lining the courtyard were soldiers with machine guns.

The crowd quieted as several German officers strode out and faced their captives. One came forward.

Someone behind Alexander whispered, "That's Danneker." Danneker was the Gestapo head of Jewish Affairs in France—the man in charge of their fate. He was flanked by the French Commandant of the camp.

Danneker barked an order in German. Alexander heard the words "three hundred men." The Commandant repeated the order in French and the gendarmes began moving among the prisoners, pulling men out of the lines and sending them to stand along the sides. Alexander held his breath as a gendarme passed him and grabbed Felix by the arm, shoving him along with his stick. Felix opened his mouth to say something, but before any words could emerge the policeman slapped him and gave him a kick to move him faster.

When they had gathered the required number, Danneker nodded his head at one of his underlings and the gendarmes began moving the chosen men out toward the exit, followed by the machine gunners. Felix looked back for a moment and Alexander could see his thin white face, his mouth open as he stumbled and turned to follow the rest of the men.

The remaining prisoners were hustled back to their rooms. At first, they just huddled on their beds, too shocked to speak, or even think clearly.

Finally, someone said what many of them were thinking, "Why now? Why them?"

"Because of the Americans." It was Armand's matter-of-fact voice.

"The Americans?"

"They're angry that the Americans have come into the war. So three hundred hostages from the Jews at Drancy have to pay for it."

"But the Americans won't know about what happens here! And will they care if they do?"

"Just so," said Armand, and that was the end of the conversation.

Alexander couldn't stop thinking about that last glimpse of Felix's terrified face. From the start, in the bus taking them from the cafe to the Paris jail, Felix had been annoying and ridiculous, whining and protesting that there was a mistake, that his papers were in order. And now he was gone, and Alexander would most likely never see him again. It was almost as though Felix had been a character in a bad story, a caricature who appeared to create a diversion and then was quickly disposed of when he was of no use. No, it wasn't that—that implied there was an author with a plan for each of them in the story. Felix had been here, had been with them, with him, and now he was gone. There was no reason, no plan, at least no plan that had anything to do with *Felix*. And there was no plan especially for him, Alexander, either. He was here, now, and whatever might happen next was completely random. The next time the gendarme's eyes might alight on him, and it would be his face looking back at the others.

Two days later, a detachment from the Wehrmacht arrived at the camp. This time they didn't bring all the prisoners down to the courtyard. A soldier came around with a gendarme and read names from a list.

"Joseph Handelsman." Handelsman had owned a small bookstore near the Sorbonne on the left bank. "Bring your belongings. Albert Buchalter."

The man who had shown them to the latrines that first morning, who had introduced himself and given advice on how to navigate camp life. "Take your belongings." The two men gathered their few possessions and walked to the door. "Gabriel Epstein."

Buchalter answered, "He's dead. Died almost two weeks ago."

The German officer looked at Buchalter suspiciously. "Are you sure?"

Buchalter looked back at him. "Why would I lie?"

The officer shrugged, as if to say, "Who knows what a Jew will do?" and then walked out of the room, followed by the two prisoners and the gendarme.

"Why Handelsman and Buchalter?"

"Why anyone? Why the three hundred men on Friday?"

"That was clearly random; any three hundred men would do. But this time they had a list with names on it. They wanted those particular men. Why?"

"Who knows? Maybe they made the list randomly. Danneker said, 'I want this many Jews,' and someone goes down a list and marks off that number. There's nothing we can do to not be chosen, to not be on the next list."

They heard via the Outhouse Radio that eight of the men taken by the Wehrmacht were well-known Jews—lawyers mostly. Did that mean the men who were taken were going to be treated better or worse? No one was sure.

It was the first night of Chanuka. No candles of course, but the observant sang the traditional songs even though they couldn't say the blessings.

"A miracle would be nice right now."

"But maybe something other than oil for the Temple."

"A few latkes maybe?"

"Rather than oil or latkes, we could use Judah Maccabee."

And then, an amazing development, maybe a miracle of sorts. Albert Buchalter came back. He told them what had happened.

"They took us to Sante, a camp where they already had another fifty prisoners from somewhere else. They told us we would all be shot the next day because we were 'Judeo-communists.' We were allowed to write letters to our families and given a meal of stewed cabbage. They went through their lists and that's when they discovered a mistake. Their list had an Albert Buchalter who was born on April 22, 1900. I was born on May 3, 1906. I

A Small Door

was the wrong Albert Buchalter! You'd think one Jew would be as good as another when it came to execution on a made up charge, but these Germans have their standards. They brought me back here and took the April 22, 1900 Buchalter, poor bastard. They've all been shot."

He went back to his old bunk and they all were quiet. Absurdity is only amusing when it's not a matter of your own life and death.

December ended and the new year began. It was hard not to hope that 1942 might bring better times, but Alexander was not too optimistic. The postcards and parcels from Elise and the Bernheims kept him from feeling utterly cut off from the outside world. He wondered about the rest of the family in Cuba, and about what was happening in Brussels. Was the university still open? Professor Vermeulen, Lucas, and the others working with the Resistance, were they safe? Some war news filtered in to the prisoners, and some heard from their families how much more difficult daily life had become. Some men stopped getting parcels; their families had left Paris, gone into hiding, or had nothing to send.

At the end of January, Danneker returned, and they were all brought down to the courtyard again. This time he made an announcement. Volunteers were needed to do farm work in northern France. He promised good food, comfortable housing, and pay. Alexander knew it had to be a trick, but enough men volunteered that Danneker was satisfied. Of course, they never found out if those men got what they were promised.

The first week in February, another fifty or so men were taken away, again from a list. None of them returned, and no one had any illusions about what had happened to them. With his first February package, Alexander got a postcard from Elise's uncle. Elise and her mother had been "detained" and he was working to get them released.

Alexander was frantic. And filled with guilt. Had they been taken because of their contact with him? He could barely eat or sleep.

Lev noticed and asked him what was wrong. "I mean, what new is wrong? Aside from everything else that has been bad from the beginning." Alexander told him. "Are they Jewish?" Alexander nodded. "Then it probably has nothing to do with you. They would be in trouble no matter what."

"I can't help but feel responsible ..."

"Don't. Feel bad for them, worry about them, but don't feel guilty. None of us are blameless in life, but we are not to blame for what's happening now. You might as well blame your parents for having you, and then making it worse by circumcising you."

At the end of the month, Alexander got his last postcard from Elise.

"We are well. Mother and I are planning a little holiday. I hope you are well and look forward to seeing you. Love, Elise."

From that, Alexander understood that they were going into hiding and would not be able to contact him again. Though he missed the cards and parcels, he was calmer knowing she was safe. He would see her when all this was over. He just had to make it through.

March came, but there was little change in the weather. It was still cold and raw and frequently raining, the kind of freezing rain that chills you through even if you're warmly dressed, which of course none of them were. Alexander's dripping nose led to a cough, which made sleeping even more difficult. No sooner did he lie down than he began to cough. At least he didn't have to worry about disturbing the others. The room was filled with a discordant symphony of coughs, sneezes, snores, and groans.

The holiday of Purim came on March 3. There was none of the joyous gaiety that usually accompanied the holiday, but the observant recited the story of Esther from memory. On Chanuka they had wished for a Judah Maccabee, now they hoped, with even less likelihood of success, for another Queen Esther to plead for their lives from Haman/Hitler. No luck.

March was almost over when a gendarme came to the door of the room. "Gather your belongings and come down to the courtyard. Quickly!"

They did as they were told. Everyone was tired; they had been worn down by the months of cold and hunger, the times when prisoners had been pulled from among them and sent away, never to return. Nicolas' jokes came less frequently, and few had the energy to argue or ask questions.

This time it wasn't the whole camp lined up, just the occupants of several rooms. They were marched out of the camp gates. Alexander looked around. The streets were empty of people. No one was about, and there were no buses or lorries waiting for them. A whisper went down the line from the men at the front—"the train station!"

At the station, was a long line of third class carriages, each one guarded by two armed French gendarmes. They were bundled into the train and the doors were shut. Someone dared to ask the gendarmes where they were going.

"You'll see soon enough," was the answer. The train jerked and began moving. Alexander was by the window. Despite the anxious uncertainty, he looked hungrily out of the train. He had been at Drancy for six months and the outside world was still here!

"Which direction are we going?" whispered Nicolas.

"North, I think," Lev said from behind him.

As they passed through familiar stations without stopping, Alexander knew. This was a route he had traveled before.

"We're on the way to Belgium," he said. They knew what that meant.

Germany.

16

Alexander ~ March 1942, Northern France

It was the most basic of third class carriages—wooden benches, no padding, bare floors. But it was clean and there were large windows. And at the end of the car was a drinking faucet and a toilet with a door.

At 6:40, just as it was getting dark, the train came into the station at Compiègne. The men looked at each other. There was another camp at Compiègne. Was that where they were being taken? Their train was shuttled off to a siding. The gendarmes took turns taking breaks off the train to smoke, get food, walk around.

The prisoners speculated among themselves. Surely the train would have stayed on the platform if they were being taken off? Was it better to be taken off the train or not? No one had any illusions they were being freed. But it was better to stay in France than be shipped to Germany. Even if Compiègne was worse than Drancy, they would still be in France.

After almost an hour's wait, the train was shunted back to the platform. More cars were coupled to the train, and a long line of prisoners guarded by French gendarmes were led along the platform and loaded onto the new cars. They would not be going to the camp in Compiègne.

An hour after it had arrived, the train left. Around nine, they pulled into Laon, where they stayed for less than twenty minutes. It was after ten when the train entered the station at Reims and was shunted into a siding. Their guards told them that the train was stopping for the night.

There was little conversation among the men. No one wanted to voice the conclusion, by now fairly clear, that they were headed to Germany. They tried to sleep, lying on the benches or the floor, using their few belongings as covers and pillows.

By daylight, everyone was awake. The gendarmes had taken shifts for breakfast, but there was no food given to the prisoners. Nicolas asked when their morning "soup" would be served.

"You'll eat when you get there," was the answer.

"When we get where?" No answer.

Suddenly, there was the sound of running feet and yelling outside of the train. One of the gendarmes went to the exit. From the windows, they could see police, railway workers, and German soldiers rushing over the tracks.

The guard came back into the car. "Close the shades," he ordered. Then he called the roll for the first time since they had left Drancy.

"Why are they calling the roll? We haven't moved. Where could we have gone?" whispered Nicolas from behind Alexander.

"No talking!" The guards, who had been taking their duties fairly easily with their charges corralled within the railway carriage, became more vigilant, walking back and forth along the aisle.

Finally, soon after nine in the morning, the train was shunted back to the main track and began moving again. They were allowed to partially lift the shades. They seemed to be going northeast, through Alsace. The guards' vigilance relaxed slightly and the men began whispering, speculating about what might have happened at Reims. It wasn't until several hours later that they learned, via the rumor mill that could never be completely stamped out no matter how hard the authorities tried, that someone had jumped from the train and escaped. The thought cheered them no end.

"They were stupid not to guard the train more thoroughly, at least while we are still in France," said Lev to Alexander. He nodded, and they both looked glum. Hard as it was to think of doing what that man had done, it was impossible to think of escaping once they were in Germany. In France, it was possible to blend into the population, but in Germany?

"Do you speak German?" Lev asked.

"Yes," Alexander answered, "but I have no idea if it will help."

"Who knows what will help, or make any difference. I thought being a Pole rather than being French, or Belgian," he said, looking at Alexander, "was worse, but it turned out it didn't make a difference because I'm a Jew."

"I was born in England," Alexander said softly. "My father is Belgian, but I'm legally British."

Lev stared at him. "Tell them," he whispered fiercely. "Maybe they'll just intern you with other British nationals."

Alexander shook his head. "Why would they believe me? My papers say

I am Belgian. Nothing says I was born in England." He laughed bitterly. "It seemed too dangerous to be British."

"How did you come to be born in England?" Albert Buchalter, sitting behind them with Nicolas, asked curiously.

"My parents went there during the last war. My mother grew up in London; all her family are there."

"Then why didn't you go there this time?"

"We tried. Couldn't get across."

"And you, how did you come to be in Paris?" Buchalter asked Lev.

"My professor in Warsaw had contacts at the Sorbonne. My family pushed me to go there once the war started. They thought I'd be able to send for them later if things got too bad in Poland." There was a brief silence as they all thought about what might be happening to Lev's family now.

Prompted by more questions, the men began to share their stories with each other. Lev's parents had both been teachers. He was twenty-six, like Alexander, and had two younger sisters. Nicolas was, to everyone's surprise, an accountant. If anyone seemed unlikely to spend his days with dry figures, it was Nicolas. He was married to a non-Jewish woman. His wife had gone to stay with her grandparents in the country when he had been imprisoned. He was an orphan with no other close family.

Albert Buchalter had been a journalist, writing for a daily paper until it was closed down. As a Jew and someone who had written for a closed publication, he couldn't get another job. He was married and had a small son. Before he was arrested, he and his wife had made arrangements for her and the child to go into hiding if anything happened to him.

The train made one more station stop near Strasbourg in Alsace. Then they traveled continuously from the afternoon of March 28 into the night of March 29. Their guards were rotated, giving the gendarmes time off, but there were always at least two armed guards in the car. There was water, but they were given no food. They slept, talked, and slept again. No more speculating about where they were going. Some places were recognizable— the train went through Stuttgart and Nuremberg and continued on. The next big city was Pilsen, in Czechoslovakia, and then Prague. Still, the train traveled on through the night of the 29th.

As dawn broke on March 30, Lev said, "I think we're in Poland."

They came to a shuddering halt. Through the window, Alexander could see the end of the tracks, an open area, and iron entrance gates with the words "ARBEIT MACHT FREI."

"What does it mean?" whispered Lev.

Alexander answered, "Work sets you free."

"And I thought the Germans had no sense of humor," was Nicolas' comment.

They were hurried off the train. Alexander was tired, terribly tired, and disoriented from lack of food. Many of the men stumbled, their legs cramped from the long journey and weak from fasting.

Buchalter whispered fiercely, "Look strong! Stand straight."

They were lined up and led into the camp and into a low barrack filled with wooden bunks. About a third of the bunks were already filled with men even dirtier and more gaunt than they were. They claimed unoccupied beds and sat down, numb. The man in the bed next to Alexander's gave him a welcoming nod and said, "Welcome to Auschwitz, hell's training ground."

The new arrivals were pushed out of the barrack and lined up for roll call. As their names were called, each man was asked his trade or profession. What was the right answer? Something manual that might be useful to the Germans? But what would happen when they found out you actually knew nothing about carpentry or masonry? What else might be helpful? Some men couldn't think fast enough to lie. When Sylvain said he was a French teacher, the soldier laughed and said, "We'll see how quickly you can dig ditches."

Each prisoner was assigned to a "kommando" or work group, with its own prisoner leader, or "kapo." When they learned that Lucien was a doctor, they assigned him to the prisoners' hospital. He said quickly, "There's a pharmacist here. He should be able to help me."

"We'll decide who works where. But who is this man?"

Lucien pointed to Alexander.

"Name?"

"Brody, Alexander."

"And you're a pharmacist?"

Alexander nodded, "Yes."

"You'll work in the hospital kommando."

When they were sent back to their hut, Alexander thanked Lucien, who shrugged. "If we don't try to help each other, we're finished."

Alexander heard his name called out. He turned and saw Willy, his neighbor from the Paris lodging house.

"I thought you got away."

"I thought so too. I had all the papers and was on my way out of Paris when I was stopped at a routine checkpoint. There had been Resistance activity in the area and they were looking out for anything suspicious. They decided my papers didn't match my French accent. When they realized I was Austrian, they sent me straight here."

"How did they figure out you were Austrian?"

"The man who faked my papers was with me; he told them in hopes they wouldn't deport him."

"Did they?"

"They were going to, and he tried to run. They shot him." They were both silent for a moment. "What happened to you?"

"I was in a cafe getting my papers and there was a raid. They sent us to a French prison, then Drancy, now here."

"What kommando are you with?"

"The hospital. They think I'm a pharmacist."

"Good, you'll be inside. I'm in the kitchen. No extra food, but it's out of the weather."

The food was similar to what they had been given at Drancy: thin soup, and dry, sour bread. Their clothes were taken and they were given uniforms to wear, thin striped pants and shirts. Their shoes were left to them.

As he and Lucien walked over to the hospital block early in the morning, Alexander was too preoccupied to notice much of the surroundings. What would happen if they realized he wasn't really a pharmacist? Would Lucien be in trouble too?

The hospital was barely worthy of the name. The patients lay on iron beds, though unlike the wooden ones in the barracks, they had bedding. But they were clearly still prisoners. They wore the same clothes as Alexander and Lucien. There were very few of the medical supplies that one would expect in a hospital. There was one tap in a sink at the end of the room, but no piles of clean linen, and little soap or disinfectant.

The doctor in charge was an SS officer, but he spent very little time dealing with the patients, or with the prisoners like Lucien and Alexander working in the hospital. Their real supervisor was the kapo, a Polish prisoner who did little work himself but made sure they were always busy.

Alexander needn't have worried about not being a real pharmacist. They were put to work emptying bedpans and sweeping and moving trash, mostly discarded bandages. The smell was horrendous; he struggled not to gag. They were watched all the time, not by the doctor, but by the kapo. If they worked too slowly or missed something, the kapo shoved them and scolded them in Polish. Alexander had no idea what he was saying, but it didn't matter—he realized quickly that if he stood still or didn't seem to be working, the kapo would hit him.

When the kapo wasn't watching, Lucien tried to help the patients. There was little he could do medically, but he offered reassurance and attempted to make them more comfortable. If the kapo caught him talking to the sick, examining them, bringing them water, or shifting someone to ease their discomfort, he yelled at him or struck him.

One of the other prisoners in the kommando was a Czech named Elias, who spoke enough German for Alexander to converse with him. He had been there for six months and, in whispered conversations when they happened to be working side by side, explained how to get by.

"Never look like you're not working or like you don't know what to do. Don't ask any questions. This kapo isn't too bad, his beatings are mostly for show. He's worse when the doctor is watching or if he thinks someone might snitch to the officer. And watch out for Marek," he indicated the prisoner working at the end of the room.

"Why?"

"He'd give away his mother if it got him more food. The worst snitch you can imagine."

Listening to the other prisoners in his barracks, Alexander realized that he was very lucky to be in the hospital kommando. Lev had been sent to clean latrines, which, though it sounded miserable, was considered one of the better jobs since the latrines were roofed and sheltered from the weather and the kapo was tolerable. Nicolas and Sylvain were doing hard labor, clearing stone from an area for construction. By the end of the first week, Nicolas had stopped joking and Sylvain was barely speaking, crawling onto his bed each night, silent.

Alexander was so exhausted from the work and the poor food that he barely had time to think about how miserable he was. He fell asleep almost as soon as he lay down, and had few dreams, at least none that he remembered. He had never been so tired in his life. By the second week, he had lice, despite the fact that his head had been shaved.

The itching was maddening, and he remarked to Lev, "My mother would be mortified to hear I had lice. According to her, people like us don't get lice."

"They're not lice, they're insect members of the SS, 'Pediculus humanis capitis germanicus.' They specialize in Jewish blood."

Next he developed a rash on his torso and legs.

"Malnutrition," said Lucien tersely, when he showed him the rash. "We're going to be textbook cases."

Thoughts about Elise and his family were fleeting and painful. In the Paris prison, he had looked forward to release, thinking only of the future. In Drancy too, he imagined the end of the war, especially after they heard that the Americans had joined the Allies. But now all he could do was get through each day. He told himself that that was his task: to survive each day. Each day that he continued alive, and himself, was some kind of victory over the Germans, and maybe, though he was almost afraid to put it into words, one step closer to the end of the war.

Many of the men were losing heart, turning in on themselves, giving up, like Sylvain. Others had ways of staying sane and as strong as possible. Lev made up taxonomic names for the insects, German functionaries, and kapos. Albert Buchalter asked each of them about the work they did and what they noticed in the camp, as though he were still a reporter. He was the one who learned and told the rest of them what the greasy black smoke was that they often saw in the sky, and why so many trains seemed to arrive at Auschwitz and yet they didn't see more prisoners around.

And Lucien, Lucien tried to stay a doctor, even as he emptied bedpans and swept the floor. One time, when the kapo had kicked him for spending too long near one of the dying patients, Alexander asked him why he did it.

A Small Door

"You know he's going to punish you, and the man is dying anyway. Why do you put yourself in danger?"

"Because I'm a doctor."

"What good will your being a doctor be if the kapo beats you to death?"

"I took an oath, the Hippocratic Oath. If I don't live up to my oath, who am I?"

"Alive? I don't mean to be flippant, but what value is being a doctor if you're dead?"

"My death here is likely anyway. I might as well live what little time I have left with some integrity, some purpose."

Alexander didn't know what living in Auschwitz with integrity and purpose meant for him. Just staying alive to see Elise and his family seemed an overwhelming task. Maybe that would have to be enough. To survive.

Surviving was the goal of every prisoner, except those who had already given up. The way to survive was to get extra food and avoid physical abuse. How did one get more food? Alexander soon learned about the camp practice of "organizing." Organizing was stealing or smuggling valuables that could be bartered for food or privileges. But that, like everything else in Auschwitz, could be very dangerous, as Alexander would soon learn.

The hospital patients were sometimes given extra food. Not much, and not any better quality, but it was something. It was either distributed right away or kept locked up. Alexander assumed that only the German doctor had the key.

Both Lucien and Alexander suspected that Marek stole food from the patients who were too weak to eat it, but they had never actually witnessed it. Even if he had seen Marek doing it, Alexander wouldn't have reported it, but someone else must have, because one morning the kapo was dragging Marek from his sweeping as the man protested that he was innocent and had done nothing.

It made no difference. The kapo picked up a stick and began beating Marek right in the middle of the hospital room. Elias, Lucien, and Alexander retreated to the farthest corners to avoid being seen. Marek was crouched on the ground, his arms folded over his head to protect it. The kapo began kicking as well as beating with the stick. Blood and snot were pouring from Marek's face. The noise brought in the German doctor.

"What's going on?"

"He stole food from the patients."

"Stupid Jew—stealing from the sick. Why did you steal from your own people?"

Marek could barely speak, but he managed to squeak out, "The store cabinet was unlocked."

The officer turned on the kapo. "How could that be?" he shouted.

"But sir, I don't—" Before the man could continue, the officer hit him across the mouth. Then he pulled out his pistol and shot the kapo in the head. The man collapsed like a rag doll.

Alexander was frozen in place. The officer wheeled around and saw the three men at the other end of the room.

"Take out this trash," he barked, indicating the kapo with his foot. Elias nudged Alexander and Lucien to follow him and they picked up the dead kapo and carried him to the back door of the hospital, where the dead patients were put until they were collected. Meanwhile, the officer had shouted to someone in front of the hospital. A soldier came and, pointing his gun at Marek, told him to get up. Marek managed to stagger to his feet. The soldier hustled him to the door.

The officer barely looked at the three men as they came back from their chore. "Get back to work," he spat, and went into his office.

After a few moments, Alexander asked Elias, "What will happen to Marek?"

"The gas chambers."

A few days later, there was a "selection" at morning roll call. They were lined up and an SS doctor walked down the line and looked at each one of them, deciding whether they were fit enough to continue working. Alexander was exhausted, but without even thinking, he forced himself to stand straight and look ahead when the doctor came by him. He didn't make eye contact, just stared into the distance, seeing nothing. The doctor passed. But when he got to Nicolas, he gestured for him to get out of the line.

When the inspection was over, the men selected were marched off in the direction of the gas chambers, Nicolas with them. Nicolas, who had talked back to the gendarmes in the Paris prison and the guards at Drancy. He had even joked when they arrived at the entrance to Auschwitz.

Back in the barracks, Armand came up to him and slipped him an extra piece of bread.

"How?"

"Organizing." He saw Alexander hesitate and said gruffly, "Eat it. We can't afford to be fussy. To survive, you've got to eat what comes your way."

"Thank you." Alexander forced himself to chew on the dry, stale bread. Armand watched him.

"Don't let them win."

There was a new kapo at the hospital, another Polish non-Jew. He wasn't as bad as some of the kapos they heard about, but he was quick to strike when he thought one of the men wasn't working hard enough. The more Alexander heard, the more he realized how "lucky" he was to be in the hospital. He couldn't see how he looked, but some of the other men, like Sylvain and Willy, were looking more and more like walking skeletons. The hospital was indoors, and the work, though constant and unpleasant, didn't require the physical strength that he didn't have.

Alexander and Elias were emptying bedpans to give Lucien a little time to comfort a dying prisoner when the German doctor came in to look for the kapo.

"What are you doing?" he shouted at Lucien.

"Just moving his leg a bit." Lucien knew to give as little information as possible and not look directly at the German.

"You've been told not to try and treat the patients! You Jews are just covering for each other!" Lucien said nothing. "Arrogant Jewish doctors! You think you know better than anyone else." When Lucien still said nothing, the officer was even more infuriated. He pulled off his belt and began whipping Lucien. "That'll teach you to know your place, Jewish swine!"

The breath caught in Alexander's throat, but he could do nothing. Anything he did or said would only make things worse for Lucien, and for him. He only hoped the madman wouldn't kill Lucien.

Finally, the officer stopped, and before leaving to go back to his office, said, "If I catch you practicing medicine again, it'll be even worse."

The kapo came back in and glared at them all. Lucien dragged himself up and crawled over to the patient's bed.

Elias hissed, "Lucien, no!"

Lucien looked up at him. "He's dead."

At the end of their shift, Alexander and Elias supported Lucien back to the barracks. Elias kept telling Lucien he had to be more careful. Alexander said nothing. He knew Lucien wouldn't change.

Alexander crawled into his bunk. His body ached as though he had been beaten. He fell asleep and woke up coughing and disoriented. For a moment, he thought he was back home in Antwerp, in bed with bronchitis. Growing up, he had gotten sick with it every winter. Then he saw Lev in the next bunk and remembered where he was.

The next day, when he returned from the hospital, Willy was gone.

"He never woke up," said Lev. "Died in his sleep, lucky fellow."

Alexander shook his head. "No, he must have gotten his papers and left. He told me he'd see me in New York."

Lev looked at him oddly. "What are you saying?"

"I don't know." Alexander tried to shake his head, but it was pounding. He shivered and started coughing.

"Get into bed. I'll bring you your food." Alexander climbed into the bunk. He couldn't stop shivering, and as soon as he lay down, he began coughing again. Lev brought him his bread, but he couldn't eat.

They dragged him out for roll call and managed to prop him up between Lev and Armand. He was able to stand long enough to satisfy the soldier taking the roll. In the hospital, he swept whenever the kapo was watching him and used the broom to help support himself. Elias watched him and the battered Lucien worriedly, and just barely got them back to the barrack at the end of their shift. Lev brought his food.

"Just need to sleep," he said, and closed his eyes. Despite the coughing, he drifted off. He would sleep, then wake in a violent fit of coughing and retching, then fall back asleep in exhaustion. He shivered, then felt like he was burning, then started shivering again, his teeth chattering.

He fell asleep again and dreamt. He was in his bed in Antwerp with Daniel in the other bed. As on so many nights, he was telling Daniel about something, maybe an experiment in the lab or a joke one of his lecturers had told, or about some odd character he had met in Brussels that he knew his brother would get a laugh out of. He wasn't sure what he was saying, and every once in a while, Daniel would say "mmm" or something like that so Alexander knew he was still listening and not yet asleep. Daniel was a good listener, the best. Usually at night Alexander would talk first, and then Daniel would tell him what he had been doing, who he had been seeing. They were close as brothers, though, like all brothers, they argued. Finally, Alexander finished talking. He drifted at the edge of sleep, waiting for his brother to speak.

17

Rachel ~ July 1942, Havana

It was not even 7:30 in the morning and already the air felt thick and steamy. In the year since they had arrived in Cuba, Rachel had learned that if she walked too quickly she would arrive at work dripping with sweat. A group of workmen repairing the road whistled and called out a compliment. She smiled and kept walking. She never felt threatened in Havana by the comments men made. It was just part of being in Cuba. She glanced at her watch. Good, she would be early. Not too early, but early enough to get settled at her machine and chat with her friend Stella before they had to start working.

It felt good to be back at the diamond factory, where she spent her days polishing diamonds. Especially after yesterday.

In November, when they had been in Cuba for four months, Rachel came home to find Mother in tears, and Father trying in vain to comfort her.

"What happened? Is it Daniel?" Her mother shook her head. "Is something wrong with Lena? One of the children?" Father handed her a letter. She looked at the signature.

"Who is Albert?"

"Mimi Bernheim's brother-in-law," Father answered. Oh. She realized the letter must be about Alexander. Or maybe not, maybe just about the Bernheims. She felt ashamed of the momentary lessening of the tension in her stomach. No, if Mamma was crying, it must be Alexander. Rachel turned to read the letter.

"My dear Freda,

Mimi wants me to write to you that your son is in perfect health and has a perfect morale..."

"If Alexander is in perfect health and morale, why is Albert writing and not Alexander?"

"Read on."

"... but he cannot write for the present. It seems that his papers were not in perfect

order and that he got in trouble therefore. Everything that can be done for him is done, through my family in Paris, and, Mimi adds, you could not do better.

Mimi wants you not to worry, she hopes that he will be set free very soon. Of course, as soon as I know of anything I will let you know ..."

"What does he mean, everything that can be done for him is done?"

"I expect they are contacting a lawyer, trying to use connections ..."

Rachel looked at her father. This was why he didn't want Alexander to go back to Belgium or stop in Paris on the way back. He was afraid; and rightly so.

"Is there anything we can do?" Father looked uncertain. "I'll ask at the Joint Distribution Committee tomorrow when I go to work. Maybe the Red Cross can help. There must be something."

"We need to write to Lena and Freddy. And Daniel."

She nodded. "I'll write Daniel, you take care of Lena and Freddy." She turned to her mother. "I'll make tea. While you drink it, I'll write to Daniel, then you can add on to the letter."

The months stretched on and they didn't get the visas for America. Rachel left the job with the Joint Distribution Committee; it was just too upsetting listening to the new refugees telling their stories, hearing about journeys much more terrifying than theirs had been.

The diamond factories opened and Rachel got a job polishing diamonds, making much more money than before. Her father managed to do some business but never earned enough to support them. They lived on Rachel's wages, help from Freddy, and what Daniel sent from his army pay.

For months, there was no more news of Alexander, neither through the Bernheims nor from anywhere else. The Joint Distribution Committee and the Red Cross were unable to get information. In September 1942, they received another letter from Albert, which had taken almost a month to get there.

"My dear Freda,

First of all I want to give you a glimpse of good news."

Rachel caught her breath. Maybe he was free!

"Alexander left the camp as a sanitary help, it is considered the best for him in his case. Impossible to get further news."

"If he left the camp, does that mean he's free?"

"No. They sent him to a different camp." She knew that couldn't be good. But what did sanitary help mean? She didn't ask.

"I heard of this as Mimi and her daughter Elise were for a month at Drancy."

"Oh no!" Rachel and her mother exclaimed together.

"Mimi's husband managed to get them out, God knows how, after a month's stay. They are at home now, safe. Alexander's occupation will spare him some hard work and give him certain favors. Be brave and hope for the best, every one of us has now his burden, and none of us feels safe. Be sure that nobody could have done anything for him, even had you known of his troubles in time, it was not a case to arrange with money. Be sure that as soon as I know of anything I will let you know, and cable if there is anything of importance."

"We should have waited for him in Bayonne. We never should have left without him." Mother was crying again.

"And risked everyone? We've been through this before, Freda. We are safe. And more important, Rachel and Beatrice and Maurice and Louise are safe. We could have all ended up in camps. We had to leave."

"And Daniel? Daniel isn't safe!"

"Daniel and Alexander are adults, men. They made their own decisions." Father took Mamma's hand. "We can only pray. And hope for the best. There's nothing else we can do. Just hope the war ends soon."

Once a month, her parents went to the American Consulate to find out if there was any progress on their request for visas to the United States. Each month, they were asked the same questions.

"Have you heard from your son, Alexander?"

"No."

"Have any Germans tried to contact you?"

"No."

"When did you last see your son?"

"November 1940."

"Where was that?"

"In Paris."

"When did you last hear from your son?"

"We received a postcard in July 1941."

"Where were you when you heard from him?"

"In Spain, Bilbao."

"Where was he?"

"In Belgium."

And on it went. Pa answered all the questions, with Mother just sitting next to him, listening. At the end of the questions, Pa would ask, "And is there any news about our visas?"

And the official would answer, "I'm afraid not, sir."

After the first time, Rachel asked Pa, "Why do they ask you all those questions about Alexander? Are they trying to help find him?" Pa shook his head. "Then why?"

"They think the Germans will try to get in touch with me to use me as a spy in return for Alexander's safety." By now, Mother was crying.

"That's insane! What could you spy on?"

He shrugged. "That's why they won't give us visas. We're a security risk."

Mother was rocking back and forth and Rachel had to try and comfort her while her father sat at the kitchen table, staring at his hands.

Yesterday was the worst yet. The consulate had been crowded and they had had to wait much longer than usual. Between the heat and the wait, her parents were even more on edge than usual. Neither of them had been able to eat that day. A new official was asking the questions and he was brusque and impatient, barely giving Pa a chance to answer. And of course, the session had ended the same as always—no visa.

Rachel was already home from work when they got back to the apartment. Mamma fell apart immediately. She wasn't just crying, she was hysterical, wailing and saying Alexander's name over and over. Usually Pa just sat or went to another room, leaving Rachel to soothe her.

But this time, he turned to Mamma. "Stop it! Stop now! Your crying won't bring him back!" By now, he was almost yelling, in his own way nearly as hysterical as she was. Confronted with two hysterical parents, Rachel didn't think, she just acted. Turning to her father, she slapped him.

Silence.

"I'm sorry," she whispered. Pa nodded slightly and walked out of the room. Rachel put her arms around her mother, who was now weeping softly.

After a few minutes, the crying stopped and Rachel asked, "Do you want me to make supper?" In answer, Mother stood and together they put together the meal, without speaking. The three of them ate together, or rather pretended to eat, as no one was hungry.

When she began clearing the table, Rachel said to her mother, "Why don't you go to bed, Mamma? I'll do the washing up." Mother got up and left Rachel and her father alone in the room.

She knew she had to say something, though she had no idea what. She had said she was sorry, but that didn't feel like enough. "Pa ..." she started.

"Don't," he answered. "You don't need to say anything. You did the right thing. *I'm* sorry." And he walked over to the armchair and picked up the newspaper.

Rachel finished cleaning up and said goodnight to her father. She lay in bed, awake, for a long time.

The war went on. There was no more news of Alexander. Daniel sent letters when he could, from Canada, and then from England. And the monthly visits to the consulate continued, with no better results.

There were many young Jewish refugees in Havana waiting out the war, working in the diamond factories or going to school. Most of them had had difficult journeys to get to Cuba, some were with their parents, but others had traveled on their own, sent ahead by families who didn't or couldn't afford to leave. Many of them were like Rachel, living a normal life but anxious and guilty about those left behind. Some of the young men did what Daniel had done, signing up or rejoining the armed forces so they could fight.

They went to the beach in big groups, to the clubs to hear music and go dancing. On weekends, they often went out to the country, camping. And after a while, some began to pair off.

The war news began to get better. And then in June, 1944, the Allies invaded and the Germans were finally in retreat. Rachel sat by the radio with her parents, listening to the news.

"Maybe Daniel is with them."

"Better he should go later, when it's safer." Nobody wanted to remind Mother that there was precious little safety in combat.

Over the summer, everyone followed the news avidly, marking on both mental and physical maps the progress of Canadian and British troops through northern France into Belgium.

Once Paris was liberated, Daniel was able to go there on leave. He spent most of his time talking to the Bernheims and trying to find out what had happened to Alexander. After Mimi and Elise had been released from Drancy, they had been warned by non-Jewish friends to "disappear," and had gone into hiding until the liberation. Daniel wrote his family what they knew about Alexander.

"When he came to Paris, he was of course without regular papers, and without a ration card ... He was overconfident. The Bernheims were more afraid for him than he was for himself, but didn't want to take a 'you've got to get out of Paris at once' line, because they didn't want to appear as if they wanted to get rid of him ... He was at Drancy until he was sent away. This was either the 24th or the 26th of March, 1942, with a group of doctors—he was taken away as a pharmacist. That is where our hope lies. If they considered him as useful, then his chances are good."

"The Germans would want to use his skills," Mother said hopefully. Father said nothing, but Rachel saw her mother's anxious look, and nodded. "We can hope," Mother added.

But when she had gone to bed and Rachel sat alone with Father, he said to her, almost as if he were speaking to himself, "He won't be back."

"Do you think he's ..." She couldn't bring herself to say the word "dead" out loud.

Pa only repeated, "He won't be back."

"But there's some hope. Daniel said there's hope."

"Daniel and Mother can hope."

Rachel looked at her father, slumped in the hard chair he always chose to sit in. She understood. He couldn't bear to hope any more.

In September came the announcement that Antwerp had been liberated, and a few weeks later a jubilant letter from Daniel. He had been with the troops that freed Antwerp. Bonmama and Tante Rosa were well, despite their long spell hidden in the apartment.

"Not good news about Uncle Itzik. After six months of being shut in the apartment, he couldn't take it anymore. He went out for a walk and never returned. We'll try to trace him, but it seems unlikely we'll be able to find out anything."

Rachel met Jules Grunwald on one of the youth group camping trips. They stayed up all night talking, and that was the beginning for them. He was from Antwerp too, and though they didn't know each other there, their families did, which made Rachel's parents happy. They knew they weren't going to "make a match" for her like they had with Lena, but Jules came from a "good" family.

In May 1945, the war in Europe was officially over. Jules and Rachel, like many of their friends, could get married and go on with their lives. The American visas finally came through and Rachel's parents left for New York soon after the wedding. Father managed to do some business in New York's diamond district, working again with his brother-in-law Uncle Eugene. He never went back to Europe, couldn't bear to think of it, and left it to Daniel to see to the sale of the house in Antwerp and salvage whatever had been left of their possessions.

Jules and Rachel moved to New York after his family decided to return to Belgium. She needed to be near her sister and cousins. Rachel was ready for her life to begin. Another door to walk through.

Epilogue

Rachel ~ August 1949

The customs and immigration line snaked around the narrow hall. First class passengers had been interviewed on board the ship, but Rachel had to wait. Her luggage was beside her, two heavy suitcases. Her clothes were packed tightly into part of one, the rest was filled with everything Mother and Lena had bought from the lists the family had sent. Household goods and clothes that were prohibitively expensive, difficult, or impossible to get in England or Belgium, a few of them still rationed. Her passport and return ticket were in her handbag, the smuggled diamonds that would pay back the money loaned for her passage sewn into the hem of her raincoat.

At last, it was her turn. She handed the official her passport. He looked through it, looked at her, asked her where she was going and what was the reason for her visit. After Rachel explained that she was visiting relatives in London, he looked at her again. She could almost see him running through the checklist in his head—Belgian passport, American clothes, Jewish name (and nose), English accent—another one of the confusing human flotsam left over from the war.

"Anything to declare, ma'am?"

"Only gifts for family—stockings, treats, things like that."

"If you speak calmly and normally, no one will ask questions, no one will suspect you," everyone had told her. It was hard not to imagine that the mild blue eyes could see through her coat to the smuggled diamonds. But he waved her on and then she was safe on the train on her way to London, then Belgium to see Daniel and her in-laws, then Paris.

She looked out the train window at the English countryside. Everything was green in the late summer light, that unique light and greenness of Northern Europe. Not at all like the brilliant tropical green and bright sun in Cuba or the patches of green she saw in the New York City parks baking in the hot, humid summer air. She was enjoying the gentle warmth that reminded her of childhood summers. But who was she now?

There was always that difference between her name in French and in English. In French, "Rachel" had a softness—the smooth sound of the ch, like sh in English, followed by the slightly elongated "el" that just faded away at the end. The French Rachel might recline on a chaise, gentle and feminine. English Rachel stood up straight—the sharp "ch" neatly cutting the name in half, and the quick, clipped "el" with the barely pronounced vowel.

Where French Rachel might smile and cajole, English Rachel spoke plainly and said what she thought. Which was she? Oh, English Rachel without a doubt. Years of schooling in French, years of hearing her name in French, did not change who she was.

And she wasn't "Rokhel," the Yiddish version her brothers used when they teased her. That was done now too.

It was an express train, and didn't stop at the small country stations they passed through. The compartment was filled with travelers who had disembarked at Southampton, mostly foreigners and better off British people, and no one else got on until Eastleigh.

A couple boarded the train and sat down. The woman was carrying a battered handbag and an even more worn carpetbag. The man had one too. They were both quite thin and their clothes looked shabby and several years out of fashion. When they took off their hats, Rachel was surprised to see that they didn't have gray hair. She looked at their faces again. They weren't as old as she had thought, just worn and tired.

She read the station names: Eastleigh, Winchester, Basingstoke, Woking. The train slowed as they reached the outskirts of London before Clapham Junction. Her breath caught in her throat. She knew England had been bombed, of course. She knew what bombed streets and buildings looked like up close, she had been through bombings in France, huddled in shelters or doorways or watching out of windows. But she thought that was behind her. In Cuba and in America, the war was someplace else, or over, and if it existed outside of her mind, in public, it was in words on the radio or in the newspaper or in black and white images in newsreels. Passing through the edges of London where so many bomb sites had been cleared but not rebuilt, she was thrown back in time again.

Rachel had thought she was returning to England of 1939 or earlier, that safe, jolly place she loved to visit, where everyone spoke the language of home and she had wonderful aunts and uncles and cousins. She hadn't even realized that that was what she was expecting until she saw what it really looked like, a battered, beaten down place filled with tired people. And they had won the war! For the first time, she realized that the family would be changed too. What would she find?

She was back in England, a "normal" peacetime England, but an England changed by six years of war and three years of exhausted peace. Victoria Station looked dingy compared to the brightness of Penn Station and Grand Central in New York. There were the same crowds rushing on and off the platforms, the same echoing noise made by many people in huge, cavernous spaces. The clothes people wore were older and less smart and, after Cuba and New York, it startled her to realize that all the faces she saw were white. The variety of skin colors had become so familiar.

"Rachel, Rachel!" And at once, she was enveloped in a familiar embrace. When she caught her breath and stepped back to look at the face of her mother's older sister, Auntie Minnie, she nearly cried. Auntie Minnie sniffed, her only concession to sentimentality, and began to organize. "You must be exhausted. Where is the rest of your luggage? Let's get you to a taxi and then home. What you need is a cup of tea and a rest." Before Rachel could begin to answer that she wasn't tired, she had only taken the train from Southampton after a restful sea voyage, Auntie Minnie had summoned the porter, directed him to the taxi rank, and deposited herself, Rachel, and all her belongings in a black London cab. After giving the cabbie her North London address, she began speaking, giving a guided tour of the wartime fate of all the streets and buildings.

They passed streets where half the buildings had been destroyed and rebuilt, and others with gaping holes like missing teeth, where rubble had been cleared but nothing else done. There were construction sites and whole untouched streets, where, except for the clothes, one could imagine it was still 1939.

Auntie Minnie was proud of how carefully she had husbanded her rationed supplies to provide a bountiful welcome. Four years after the war had ended, there was still rationing and all the paraphernalia that went with it—ration books and stamps, rumors about where scarce foodstuffs could be had, long queues outside of shops early in the morning.

Her aunt wasn't quite as good a cook as her mother, but it was lovely to be eating the familiar food in the dining room she knew so well from before the war. Uncle and Auntie's well cared for furniture, the plates and silverware that had belonged to Rachel's grandparents, the white embroidered damask tablecloth over the table pad, the silver candlesticks and Bohemian glass decanters on the sideboard, all lulled her into a half dream of the past.

But it wasn't the past. Though the house looked as beautifully tended as before, Auntie was visibly older, with more gray hair and more lines, both from age and worry, on her familiar face. *Mamma must look much older too, but I don't notice it because I saw it happening gradually,* she thought. And suddenly the picture of her parents as they were now appeared in her mind—thinner (though both had always been slim), grayer, and most of all sadder, less apt to smile or laugh.

And Rachel was not the same, tempting as it was to slip back into her younger self. Of course, Auntie Minnie still saw her as Freda's youngest child, the seventeen-year-old girl who had been sent back to Belgium in 1939.

Auntie Minnie was catching her up on all the family news, telling her where everyone was and when Rachel would be able to see them. Minnie's two oldest children, Joseph and Anne with their son, and Martin and Edith with their little girls, would come the next night for Shabbos, but Flora and her husband Harry Sparks (always called by his whole name to distinguish him from his father-in-law, also named Harry), lived in Oxford now and wouldn't be able to come until Sunday. "And Linnie will be home soon," added Auntie, "she's working for the World Jewish Relief."

Linnie had never wanted anything but to be married and have many children. "At least six," she used to say, and all the cousins would laugh at her. Linnie's husband Michael had been killed in Italy before she could have any of those six children, and now she was living with her parents and had a job.

"Irene said to ring when you've settled in. Of course, you'll want to see her. They're living in Cambridge." Irene had been Rachel's closest friend among the London cousins; they were a month apart in age and spent many holidays together. She had married a German refugee, Emil, who came to England right before the war. He was very bright and had gotten a scholar-

A Small Door

ship to Cambridge, paid for by a Jewish organization, after he was demobilized. He was a chemist, like Alexander.

The train from Brussels to Paris didn't go by way of the coast, so it wasn't until Lille that the journey began to retrace Rachel's steps from 1940. Rachel stared out the window, not sure what she expected to see.

Everywhere here in Europe, she was not seeing double, but *being* double, experiencing doubleness.

In London, she had been back in the late summer of 1939. In Paris, it would be the fall of 1940. And in Antwerp—her whole childhood and growing up.

She wanted to be back in New York and wholly in the present, going forward with Jules.

Who could she rely on now? No one except Jules and herself. Not Mamma, not for as long as she could remember. Not her father, not since she had been the one earning money, not since Alexander was gone. Not Lena, though she could now be a friend rather than just a much older sister. Lena seemed so fragile, almost brittle, with the burdens of her own life, and the burden of not having been there.

Lena was so much older, but since Rachel had grown up and married, they had become real sisters and friends. She knew some of the pain of Lena's marriage, and her difficult feelings about their parents. But she hadn't lived Lena's life, felt Lena's pains and joys. And though Lena would always listen to her when she spoke about what the family had gone through in France, she knew that Lena felt guilty that she had escaped their fate, and that she had been unable to help them, or save Alexander. They all felt that.

And not Daniel. On the floor of that hotel room in Lille, Rachel had listened as Daniel told her about the retreat before the German advance. She shook inside, sick with imagining the horrors he described, but she listened because she knew he had to tell someone. But now, he couldn't listen to her. Who knew what he had seen since Paris, on D-Day, and after? Did he tell anyone? Or did he keep it locked deep inside him? She couldn't talk to him now about anything but the most mundane family news. Not about Lena or Father, and especially not about Alexander.

Daniel had told her about his first experiences of combat, but what really went on in his head—and what had changed him from the brother she had known growing up—she had no idea. Daniel had always been a dreamer, absent minded. You could tell him to go upstairs to get something and fifteen minutes later, when he hadn't come down, you'd find him standing in the middle of the room, lost in his own thoughts. Or he'd sit at the dinner table, slowly eating his soup, staring absently at the salt cellar while everyone else had gone on to the next course. But he wasn't always quiet. When he had something he wanted to tell you about, some funny incident he had seen or some information he had read, he could talk for a long time. He was a good storyteller and he would have been a good teacher because he explained things very clearly with just the right amount of detail.

But now he was different. He didn't seem absent minded, but truly absent. As though he wasn't daydreaming, but had walled himself into some part of his mind that was terribly far away, where no one could reach him. And when he talked, it was often about something he had read in the news or some unimportant daily occurrence, and you couldn't get him to say anything about what might really touch him, or you.

When Rachel tried to talk to him about the parents or Lena in a less superficial way, he listened, but instead of telling her what he really felt or responding in some genuine way, he led the conversation in a general or trivial direction, letting it skitter away from what she wanted to talk about. When they were growing up, he could be equally elusive when he didn't want to do something—born between a strong-willed and confident older brother and an equally strong-willed little sister, he asserted himself by not asserting himself, by eluding them. There were times when Rachel had been so angry with him she just wanted to shake him, to get him to pay attention to her.

Now she wanted to shake him again, to make him look at her and really listen, but she was afraid to. Like with Lena, there was an underlying fragility to him, and she was afraid to push too hard. He didn't make her angry, she felt more sad and frightened. Part of her wanted to say, "Where are you? Where is my brother?"

The one time he had given her a straight answer was when she told him that she was going to Paris to find out what had really happened to Alexander.

"Don't tell me," he said. "I want to think he fell or jumped off the train, hit his head, and lost his memory. Don't tell me anything."

Rachel felt like she had lost both of her brothers, and didn't know how or where to get them back.

In some ways, she understood what Daniel said. She didn't read the accounts of the camps and the other atrocities that were being published. She didn't want to be able to picture it, to picture Alexander there. But even though she tried not to think about it in detail, she often found herself wondering what Alexander had thought or felt. Had he expected to come through it all and be reunited with them or had he known he could never survive? Rachel assumed he had been frightened, how could someone not be frightened? But she had never seen him frightened. He was her big brother, and he had certainly never shared any fears with her. She could imagine him angry or defiant or even scornful, but not frightened or despairing.

But how could one imagine the feelings of people in such an unimaginable situation, even people one knew so well? They had grown up in the same house, with the same parents, and she felt she knew her sister and brothers as well as she knew anyone, but did she really? She could describe them, not just physically, and predict how they might react in many situations, but how well did she really know them?

Maybe that's what always happened to siblings when they grew up and left home. Their shared life ended and they grew different, apart. Maybe she had never really known them deeply, only assumed she did.

Was it that Rachel couldn't imagine what Alexander had felt and experienced, or that she didn't want to? Did she, like Daniel, not want to know too much? But she had been forced to know, forced to come to Paris and find out what had happened to Alexander. She was the one who had to face things, take care of business, find out what needed to be done to get the money to support the parents, just like she had to earn the money and be strong for them in Havana.

There was nothing to distinguish it from the neighboring doorways. A bit shabby, but most of Paris was a bit shabby now. She checked the building number and read the sign. She opened the door. Another sign, and a dog sitting watchfully by a faded stuffed chair.

"Je viens, je viens," the concierge rasped, her slippers slapping on the tiled floor. With something between a wheeze and a sigh, she dropped into the chair. She glanced at Rachel and said, "Par là," indicating by just the slightest movement of her head the way down the corridor.

It was a short hallway, too short, and then another door, ajar. She knocked. "Entrez."

A thin dark woman sat at the reception desk, though "reception" was a rather grand name for the battered desk with a telephone and two rickety chairs in front of it. The woman looked her over and she saw a flicker of the wistful envy she had seen in the faces of other young women.

"I have an appointment. Rachel Grunwald." The woman nodded and stood up. Rachel followed her into the inner office, an equally threadbare room where almost every surface was covered with papers and brown folders. The man behind the desk stood and held out his hand.

"Madame Grunwald, David Blumenthal." The man who had answered her letter and given her this appointment. She was aware of the feel of his hand, warm and dry, and the dusty undersmell of the room; everything else seemed very far away. Rachel swallowed hard and willed herself to be present, to be calm. "Please sit down, madame." He looked to be just a little older than her, thin (everybody here was thin), and tired. He must see people like her every day. Thinking about him helped steady her. Thinking about anything other than what she was here for. But now he was speaking to her, telling her what she had come to hear.

"We have the information for you. It's lucky," he half-smiled, ruefully, "Most of the time we have hardly any details. But early in the war, when your brother was taken, the Germans kept more complete records." Rachel thought of Alexander's careful scientific notebooks: reports of experiments; inexplicable information in his indecipherable handwriting—the orderly accounts that recorded the smelly messes he created in the laboratory. David Blumenthal continued, "Since you were able to tell me when your brother was at Drancy and approximately when he was deported from there, we could trace what happened to him."

In spite of her efforts at control, she must have changed color.

"Can I get you something, madame? A glass of water perhaps?"

She shook her head. "No, thank you."

He went on, looking down at the papers in front of him, not at her. She was grateful for that.

"Alexander Brody was deported from Drancy to Auschwitz on March 27, 1942. He died there on May 14."

The room shifted and swam.

"The toilet ..."

The receptionist must have been waiting at the door. Holding Rachel's elbow, she led her to the tiny closet, where Rachel was blessedly alone while her insides cramped and emptied and cramped again. She splashed cold water on her face but didn't look in the mirror.

"Pardonnez-moi," she began when she returned.

David Blumenthal shook his head and held the chair for her.

She swallowed hard, took a breath, and said, "Tell me everything. I need to know. My parents ..."

He nodded and went on. "One of the men who was in the camp with your brother survived. He gave us details about many of the men who died." He looked carefully at her. She nodded. "The men in his transport were not sent to the gas chambers. They were made to do hard labor. The food was bad, and there wasn't much of it. They didn't have proper clothes."

She remembered Alexander's dark brown winter coat, the one they had bought here in Paris to replace the coat left in Antwerp. It had a wide collar you could turn up almost over the ears against the wind. If only he'd had his coat. If only.

"Your brother caught pneumonia." He'd always had weak lungs. Every winter he had a cold that turned into bronchitis with weeks of coughing. Mamma always nagged him to wrap up well.

There wasn't much more to tell. There were a few pieces of paper in one of the brown folders. The name and address of the man who'd been with Alexander in the camp, but with no guarantee he'd still be at that address. "He was planning to emigrate to Israel, or maybe America," Blumenthal explained. She was almost glad he would be difficult to contact. There were the forms to be filled out so Pa and Ma could get reparations money. And the piece of paper she had come to get, the single typed sheet that stated that Alexander Brody, born on September 12, 1915, in London, died at Auschwitz in Upper Silesia, on the 14th of May, 1942. A death certificate.

She didn't remember how she got out of the office, though she must have thanked M. Blumenthal and shook his hand again. He must have told her how sorry he was, and she probably said that it was good to know for sure. She must have walked past the receptionist, who might have wished her a good day, and past the concierge and her dog. The door must have closed behind her, and she must have walked away from the building, down the Paris sidewalk, past other buildings and the cafe at the corner, clutching the brown folder with the paper that said that Alexander Brody, her brother, had died at Auschwitz in Upper Silesia, on May 14, 1942, seven years before.

Somehow, she found herself, as one always does in Paris, by the river. She looked down at the water. She just stood there on the quai, looking down at the Seine, trying to stop the words repeating themselves over and over in her head. *Alexander is dead.*

She had known he was dead. They had all known, if not for all those years, certainly since the war had ended and they had heard of families being reunited, lost relatives seeming to return from oblivion, and they had heard nothing. Her father, who never mentioned Alexander's name, and her mother, who left the room when she heard of other women's children who had returned to them, knew he was dead.

But Rachel was the one who had been told "Your brother is dead." Rachel was the one holding the piece of paper that made it true: the death certificate. She stood there, looking first at the brown river moving past, then at the people walking past it, some alone, some in couples, some with small children, some so old that they had lived through both wars, and none of them, not the river or the couples or the old people, knew or cared that Alexander was now really, truly dead. She was there, where they had all been together, and now she was alone, and they would never all be together again.

But finally she turned away from the river and walked back into the city, to go back to New York, back to her life.

A Small Door

Author's Note

This story is based on the journey taken by my mother and her family when they left Belgium in May 1940, and traveled through France and Spain to reach safety in Cuba. When they arrived in Havana, my grandfather, Louis Eckstein, wrote an account of their experience for his older daughter in New York. Though he had been born in Hungary and educated only through the eighth grade in Belgium, he wrote the account in one hundred pages of fluent and evocative English. An acute observer who had read widely in history and economics, he wrote about not only his own family's experience, but the conditions he saw around him. Since it was still wartime, he left out many names of people and places. Though he spoke of his own impressions, he revealed little of his feelings and didn't disclose the names of family members. I could not have written this book without his text.

My mother, Esther Eckstein Lowy, told me many stories about what she called their "flight." In 2011, my daughter, Matilda Feder, wrote a college paper about the flight. She interviewed her grandmother extensively, did research, and went through photographs and documents. I am indebted to her for that work, and for her support throughout the writing of this book.

We were lucky to have photos and documents—identity cards, ration books, and letters—to make the stories come alive. In 2016, my husband and I went to France to retrace the steps the family had taken in 1940 and 1941. My cousin, the late Anne Eckstein, traveled with us from her home in Brussels to look for where the farm near Carly might have been. I treasure the memory of that trip, and the conversations about the family we had.

The Centre Jean Moulin in Bordeaux has an amazing collection of posters, photographs, and other materials about the Occupation and the Resistance. In Bayonne, we were able to identify the hotel where the family probably stayed using my grandfather's descriptions, and then to cross through the Pyrenees to the huge, abandoned train station at Canfranc.

Though the book is based on a true story, and much research went into the writing, it is a <u>novel</u>. The characters are fictional, and though their circumstances resemble those of the real people who inspired me, they are my creation. I have imagined incidents and, of course, conversations. Many of my cousins have been interested in the progress of the book, and I want to assure them that the foibles of my characters do not reflect on the real strength and courage of their parents. The book is dedicated to my grandfather, mother, and uncle, but the dedication could easily expand to Granny, Mark, Judy, Irene, Ruth, Menachem, and Uncle Elie. And to all the others, those who escaped, and those who didn't. I want especially to mention Mme. Bayens, the mother of my uncle's university friend, who risked her life traveling from Brussels to Antwerp each week to bring food to my great grandmother and great aunt. Mme. Goossens is based on her.

About the Author

M ichele Lowy was born in Manhattan and grew up in Queens. She has lived in Brooklyn, Oak Park, Illinois, and New Jersey, with briefer stints in Pittsburgh and Madison, Wisconsin. After graduating from Barnard College and Bank Street College of Education, she taught elementary and middle school for many years. She has three adult children and lives in Middlebury, Vermont with her husband, a Unitarian Universalist minister, her perfect cat, and her not so perfect dog.